IT WAS AS IF HE OWNED THE SKY . . .

His naked torso glistened with sweat as the late sun kissed his skin, turning it to a beautiful, deep, even shade of bronze. His jet-black hair was pulled back into a ponytail trailing down the middle of his back almost to his waist held by a leather thong. She watched the hard muscles in his arms and back tense when he raised the ax.

The act of chopping wood seemed very sensual to Jessie as she watched his body flex and relax, tracing the route of a glowing bead of sweat down his back and around to his hip where his jeans dipped precariously low.

A loud crack broke her reverie and she noticed two halves of the newly split log. All noise ceased abruptly, throwing the forest into eerie silence. When Jessica looked at the man's face, she found herself swimming in a sea of darkness. His face was comprised of sharp angles and planes. His nose was perfect, highlighted by severe cheekbones, his chin fine and strong. From ten feet away she could feel his presence permeate the air. "Can I help you?" the deep voice asked, seeming to vibrate through her. He wiped his brow with his forearm, tilting his head toward the sun as if basking in it. It was as if he owned the sky.

With easy effort he flicked the ax into the tree stump and started toward her with a slow swagger. He pulled a shirt off the pile of logs nearby and covered his sinewy muscles.

It was then that she found her voice.

Come With Me

J. S. Hawley

Kensington Publishing Corp.
http://www.kensingtonbooks.com

DAFINA BOOKS are published by

Kensington Publishing Corp.
850 Third Avenue
New York, NY 10022

All Kensington Titles, Imprints, and Distributed Lines are available at special quantity discounts for bulk purchases for sales promotions, premiums, fund-raising, and educational or institutional use. Special book excerpts or customized printings can also be created to fit specific needs. For details, write or phone the office of the Kensington special sales manager: Kensington Publishing Corp., 850 Third Avenue, New York, NY 10022, attn: Special Sales Department, Phone: 1-800-221-2647.

First Dafina mass market printing: January 2007
10 9 8 7 6 5 4 3 2 1

Printed in the United States of America

Acknowledgments

Every person who has touched my life has shaped it. In some ways, my stories reverberate with theirs.

Be patient with me, I have a village to thank.

To my CBP Village: 261, CEAR, 254, TP, RP, VG, OB, KC, ER, JT, CP, DM, LG, JC, FA, BG, SC, AT, JC, AC, LP, GH and DS. And to all the initials I left out, I know I owe ya BIG.

To my close Peeps: Nik, Pam, EBS, Paula, LeeZa, Baron, Ricky S., Poppa Mickey, Susan, Sylvia P., Dr. PF and the Godfather Phil Ward. Special thanks to R.O. (webmaster), Charles Nolan (photographer), Rivo (computer tech), Yvonne (Skylark), Rosedale Sports Association, Dawn's Daycare, K. Holmes, Reverend P. Evans (Christ for the World Chapel, JFKIA) and St. Mary Magdalene, RC Church.

And, of course, to Steph, Tasha and Sulay Hernandez (my patient editor): Thanks, ladies.

And Shari (and HH, Jus, Jareck and Jai, my bestest friend and her fam).

Cynthia Haye . . . *psst, psst,* call me.

And Eugene Thorpe (HIU—I love it, I love it, I love it). The Village that raised me—I give thanks to the Most High Creator, my aunt (Mah Oba) and my sistah

(DLH) and my nephews (DJA and JMA), my cuzes, (ST and DST), CP (the firebug) and to Aunt Tootsie.

And my mother, Doretha Hawley, for helping me to be a girl, teaching me how to be a woman and showing me how to be a mother. And the testament to my mother's mothering, my spiritual reminders: my daughters, ASH-A and CJH.

Chapter 1

Jessica Bishop's private office was on the top floor of the Wiltshire building. It was an old and dignified building on 2nd Avenue in lower Manhattan. Looking up to the roof, she admired the gargoyles that stood protecting the demesne from evil. Despite all the modern towers threatening to converge on the building, the gargoyles kept them at bay with huge wings, clawed feet and staring stone eyes. To Jessica they were beautiful and she was awed by the fact that the offices of Utopia were housed on the two uppermost floors in this historical building.

In the small entry hall, her heels tapped on the blue and white marble floor. In the center stood a mirrored scroll table. Above it hung a chandelier that caught the outside sunlight in thousands of rainbow-colored refractions, creating a twinkling minilight show in an otherwise sterile entranceway. On the table was a wrought iron jardinière, with a hammered pewter vase for fresh flowers that she replaced weekly. Jessica walked slowly past the preserved antique furnishings in the rotunda.

A slight sadness began to roll over her. Jessica quickly put that feeling away. It had no place in Utopia. Over the course of the last few years the sadness seemed to be with her more frequently. Inevitably it came with other, more intense feelings that left her helpless to stop them and empty in the end. "No," she whispered to herself, "not today." She forced her feet to physically move away from the feeling and her mind followed. "I have work to do," she reminded herself.

She had redesigned the space a year after they moved in. She kept the old, weathered hardwood floors, buffed and glazed to maintain their glamorous character. The upper half of the walls had mirrors with a faded rose tint. The lower half was dark cherry wood that had aged to an appealing burgundy. She enthusiastically took classes in woodworking and then sanded and finished the walls herself. She found dainty two-seat settees that she reupholstered in expensive and ancient red velvet she had acquired. Between them she placed a beautiful tea table. Against the adjacent wall were a duet seat, a single chair and a glass-topped coffee table. The small exit hall to the elevators held an apothecary table from an era long gone, just like the rest of the Wiltshire.

She entered the old-fashioned cage elevator, hit the button for the eleventh floor and mentally ran through her itinerary on the way up. The door slid open into an ultramodern reception area of glass, polished wood and gleaming metal surfaces. The blond hardwood floor was laid like a half moon. Off to the right-hand side of the main doors, stopping short of the plush emerald carpeting, there was a high, blond wood security desk. A hidden hallway behind it held the security offices, payroll, human resources, and other business offices, all accessible from another entrance.

The smallest incidental in design was a selling point for her company. It was a way for potential clients to see what Utopia was capable of creating.

At seven in the morning it was silent and still, like a Catholic church. She popped in and out of each of the large spaces, looking at files, her big dark brown eyes taking a cursory glance at different accounts in their various states of progress. Her manicured nails, polished in a soft beige hue, drifted over file folders that matched the shade of her skin. The folders contained several active and lucrative accounts of the most noteworthy socialites in the state. Names like Bauer, Van Heusen, Vanderbilt and Tanaka flashed through her mind. Images of events she was organizing formed as she glimpsed the file notes. The small luxury of being familiar with all the accounts in such a large firm gave her a sense of order and completion.

At 10 AM the offices would open and hum with efficient activity, but now she could look over the work at her own pace without people interrupting her. Jessica jotted down a few notes, then picked her way through a few more cubicles. Each office was basically the same, but she encouraged each employee to bring a dash of themselves to their space. This was just another way for Jessica to learn about the personalities of her staffers, and help make them appreciate themselves and their individuality. It helped in the business not to stifle anyone's ideas, and to embrace, enhance and experiment. It made employees more productive if every bit of office space subtly suggested, *Come sit, work, relax, be inspired.*

She opened the door to the executive suite. Classic

opulence welcomed her. She allowed her eyes a glance toward her partner's office to the far right.

For most, Utopia was a testing ground for ideas. No one had to worry about making a mistake here. This was a place to learn. For Jessica it had always been a way to try new and fantastic things.

Most of Jessica's unorthodox methods came from listening to the complaints of her parents growing up. The long hours, the bitterness of their coworkers, the temperamental bosses and rotten pay were at the top. Both her parents worked and she would listen to them gripe for at least the first twenty minutes when they arrived home. After that they became the attentive parents she adored. Jessica always felt her parents had worked just to raise their four offspring. But they always made ends meet and managed to spare them the small extras that made life worth living, as far as a kid was concerned, and stayed in love the entire time. Jessica had had a good childhood that produced happy memories. She wanted to provide the same for her employees.

Her older brother, Gideon, had his own business. Her older sister, Naomi, was a personal shopper; and her little brother, Joshua, was doing whatever it was twentysomethings did when they weren't going to college. Her parents boasted constantly about each of their children. But Jessica was the name and the face that her parents were asked about the most.

She was in the media often, hosting parties for entertainment greats, money moguls and political figures. Jessica had become a celebrity in her own right. At a comparably young age, she garnered recognition due to her work ethic, sex and race. Jessica felt the weight of her success in every stride in her pretty, electric-purple, alligator, four-inch pumps. She saw her accomplishments through her sunglasses. She tugged at her silk scarf, and swung her mud-brown leather, fringed Chloe poncho to one shoulder.

Jessica Bishop always dressed for her role as CEO in tailored suits. She wasn't thin, or voluptuous. She was what was considered "big-boned" or "healthy." She was far from cookie-cutter, and she hated the drab traditional blue, black, brown and grays that punctuated the business world. Today she had dressed for her meeting with exquisite care, choosing a deep plum-colored pants suit, with flowing lines and high cummerbund-like waist that trimmed and flattered her ample hips. The shirt was a lilac satin, worn with a purple tie, bearing a light violet mosaic that matched her specially dyed shoes. The outfit was a bold statement of originality, with a comfort factor to take her from day to night, which was ideal in her profession.

She always dressed appropriately for every occasion. Her hair was always styled, even when pulled back into its traditional ponytail. Her nails were always manicured, her toes pedicured and her makeup minimal yet flattering. To anyone who spoke to her she was well mannered and professional. She was truthful without being hurtful and took no one's attitude for granted. Jesse was always in control, she couldn't afford not to be. Her clients adored her, and her staff respected her.

In the beginning, nothing had been sweeter than leaving work exhausted, going to bed and waking up enthused and ready for it all to start again. Jessica preened under the pressures of work, while thoughts of her family flitted at the fringes of her mind. And then the unthinkable happened and despite the therapy, she frequently felt a growing sense of malaise, and her ability to shake it off was becoming less effective. Usually she sought to slow down after a hectic day at work, her mind needing a respite, but now if she slowed her mind she felt empty, spiritually bereft. By the time she reached the rear of the executive suites she needed a mental-health moment to exhale, a slight frown marring her face.

Jessica put her notes and files into her bag. Soft music from Marvin Gaye greeted Jessica's sensitive ears. She closed her eyes and inhaled. The sweet scent of warmed cinnamon encapsulated her, relaxed away her new tensions, when her eyes suddenly flew open. "Phaedra!"

Chapter 2

"Yes," Phaedra Belle answered as she emerged from the kitchen alcove on the left, holding a steaming cup of Utopia special-blend café latte out to Jessica. "I smell eggs, and bacon, and"—sniffing the air with a look of distaste added—"and what, ham?"

"Yes," Phaedra responded again as she started back to the reception desk. "They're here. Having breakfast upstairs."

"No, get out . . ." Jessica said in an anguished whisper. Panicked denial shot through her. She laid her briefcase on the desk, cradling the mug in two hands. "They can't be here already?" she whispered, alternately sipping and blowing on the delicious brew.

"They can and they are," Phaedra answered, pushing a tray of warmed pastries toward her boss.

"What time?"

"Dunno."

"You didn't see them?"

"Nope."

"They got here before you?"

"Yuuuuuup." Phaedra dragged out the word as if to say, *Oooooh, dey in treble.*

Phaedra had been Jessica's personal secretary ever since they moved into the Wiltshire, five years ago. She usually came in only minutes before Jessica's 6:45 AM arrival to turn on the music, warm pastries in the kitchenette and make the coffee. Phaedra was gone by 2:15 so she could meet up with her children on their way home from school. At 10 AM another secretary took over the eleventh-floor desk, but only Douglas, her partner, and Phaedra were allowed in Jessica's office.

Now that Phaedra was able to take on new and more challenging responsibilities, Jessica found she very rarely had to work late in the office. This eased her mind considerably and Phaedra knew it.

Phaedra and Jessica met years before in a meditation class. Although Phaedra was a divorcée with children, the two women shared a camaraderie, beginning with a love of soft instrumental music, B-movies, rich coffees and sweet pastries.

The early-morning quiet at the office helped them center themselves, talk a bit and get scads of work done before anyone set foot into the inner sanctum that they had built for themselves. A winding staircase led up to the twelfth floor, which held Phaedra's secretarial area, Jessica's glass-walled office and a sample food-tasting den that could be set up like a mock ballroom. There was also a full-service kitchen. Everything was done in the soft tones of the signature Utopia colors of ice-green, forest green and rich, creamy gold.

Jessica couldn't remember the last time anyone had gone up those stairs before her. No one—not the cleaning staff, not the regular staff, not Phaedra, not even the man who financed the operation. "I've never known anyone to get here before us," Jessica mused.

"True dat," Phaedra agreed, watching her boss.

"It's his business too, he can go anywhere he likes anytime he likes."

Phaedra wasn't fooled. Jessica loved her morning routine; it helped make the unpredictable less upsetting and easier to handle. Phaedra agreed with the philosophy. Starting out her morning with the children on a fairly tight schedule with room for error got them out of the house prepared and on time for school. Utopia was Phaedra's retreat, her alone time, and the minute her boss/friend came they quietly went about their tasks, alone but together. Utopia was Jessica's child. She tended it lovingly and with care for the day ahead, preparing it and herself for whatever may come. Lately her boss/friend seemed to cling to her routine more than usual.

A white-jacketed waiter came flying down the stairs. He snatched up something from the kitchenette and faced them.

"James, what is going on up there?" she asked. Confusion stained his face.

"Breakfast."

As usual he looked strong and spry for an eighty-six-year-old man. He was tall and didn't slouch, possessed a full head of Brillo-like, silver-gray hair, with weathered, wheat-colored skin, and strong arms and hands. He was the manager of her seniors wait staff: retirees who wanted an easy, well-paying, flexible job to supplement their income and keep the boredom at bay.

James Dale then shocked Jessica by dropping a kiss onto her head. "I know your daddy wouldn't have no problem with me doing that and I'm sure you needed it. You haven't looked none too happy lately, you let me and Stel know if there's anything we can do." Mr. Dale disappeared up the steps.

"That man is brave," Phaedra said, her eyes once again riveted to the ceiling.

"I'm going to finish my coffee before I go in."

"Fine."

"Fine?"

"Yesum, I knows wat sides my bread be buttered on."

"Stop that." Jessica playfully swatted at Phae. "Phaedra?"

"Yeah."

"Does everyone believe what James believes?"

"No. No one knows you that well."

"James and Stella know me well enough."

"James is a 'crazy ol' coot' if you ask Stella. And Stella's 'a pushy ol' gossip' if you ask James."

"And you?"

"I'd like to believe I'm your friend," Phaedra said.

"You are."

"Well, good, because I agree with the 'old coot' and the 'pushy gossip.'" After a pause Phaedra said, "I don't think any of us would have bounced back from something like that as well as you. That's what makes you special."

Jessica changed the subject. "What do you think they're talking about up there?"

"Dunno."

"What else do you know, friend?"

Phaedra looked over at her friend and boss. She placed a hand on Jessica's shoulder. "Slap me if you want, but your mama might say you need one of deese . . ." Phaedra pulled Jessica into an awkward hug as Jessica tried to get away.

"You're wrinkling my suit."

"I likey, likey." Phaedra said teasingly.

Jessica answered with a raise of her eyebrows on her way up to her office.

Phaedra laughed at how there's a little princess ballerina in every woman. Phaedra was glad Jess still had the ability to smile. Phaedra knew how hard the last few years of change had been on her boss. She only hoped the little ballerina would always be there.

Jessica made her way into her office first, flinging her cape into the closet and setting her briefcase on the desk. The big, old-fashioned, majestic mahogany desk dominated the comfortable room. The office was a sleek expression of all things old made new. She had designed the space like a traditional "old boy's club" law office. The furniture was large, heavy and scarred. Her chair, a large swivel Chippendale in burgundy leather with gold studs and gold threading, was flown in from London in its original condition. It was said to have once belonged in the office of a barrister who handled only cases destined for bedlam. The desk was documented to have come from a laird in Scotland, who had a love for young men.

Jessica sat and slowly turned her chair to look out of the large, high, wide windows. The effect was astonishing. They provided incredible light even on rainy days, cloudy days and moonlit nights, and no window dressings were needed. The ice-green walls with faint mauve trim reflected light better than most mirrors. The view of the city was entrancing, with manmade peaks and valleys, and shimmer and glimmer all around; she couldn't imagine working anywhere else.

The cheeriness of the office helped her mind slow down. She emptied her briefcase with care, refusing to be rushed or manipulated by the meeting taking place without her. As she opened the file about the issues to be discussed, her agitation returned in leaps and bounds. She tried to gather her thoughts and center herself, but she kept getting distracted. She knew it was childish to feel resentment but that didn't stop her from being upset with him for excluding her. James and Phaedra were right: things had been changing for quite some time.

The truth was that she felt lonely. Her partner had met a wonderful woman and gotten married. Now, two years later, they were expecting. His life was taking a normal progression. But, despite the architectural beauty that surrounded her, the wealth she'd amassed, the fame she acquired and the satisfaction of her occupation, she was still haunted.

Chapter 3

Jessica tried every deep-breathing technique she could think of to change the course of her thinking but nothing worked. She attempted to empty her mind, but her morning ritual had been shattered and her spiritual center knocked off its axis—all because of this mysterious newcomer meeting with her partner. It was time to become the businesswoman that everyone was in awe of. She squared her shoulders and marched across the open space. Phaedra was downstairs and Jessica could hear the Dales laughing with her as she paused near the stairs. Laughter. The laughter seemed to be the salve for her raw soul.

She opened both heavy doors to the mock ballroom with authority. Jessica was met with low masculine tones barely above a whisper. The sounds did not cease as her shoes tapped out a quick staccato across the hardwood floors. She passed by a banquet table set with their most impressive arrangement. A huge Waterford crystal punchbowl sat amid the Lenox China serving platters accentuated by the finest Fabergé silverware. Exotic fruits and aged cheeses cut in intricate designs adorned the mother-of-pearl plates. The Arte Italica cruet set held strawberry, blueberry, maple and a signature-blended Utopia syrup. A variety of pastries made up the bulk of the setting. Off to one side the burners were set on low, keeping the ham, sausage, eggs and bacon warm. Flowers of the creamiest hues adorned delicate, handblown glass strategically placed to highlight the main dishes. The scent of five coffees—of the thirty-seven types they offered—wafted in the air. She made her way to the intimate table set for two. Two, not three, she noted disdainfully.

Jessica's spine was rigid with anger as both men unfolded their tastefully suited bodies from the table without so much as glancing her way. The debonair Douglas Spiegel and company had both removed their jackets and loosened their ties, and were lounging as if they were having cocktails at the end of a long day of work. Douglas stopped talking and dabbed at his lips with a blue-and-silver-patterned napkin.

"Hey, Jess. Jess, this is Fred . . ."

"Ms. Jessica Bishop," she corrected, introducing herself and brusquely throwing out a firm handshake. She had no intention of allowing Douglas to manipulate her or the situation. Turning to Douglas she said, "I see you've arrived early."

"Yeah . . . but so are you. So, since you're here why don't we . . ." Douglas began, slightly chagrined, and offered her his chair.

"Fredrick Tyler, but call me Fred. Everyone does," he responded, taking both of her hands in his and pumping them gently.

Douglas pulled over another chair for himself, while Jessica seated herself.

"I'm not everyone, Mr. Tyler. Now, shall we get on with this interview?" Jessica nodded in his direction, and Fred nodded back.

"It's not really an interview, Fred," Doug added.

"No, you're right, this was a meet and greet," Jessica said, plucking a grape from one of the fruit platters, barely disturbing the cascading design. "This was supposed to be a meet and greet for *me and Mr. Tyler*. It's almost a shame we had to drag you from your bed so early, Douglas."

"The meeting isn't until nine. But we figured we'd meet and have breakfast, catch up with each other. Take some of the edge off. I figured breakfast at Utopia would be a nice way to introduce him to the home office. Get him familiar with our brunch and baked goods. Already he has some sug . . ."

"Well then, that's as good a place to start as any. Let's hear what Mr. Tyler would *suggest* for improvements." She was calm and in control. She was taking her upper hand and smacking them in the face with it.

Doug was never very good when it came to the high-pressure moments and so his words faltered. "No, I mean he's just had a quick look around. I just let him see it from a client's perspective."

"'Client Presentation' is one of my departments. He won't have to concern himself with that, but I would love to hear from Mr. Tyler," Jessica said, effectively cutting off Douglas. Jessica pinned Fred to his chair with a hard look. "Your focus would be food preparation, menus, hiring and training chefs and cooks. Do you have experience in those areas?"

"I have," came a smooth reply from Fred. "I also know at least as much as Douglas does about the financial end of things. We started out our careers together at the Millennium Hotel in Midtown. He taught me everything he knows about money."

"Which isn't much," Jessica and Douglas both said.

"It did, however, give me a desire to learn more.

The same way I set out opening my own restaurants is the same way I've gone about looking at this opportunity. I have been researching your company since you opened your last store four years ago and began restructuring Utopia." Jessica began taking notes. Fred and Doug shared a shrug and Fred plunged ahead. "I was glad you were able to retain the rooftop garden, even without the adults-only restaurant. The restaurant served a genuine purpose so I was sorry you couldn't salvage it. Parents could just sit comfortably, watch a movie, eat, read, dance, anything except be parents. The children were entertained in age groups like a camp. . ." Fred extolled the profitable history of the company and Jessica Bishop's drive and creative vision that got Utopia there. Jessica's pen was in constant motion. Then he mentioned the slump in the market that sent the company into an entirely new direction. " . . . The restructure was an amazing feat."

Jessica remembered that year vividly. It was the only time she thought she might have to close the doors of Utopia. She had given Douglas the floor plans for the new store when he gave her the Utopia account books. She already knew about the red figures all over the ledger, but the other businesses supported the Utopia monstrosity. She managed to beat the figures into submission over the course of a week. Doug put the plans back on her desk, along with budget-saving techniques. And throughout it all she was working the deal for the offices at the Wiltshire. They have been booked steadily since the doors opened.

She looked up and saw that Fred had stopped speaking. Jessica sat back. "It seems you have done some research." Fred smiled to himself for taming the shrew. "What else do you have to add?"

"I met with an analyst to offer insight into the future trends that might affect this company . . ." He spoke at length about stock, shares and financials before he moved into the calendar of events. "I know that you are currently booked by an Arabian sheik to hold a naming ceremony for his eighth son by his twelfth wife. You also have an Irish wake planned for a famous Welsh tennis professional's father and no less than three notable weddings in as many weeks. Money no object. So why bother with the less-elaborate events?"

"Excuse me?"

"Let go of the small accounts. Or, in order to save money you should have smaller teams for smaller events. Let staff do double duty. That way they get more experience faster."

Her staff were handlers/wedding planners/event coordinators—everyone did every job but only one at a time. More flexibility with schedules, minimal disagreements, no overspending, it was an experiment that worked when she assigned teams to handle an account. "Wouldn't you be more successful at a job if you only had one area to focus on?"

"Yes, but . . ."

"*If* we decide to take you on, we can discuss it," she said in a patronizing tone.

"Ms. Bishop, I wouldn't be at this meeting if I didn't think I could handle managing half of this company. I'm not here to tell you how to do your job or even assume that I could do the job remotely as well as you. It would take me a long time to learn the ins and outs of this conglomerate. It's a very large operation, attempting to run it with only one person at the helm could be disastrous. You need Douglas here to run his half or at least a proxy Doug. I think you'll find I'm qualified. Working with Doug on and off over the years I've picked up his techniques, so Utopia would still carry with it his unique flavor."

Jessica ripped a sheet of paper out of her pad. She was so raw with feeling she couldn't find anything redeeming in what this man had just said. She then looked Mr. Tyler up and down. His appearance was very reminiscent of a surfer-dude calendar model. Sandy blond hair in a stylish mop that fell carelessly over one eye. His tan looked like it came straight out of a bottle and his hands were soft. It seemed almost sacrilegious for a man to spend that much time trying to be pretty.

It seemed all the men she met these days were more interested in pretty: pretty girls, pretty jewelry, pretty houses, pretty cars, pretty clothes. There was a time when the majority of men could fix cars, carry heavy items, get dirty, throw out the garbage, drink scotch, open doors for a lady, watch sports and kill bugs. But Jessica knew guys who complained about back pain, got manicures, reminded you it was your turn to take out the garbage, drank bottled water, watched 007 movies and talked about James Bond's suits. Men who murdered chivalry.

"Doug isn't leaving, he's just reducing his hours." Jessica lit up the room with a perfect smile. "Could you give us a minute, Fred?" Fred walked with a type of self-confidence that made Jessica cringe. "My secretary is available if you have any questions for her."

Once the doors closed behind Fred Tyler, Doug could feel the tension in Jessica rise.

Chapter 4

"I don't like him, find someone else," Jessica said.

"Jess, that's bull. You're stalling. You're trying to keep me around longer, but it isn't going to work."

"I'm not stopping you. But he isn't the one." Jessica went back over to the table and tapped on the file she had there. "Here, look at his background check." Doug gave her the question-mark look. "Yeah, I did some of my own digging. That little book report you gave me didn't impress me much. Fred can manage money. But he's made enemies in the same circles that we do business with and that image is not good for us. He's using his friendship with you to wheedle his way in."

"People hire friends all the time. You and Phaedra for instance."

"We were just passing acquaintances when I hired her."

"It'll be cool to have a guy to hang with. Someone who gets my jokes."

"He's counting on that. You and him against me."

"Don't give me that 'I'm scheming against you

crap,' because currently I'm the outsider. Everything in this building is yours. I know you see every scrap of paper that leaves here. You earned the respect of your staff and the business world by your dedication to progressive thinking and unwavering belief in what you want this company to be and do. I know you make thousands of decisions every day that I never need to know about. I know that from the time you wake up till you go to bed, all you do is eat, breathe and shit this place. There is no one who can replace you because you *are* Utopia. Bringing in Fred is another step in helping us to keep up with our growing demands. This will work. I'm not leaving, it'll just be like a vacation. Then I'd work a part-time schedule. You'll see."

"If it doesn't work, I wouldn't even be able to use him if Utopia needs a loan, or refinance . . ."

"That can't possibly be a consideration because we can get money from anyone with just IOU written on our letterhead in crayon. But even if he did screw up, Utopia won't suffer because of it. Thirteen years, Jess, I think this place is a New York staple, like Junior's cheesecake, Nobu and City Island, and Nathan's on Coney Island. No one guy can wreck everything we've built."

"You know what? That's fine for you, but I don't like screwups. Personally my standards are set too high for some half-steppin' showman, shuckin' and jivin' his way across my stage."

"It's supposed to be *our* stage. But that, right there, is what I mean. This company hasn't been mine in a very long time. About three years now, ever since . . ."

"Since you became a family man . . ."

"No. Since I almost lost you! I can't even walk by there without thinking about what could've happened, all because you were too stubborn, because you had to make one last call or review one last list or check one last detail!"

Jessica shivered at the memory. "I don't want to talk about it."

Douglas fell back into the chair, his composure back in place. "We've been at this for years. Nothing is more important to you than Utopia. Somewhere along the line we stopped looking the same way at the same time and got knocked off track. Now we can't pull it back together. But Fred is willing and able to step in and help."

They were both quiet for a moment as Doug shifted around in his seat. He fidgeted with the silverware and the tablecloth. He was so full of energy she was amazed he could sit still long enough to eat a meal. "Look, Jess, I know he's not your ideal . . ."

"And my ideal would be?"

"A black guy."

"Maybe if he were a woman, I'd have less objection."

"So he goes against your values as a woman. As a black person. As a black woman! I can't even imagine which one of those sensibilities he encroaches on more. Fredrick Tyler is a white, Anglo, all-American, red-cheeked, apple pie–eating, good old boy. Blond hair, blue eyes, college educated, upper-class, suburbanite. Driving a flashy car, dressing like a model, world traveler. Ancestors-probably-owned-slaves kind of guy. You hate him because he's 'Da Man' you been fighting since someone told you you were black, the one you fight even in your sleep."

"And if the walls of Jericho come tumbling down I'm pretty sure he's just going to shake the dust out of his blond hair, flash his Crest whites, pick a piece of lint off his hand-spun suit, jump into his fancy sports car and bounce. Without so much as a sneak peek back lest he turn to a pillar of salt," Jessica said.

"You look at me that way?" Douglas asked, his brow slightly furrowed.

"You're black."

"Half black."

"They say if you got one-tenth black in you, you black. Besides, my problem isn't with what you are . . ."

"I'm not a 'what,' I'm your fucking friend!" Jessica flinched imperceptibly. "I don't care if you accept 'what' I am. I wouldn't trade who I am for all of Utopia. Light, dark, my skin tone doesn't make me who I am." This was an old argument for them and Douglas was tired of hearing himself talk. "You have no heart, Jess. You think of Utopia as yours, but, news flash, it took both of us to make this"—Douglas waved his hand around to encompass the room—"*our* company that you lord over. Me and my half-a-gene splice that you detest."

She exhaled. Too many years of fighting this fight. "Ideally all people of all races, cultures and religions should get along. They should learn tolerance and acceptance, one person, one event at a time. A real Utopia. I believe that . . ."

Doug smiled a proud, daddylike smile. He was proud that her views on race were expanding until she said, "But not me, not today." Jessica stood up, placing her hands on the table. "Listen to me good, Douglas Spiegel. I will not tolerate having a white man at the helm of my company even if his name comes after mine on the paperwork. Everyone will forget the work I've done and hand him all the credit and I haven't come this far to be set back that much."

She leaned in. "Banks, food importers of sugar, coffee and other raw goods—all owned by white men—are making a profit from me. Growers, farmers, even the trucking companies are white-owned, white-run companies. All of our hardware, flatware, silverware, flowers, linens come from all-white distributors. So forgive me if I'm trying to uplift *my* race with the only tool I have: Utopia." Jessica took a cleansing breath. She hadn't felt this free in a long time. "Don't get up, Doug." She put out a hand to stay him. "I can't tell you what to do with your half of the company any more than your family could tell you how to spend your share of their gazillions. I know you invested in a black company to tick them off. So get off your high-and-mighty soapbox, you used me too when it was convenient."

"That was different."

"No, it's not. You didn't compromise, so don't expect me to compromise myself, and I won't expect you not to bring Fred onboard," Jessica said. Douglas looked at his friend closer, it seemed that her eyes were getting back some of their sparkle. The weariness was receding. "Doug, I need a break."

"I'm the one who wants to leave, Jess. I was hanging on for you."

"Maybe deep down I knew that. It might just be time for us both to move on."

They sat staring at nothing in particular.

Jessica then headed to the door with as much purpose as when she had entered almost two hours ago. She threw Doug a devastatingly loving smile over her shoulder and all his anger dissipated. She said, "With all the free time I'm gonna have, your kid is gonna have one hell of a godmother."

Doug lifted his head from his hand, sure that their friendship was the only thing that mattered. "Practice being a better friend while you're at it. Damn," he said to the empty room, "I need more guy friends." Then he laughed at his own joke. Jessica could hear his laughter through the door. She knew he would be all right and for the first time in a long time her mind was free of stress and work, and the haunted feeling she'd been living with did not come.

Chapter 5

When the news of "Jessica Bishop's flight from Utopia" hit the papers Jessica was hard-pressed to find a moment alone. She spent her mornings lying in bed, her mind abuzz with activity. She spent time issuing instructions to her attorney, accountant and the bank in her pajamas. Jessica's publicist may as well have slept on her couch. She held several meetings, had a few teleconferences, gave interviews to everyone—from the *New York Times* down to a community pennysaver—and, of course, she had client calls by the droves. The socially prominent, the filthy rich, the influential, the politicians and the entertainers all wanted some of her precious few moments. Jessica went by all the businesses for a bite to eat, pictures or whatever other publicity they asked of her. She hosted a pregraduation affair for Phaedra's oldest daughter and a minifarewell party for herself.

Jessica was comfortably dressed in a taupe double-breasted blazer with dark brown pinstripes and taupe slacks to match. She invited her longtime companion, Eric Martin, but he said he wouldn't be available. She was surprised to see him enter the ballroom just as the party drew to a close. He was dressed as if they woke this morning in a similar frame of mind. He wore a brushed wool suit in chocolate brown, his shirt a soft, creamy taupe that complemented his smooth coffee skin tone and made his eyes sparkle. His head tilted in a Billy Dee Williams way and his short-cropped hair was overly gelled to create and hold his "natural" waves. The sheen glinted in the dim lighting.

He wore a miniscule diamond in his ear, a huge gold Masonic ring and a stately Hugo Boss wristwatch, otherwise he was free of adornments. Eric Del Martin didn't need flashy accessories. Almost everywhere they went together women flirted with Eric as if he was a rare gem. He was five feet ten inches tall and (Jessica guessed) weighed about one hundred and ninety-five pounds—although Eric bragged he wasn't more than one seventy. Eric claimed he worked out four days a week, and ate only vegan. Jessica was skeptical. She had seen him ingest handfuls of horse-pill-sized vitamins like they were his religion, not always the most natural brands. He was always on his way to the gym or just leaving, but never actually there when she called. She'd seen him eat meat byproducts at plenty of events they attended together, claiming he didn't know they had vegetarian choices.

He walked up to her and just that fast the sadness snuck up on her. The feeling that life was never going to be the same, that she had an empty hole in her that would never be filled, crowded the corners of her mind. She moved to Eric to escape the feeling. She practically jumped into his arms but once there the coldness still lingered.

"Are you okay?" he asked, concern furrowing his

brow. He gave her arms a friction rub to generate some heat as if he knew she was freezing.

"Tired. It's been a long night."

"I can see that," Eric said, looking at what was left of the carving stations, hors d'oeuvres carts and the champagne fountain. He was glad she didn't spare any expense, he hadn't planned to. "You're a hard woman to surprise. I wanted to be the one to do something like this for you, but as usual you have it all under control." He dropped a kiss on her forehead, missing her lips when she turned her head while reaching for her wrap. "My little control freak, perfectionist extraordinaire. A one-woman crew, never saw why you needed Douglas."

The line sounded as much like an insult to her as the "control freak" comment from Eric. Getting away from the cold feeling was more important than making Eric understand. "Let's get out of here," she said, pasting on a false smile to get Eric to cooperate.

"Where do you want to go?" he asked, no longer aware of Jessica's emotional turmoil. "It looks like you've had a full evening." He helped her with her cape and then put his arm out for her. "So, where to?"

"How about your place . . . in the Hamptons?"

He looked at her and pulled her closer. Usually he was the one to suggest the house in the Hamptons and she rarely accepted. He attributed her behavior to the recent events reshaping her life, and he was pleased with the way she clung to him. In the past he had been ensconced in working on her public image and an advertising campaign for Utopia.

After two years, Eric had taken his career and his client from the small, pop-culture advertising boutique Creative Forces, and had moved to the large, traditional, midsized firm of French/West/Vaughan. As his career bloomed their relationship moved from marketing strategy to dating. Jessica held her Utopia dealings above and apart from her relationship with him, listening to his suggestions and letting him do his job.

He handed her into his company town car, and climbed in next to her. Eric told his driver, Ansel, where they were headed, he leaned back and found Jess pressed close to the door. He felt the distance creep up between them and couldn't keep the edge out of his voice. "You hate going to the house. Why suggest it?"

"I don't hate going, I hate how far it is from work. I hate having to leave so early to stop home, change and still make it to work on time."

He moved across the seat and had her in his arms in seconds. He stroked her long hair, kissed her neck and pawed at her like a cat playing with a ball of string.

"Eric, Eric."

To him it sounded like a lustful chant, but when he looked at her he finally saw how unyielding she was. He supposed he shouldn't have been surprised, it had been months since they had been physical.

"I'm sorry, with everything that's going on my mind isn't on . . ." She let the sentence trail off.

"Maybe it would be better if I just went home," she said.

"How would that be better than spending an evening in each other's company? Here I thought you might let me comfort you for a change instead of handling 'everything' yourself."

Ansel looked in the rearview until he made eye contact with Jessica. He swung the car and headed toward her exclusive neighborhood. He didn't wait for instructions from his boss.

"I've been running at a breakneck speed for days and I may pass out before I get off the elevator." It sounded like the excuse it was, but she was starting to feel the listlessness roll over her, weighing down her limbs. Jessica had held on to a false hope that maybe he could help her escape the feeling, but he seemed to be making the problem worse. Previously their relationship was comfortable. After a year of working together he had suggested he escort her to several events, for the sake of her image. Jessica agreed, and found they liked quite a few of the same things. Within months invitations came to his firm in both names, assuming that they would appear in each other's company.

Currently they dated exclusively and Jessica loved the convenience of their relationship. It was two mutually agreeable adults, enjoying evenings that might otherwise have been boring and tedious. When it moved on to a physical relationship, it just seemed like the appropriate next step for them.

"Marry me." The words were thunderous in her ears even though they barely reached her across the seat. "Marry me and I'll carry you up to your condo. I'll give you a bath, tuck you in, and wake you with breakfast and a stunning diamond. All you have to say is yes."

Jessica was speechless. Eric was the ideal husband. He was smart, funny, social and friendly. Eric was good-looking, well groomed, and well mannered. He had a secure position within the megafirm, a six-figure salary and all the right connections. Any woman would be lucky to have him. Yet her answer was an equally quiet "no."

Chapter 6

Eric accused Jessica of elitism, leading him on, ignoring his needs, being selfish and insensitive to his feelings, turning her back on her responsibility to their race and, of course, cheating on him. None of it was true.

Her voice was flat, her eyes vacant, her time with Eric just fuzzy moments in her mind, which she vaguely recalled describing as "okay" to anyone who inquired. He claimed to be in love with her, to have invested time in establishing a solid relationship, and that taking a break from her company without consulting him was an insult to his manhood. She was livid, and he must be crazy if he believed she needed to check in with anyone before making decisions about her life.

She moved around her spacious condo. The living room had two big brown-velvet couches and a mustard-yellow chair with a brown-paisley pattern designed for her. Her kitchen was a study in blue—dark blue marble with sterling-silver accents, all of the accessories a dazzling yellow that harmonized with the dining room. It was primarily yellow with the dark blue accents. She had dispensed with an entertainment unit and got a flat panel set that hung directly on the wall, the speakers placed off to the sides. The other wall held her collectables, little gifts from her close friends. Her favorites she kept in a lit antique curio cabinet in her bedroom.

Jessica wasn't sure she was ready for a lifestyle change that left the frantic pace of her business behind, but she had known that a change was needed, that something was missing. Utopia no longer provided challenges; her life was simple and held no distractions and little else of value. She had tried to fill her time in the company of Eric, but she'd known Eric was not the one for a long time and she was tired of "okay"; it was definitely time to move on.

The phone rang just as the ding sounded on her microwave, pulling her from her maudlin mood. She considered letting the voice mail answer, but since it was her private number she decided to take a chance. She pulled a tray of Dim Sum from the industrial-sized microwave, one of the healthy, prepackaged specials offered by Utopia. Each little dumpling holding a different surprise: the Jiaozi had a spiced filling, the Goa Choi had pork with a garlic-chive mix, the Shu Mai was a shrimp wrap and the soup dumpling held crabmeat with a squirt of soup inside. "Hello," she said, slightly distracted by the delicious smells.

"Hello there, stranger." The familiar voice washed over her.

"I'm no stranger any more than you are," she answered back in the usual fashion.

"That gives you lots of room 'cause I'm lotsa strange," her brother responded. It was an old joke between them that for some reason transported them back to the days of Red Rover, Skelly and Cooties.

"Gideon Bishop, where are you calling me from?" Jessica asked. "It's close to 10 PM here in New York," she said, trying to locate a clock.

"I know. I'm with Susan and Derrick in New York." Susan was her brother's leggy blond assistant and Derrick was his sexy photographer. "I just finished a great package for Iceland. We're working on the brochure now but it shouldn't take too long, Derrick got plenty of good pics."

"So wadja git me? And if you're in New York why haven't I seen you?"

"Uh, you were busy quitting your job," Gideon teased.

"When you own the company it isn't quitting," Jessica explained. "So wadja git me?"

"A glacier."

Jessica listened to Gideon draw pictures with his words of the cool climate of a summer in Iceland, of breathtaking, ice-capped mountain peaks punctuating rolling flatlands. The most publicized tourist trap was a hotel built into the ice face of a mountain with a restaurant that served a sublime Mediterranean Bouillabaisse and Poached Salmon in Lemon Sauce. Gideon's travel-package company was going to feature glacier climbing as a "dangerously exciting sporting adventure." "So you bought me a big old friggin' glacier. Wherever shall I put it?"

"It's a minireplica in Swarovski crystal. It can fit on

the tip of one finger. It has all the character of a huge, life-size glacier with none of the pitfalls."

Jessica loved the sound of it and already found the perfect spot in one of her cabinets that could use "something." She proceeded to turn on the lights while she ate and recounted her tale to her brother. He laughed for all the wrong reasons, which to her were all the right times. She was warmed by the affection in his voice as he asked questions, but more than anything it felt as if they were little kids huddled under his blanket with a flashlight and a storybook.

"So, ya had a major hissy fit, didja?" her brother asked, poking fun at her.

"This is a little bigger than getting picked last for a team."

"Okay, so explain it to me. Last we spoke you knew Doug was bringing on someone to help run his part. The only question was if he was being hired as an exec or if he was buying in."

"Yeah, I got the answer to that: Doug decided to sell some of his shares of the company to Fred. You know, make it worth the man's while to dig in, lay stakes, maybe hang around for a while. But I'm just not that comfortable with the new guy. I don't know him."

"Yeah, well, your best friend does."

"All this change is happening so quickly," Jessica complained.

"You need a 'time out.'"

"I need to move on."

"Where are you moving to?" he asked with little concern. He knew his sister and she never let herself stay down for long.

"I don't know."

"What?" Now he was concerned. "Ever since Dad told us, 'You should always be two moves ahead of your opponent,' you have never *not known* what you were doing next."

"That was chess, this is life." Jessica sounded weary. After a moment of comfortable silence she added, "I'm thinking about getting out of the city. Maybe sublet or sell."

"That sounds extreme."

"*Veni, vidi, vici,* why hang around and watch Rome burn?"

"Very extreme. Why don't you stay at my place while you sort stuff through? Or better yet, just go and don't think about nothing."

She was grateful he didn't run the *before you make a decision you'll regret* line. She'd heard those words all too often in the past weeks.

"It's close enough to Mom and Dad that they won't worry and far enough so that you won't. It's rural and beautiful."

"Rural? Mom and Dad live in the country."

"There's a small town with basic amenities and a larger burg about twenty minutes down the highway. The weather is good now and there's a lodge that you can see from the cabin."

"Cabin? Like wood?"

"Yes, but the Wooden Lodge is like a regular hotel. I go over there and have meals or if I want some company."

"I don't like strangers."

"I know," he said softly. She was still fighting an unknown specter. "I'm mainly talking about the staff, a lot of them live on the property. Guests don't usually stray far from their own dwellings or the main lodge but every now and again you see folks walking, fishing, doing it down in the woods . . ."

"I don't think I want to be alone in the woods. Horror movies always take place in the woods."

"No one will even know you're there."

"Just the prey for an ax-wielding psycho."

"Stop it. It's nice. Go there for a few days, and leave when you want. There are big hotels in Asheville and Sayetteville, and you can be in Charlotte in a minute."

"I don't like wilderness. It gives the psycho who kills me more places to hide my rotting corpse."

He continued, ignoring her protests. "'Tycooness J. Bishop at play after leaving Utopia.' Wow, that is a really deep thought. Utopia is where everyone wants to go and you're leaving to go on one of my vacations. I've got this photographer friend who works for the local rag down there. He's so cool, you'll like him."

"I'll think about it, I'm all for giving a brother a break, 'specially you, big brother."

"Cool, I'll get you that info."

"Slow down, Speedy Gonzales, I've got to run this by my buddy Phaedra. See what she thinks." The silence stretched while Jessica cleaned up her mess.

"Phaedra and I had dinner earlier. With the kids. She happens to think I'm a genius."

"Poor, misguided woman."

Gideon and Phaedra had clicked without Jessica having to do a thing. Whenever Gideon came into town he managed to spend time with Phaedra and her children. They were both mature, responsible people and most importantly he loved her children. Phaedra had married at a young age, her husband disappeared years ago and she got an uncontested divorce. She was beautiful, inside and out, with four great kids. Even Jessica could manage them in small doses. Jessica smiled as her brother talked about their "date."

Jessica and her brother giggled just like when they were kids. It was amazing how much warmth family could bring. It was good to know they would always be there, but whatever she was going through was something she had to face alone.

Chapter 7

Gideon's directions were succinct. She'd thought about flying but she was glad she took her brother's advice. He had suggested she rent an SUV for her journey and take the scenic route. He said it was a good way to decompress. Jessica decided to trade in her cute little red PT Cruiser for a big black, off-road, all-terrain, four-wheel-drive vehicle. She had always admired the big beasts but found they clogged up the streets of New York City. Too much car to navigate through too much traffic. She rarely drove the Cruiser because the subways of New York were more practical. She got top dollar for the low-mileage, barely used, pristine vehicle, and paid top dollar on the purchase of her luxury monster truck. Renting was not an option once she sat on the heated leather seats.

Out on I-95 she found herself speeding along in a soundproof bubble. She had asked for state of the art and was given every modern automotive safety and convenience device. Free of distraction, wind noise and car vibrations, she listened to symphonies, operas and arias, and started a book on tape. She often engaged the cruise control because she found herself exceeding the speed limits.

The trip was an estimated eleven to twelve hours. She had left at 4 AM, figuring that after eight hours she would make camp and resume the trip the following day. Camp for Jessica would be a large, prominent hotel chain, because they would find her name easily within their system. She'd get a beautiful room with a view that would probably turn into a complimentary room upgrade. She'd end up in their most expensive suites and be given free meals. But then she thought about all the chefs who might recognize her name and try to sell her on some idea or venture. The peace and privacy of her trip would be shattered.

She stopped once in the morning for a Danish, coffee and to stretch her legs. At lunch she grabbed a tomato-on-wheat-toast sandwich and a berries-and-banana smoothie. She rested her eyes, listening to some R&B, then got quickly back on the road. She enjoyed the speed and the comfort of her monster machine.

As the dinner hour approached, Jessica decided it was time to look for something small, quaint, hospitable and clean, with decent food, soft beds and anonymity.

When Jessica reached the larger burg of Sayetteville she was pleasantly surprised. It was more of a big city than the basic town she was expecting. Buildings of glass and shiny steel dotted the skyline. Everything shone in the sunlight. The streets were clear of garbage and homeless people, a sort of fairy tale New York where people floated instead of walking and life was carefree.

She found a cozy restaurant for an early dinner that

served a Zinfandel-Braised Beef Short Ribs with Lemon-Sesame-Glazed Mustard Greens. Dessert was grilled fruit with a Bourbon glaze over a scoop of vanilla ice cream. Dinner was as eye-catching as it was delicious. Jessica decided to window-shop so she could give her legs and arms a stretch while walking off her meal. It wasn't long before she was back behind the wheel. The area she wanted was Sayer, so she found the interstate exit she needed and drove on.

She'd driven two more miles outside of Sayetteville when she saw the exit for Asheville. Jessica stopped at a Colonial-looking hotel called the Hampton Inn. It looked homey and tranquil yet large enough to have first-class accommodations, but before she even parked the car she overheard a gentleman telling a couple that Sayer was just up the road a bit.

"Jes you follow the signs."

She swung the SUV back onto the highway and followed the signs. Quickly she realized that "up the road a bit" out here in the sticks could be a few hundred miles. The first turnoff was an extremely rural roadway, the highway turning into two barely paved lanes. It was a tiny little one-horse town that was no great loss on her sightseeing tour, but she stopped at a supermarket to pick up provisions.

Jessica took a left over the highway and followed the road up into the trees, which turned into heavy forest. The road worsened as she drove. "Goddamn, he should have warned me there was no freakin' concrete up here." The map concurred that there would be no road if she was going the right way. Her all-terrain vehicle did as it promised. It delivered her, twenty minutes later, safe and sound to a gravel drive just outside a very charming wood cabin.

Jessica shut off the car, sat back and just let the silence envelop her. After two weeks of constant, intense activity she was content to just sit in the car looking out over the forest and expanse of green beyond. She hadn't realized that even this road trip held certain tensions.

She slowly lowered herself to the ground as if she were Dorothy in Oz, afraid that suddenly she would wake up and it would all be gone. She stood inhaling thin, crisp air while listening to the sounds of "things" shuffling around her and birds rustling the trees above her. Jessica moved to the front of the car so she could get a better look at her surroundings. Trees and grass, dirt and grass, flowers, rocks, bugs and more grass. The way the sun hovered between day and dusk struck her as picturesque. Here, spring made perfect sense. Somewhere in the woods to her left she could hear the faint sound of a water fountain. "So who needs pavement? God made dirt and dirt don't hurt."

The sound of chopping permeated her thoughts and she went in search of the culprit. Around the side of the cabin the ground had flowers of every color peeking out of tall grass. As she looked around she could see the setting sun glinting off an ax being swung in a mighty arc downward into the slight wind that was blowing. Jessica walked farther on the path and was able to get a good view of the man chopping wood.

His naked torso glistened with sweat as the late sun kissed his skin, turning it to a beautiful, deep, even shade of bronze. His jet-black hair was pulled back into a ponytail trailing down the middle of his back to his waist held by a leather thong. She unconsciously touched her own newly sheared mane. She had cut off her long, high-maintenance dark brown hair before leaving the city and went with a fun and wild, short, curly, reddish-gold bob. She pushed the hair back off her face as she watched the hard muscles in his arms and back tense when he raised the ax.

He wielded it like it was Thor's hammer. She noticed the musical rhythm the sound created as well as the easy control he exhibited. His legs were clad in blue jeans, and perspiration beaded at the waistband. The muscles in his legs strained against the fabric as he steadied himself when lifting the ax from the wood. The act of chopping wood seemed very sensual to Jessica as she watched his body flex and relax, tracing the route of a glowing bead of sweat down his back and around to his hip where his jeans dipped precariously low. A loud crack broke into her erotic reverie and she noticed the two halves of the newly split log. All noise ceased abruptly, throwing the forest into eerie silence. When Jessica looked at the man's face she found herself swimming in a sea of darkness. His face was comprised of sharp angles and planes. His nose was perfect, highlighted by severe cheekbones, his chin fine and strong. His features looked to be chiseled out of stone. He had a neat, thin line of a mustache and the hint of a beard. His lips were full and inviting. Straight dark hairs were lying flat against his chest and abdomen, going farther down than the pants would allow her to see. It reminded her of a faint shadow of a rising Phoenix. His hips were deep, sculptured cuts. From ten feet away she could feel his presence permeate the air.

"Can I help you?" the deep voice asked, seeming

to vibrate through her. He wiped his brow with his forearm, tilting his head toward the sun as if basking in it. It was as if he owned the sky. His dark eyebrows creased. "You Jesse?" She nodded stupidly when his dark eyes returned to her. "You're early. I was expecting you later tonight." With easy effort he flicked the ax into the tree stump and started toward her with a slow swagger. He pulled a shirt off the pile of logs nearby and covered his sinewy muscles. It was then that she found her voice.

"Jessica."

"Pardon me?"

"My name is Jessica Bishop," she asserted.

"Gideon Bishop told me to expect his little sister, 'Jesse,' 'Jesse Ruth,' to be precise. You bear no resemblance to the picture he showed me, you aren't little by half and now you say your name ain't Jesse. So it seems ta me you're not the one I'm looking for, so we got no business." He turned his muscled back to her, the view being so equally nice, she'd almost forgotten to stop him.

"I answer to Jessica, and I haven't been little in a long time."

"You Jesse or not?" He turned slowly to face her, and his hands halted while buttoning up his shirt, he felt very exposed under her powerful gaze. The brightness of her eyes, her smooth, pretty skin, her body with its perfect proportions seemed to move in ways that made a man stand up and notice. Her breasts were more'n a handful, plump and round. Her wide hips were etched in blue denim, her waist marking her exquisite dimensions.

She gave him such a slight shake of her head her curls didn't move.

"Have it your way." He reached for his ax.

"Fine, I'm Jesse. Pronounced with a long 'e' not that 'eh' sound you keep grunting out."

"You don't look much like your picture," the man said, rubbing the light stubble on his chin.

Jesse thought about the pictures Gideon might have and chances were good that it was a picture of them together at the opening of Utopia.

"It was probably an old picture. So if you're done with the inquisition, my bags are in the Jeep out front. I'd like some help." She turned her back on him, and moved quickly before he could catch up to her. She really wasn't ready to engage in small talk. Gideon had told her that someone would be at the cabin to meet her with the keys. He didn't give the man's name, let alone tell her he was dangerously sexy. She was certain Gideon did that on purpose.

She was prepared to deflect this man at all costs—until she realized she didn't have a key and was going to have to interact with him yet again.

"It's open," he said when he saw her hesitate at the door, as he passed by the front porch. "There's no real need to lock it. Animals don't usually try the door-knob first, and the next cabin is almost two miles away. The lodge is the closest thing. It doesn't look far but that's a good quarter-mile uphill hike. Keys are on a hook in the kitchen."

She gave a curt nod and stepped inside.

Chapter 8

From the outside, the dwelling looked like a small, rustic log cabin but the inside belied that quaint concept. It looked much like her condo, with stylish furnishings in autumnal tones and bright apricot accents. The huge entertainment unit held a Bose speaker system and flat screen television. It looked well kept but unused. It did lack a formal dining room but instead stepped up to a balcony that overlooked the valley. On that rested a beautiful, smoked-glass table with forest green chairs set for dining. Someone had already drawn back the curtains. The sliding glass door was slightly ajar and the fresh forest scents punctuated the interior. She and her brother really did share the same tastes. The balance within the room was very Feng Shui. The couches were big and roomy, the chairs overstuffed and cushy, the tables artistic and simple. She also noticed a small potbellied stove near the door when you first stepped into the recessed living room. It could probably heat the entire house. Jessica and Gideon seemed to have inherited from their parents the same love of old and new harmonizing together.

Big Joe loved his luxuries and Rachel wanted cozy comforts. They had mementos from family trips and holidays, to remind her parents that they were all young once, but not so much that the past was suffocating. There were African sculptures mixed with European art; otherwise their house had every modern gizmo from the clapper to a DVD burner. Big Joe and Rachel were content and comfortable. You could buy her parents anything and it found a useful place and a cherished existence.

Jessica moved into the kitchen. The kitchen floor and island were done in green and black marble with brass accents. Brass pots were hung up and the burners looked clean but utilized. The cabinets had wonderful glass panels and recessed lighting so you could see inside without having to open them, even at night. She pulled open more drapes and discovered the balcony extended to the far side of the kitchen so you could grill outside while enjoying the view.

The sound of baggage being dropped on the floor brought her back to the living room. "Could you please be careful?"

"Look, honey, I'm not your personal valet. You don't like the way I do things, ask someone else."

"Well, give me the name and number and I'll call someone else to come and help me."

He let out a bark of a laugh. "This isn't the Ritz-Carlton. People come out here to be left alone with nature, they don't usually request bellboys and maid service. If you wanted something even resembling a hotel you should have booked a room in the lodge . . ."

"I understand that, but . . ."

He held up a hand. "I'm not paid to listen to you either. Your brother is a good client. Sends a lot of business up here and he happens to be a great friend. As his friend he asked me to meet his little sister. I've met you." He strode out of the door, returning seconds later with two more bags that he tossed across the floor as if they were filled with cotton balls. He walked menacingly toward Jessica until she was forced to move out of his way or be stepped on. He stopped at the counter. "I keep basic provisions in the fridge but I noticed you've got plenty of stuff in the car," he said in a snide voice. "This is the only cabin with owners. It's Gideon's home so there are pots, pans, towels, sheets, toiletries and other necessities, but should you need anything more the lodge can provide it at little or no cost or you can get it in town. But from the amount of bags I caught sight of, I assume you've got yourself covered."

His sarcasm irked her. "Yeah, well, I'm a big girl. I can look out for myself."

"Good, then you can unload the rest of your stuff yourself," he replied.

"Very well," she said, mustering up her dignity, "you can go now." She held out an envelope in a shaky hand.

"What's this?" he asked in a derisive tone.

"It's for your time," she said defensively. He took out the money and gave a disgusted laugh. "Money doesn't do much good way up here, honey." Jessica saw that he pocketed the bills just the same. "Sometimes hard work is its own reward."

"Well, from the look of your worn jeans and old boots you could use it," she said, trying not to let him get the best of her.

"You expect me to chop wood in a suit?"

"No, but . . ."

"Good. At least you have that much sense."

"Fine." Jessica put her bag on a chair and went out to the car. She had had more than enough speeches from self-righteous people to last her a lifetime. She also had had more than enough people point out her flaws and she certainly didn't wish to hear about herself from a man who'd made her acquaintance less than ten minutes ago, who worked half-naked out of doors without a care for decency. Truth was, if he didn't have such a big mouth she probably would have wanted to jump all over him. *Thank God for small favors,* she thought, sending the words silently to God's ears.

As she pulled out the rest of the bags and put them on the ground she began to acquire a sheen of perspiration. She glanced at him as he stood on the wooden porch leaning against one of the supports.

"City chicks, so stubborn," he mumbled.

"I can hear you. Or was that the point of saying it aloud? And why are you still here?"

"I have to give you the rules of the lodge and give you a quick tour of the cabin."

"I'm not staying at the lodge and I can find my own way around the cabin. It isn't the Taj Mahal." She focused her strength and hefted two large bags, trying to make it look easier than it was.

"The cabin is on lodge property and there is emergency information that everyone has to have because the weather is often brutal and extreme. Trees come down, lines are out of service, riverbeds overflow and flood, wild animals wreck stuff and cabins become uninhabitable." She looked into his eyes as she bumped a bag up the steps past him but maintained her silence. He went on. "If you look by your phone in the kitchen there is a list of numbers. If you dial the first number on the list you will get the main desk at the lodge. Call for problems like stuck windows, lost keys, broken shutters and wood chopping. If you're prone to givin' away your money someone will be down to show you how to start a fire if ya lose power and show you basic first aid."

With her anger fueling her, she was able to get two more bags inside with less effort. He offered no help and continued after her. "Any repairs we can handle. There's a separate extension for the restaurant. You can call for reservations, pick up orders and, in some cases, get a delivery. This cabin is special because I've modernized it. It's the only one with ground electricity but there is a functioning generator. I maintain it so that it cuts on automatically if the power goes out. Bigger storms will take that out too, so we keep battery-powered stuff in each cabin for those occasions," he said while following her into the cabin.

When she released another heavy bag he grabbed her arm and pulled her along on what she supposed was the tour. "In this pantry is candles and wood, on the shelves you also have lanterns, a battery-operated radio and TV. There's a two-way that runs on batteries as well and is connected to the lodge; always turn it on during a storm even if you're okay. We call to check in and to update you on the length and severity of the storm and give you any other special instructions. The police can also get in touch with you through this means if evacuation is necessary. We've only had two evacs in my four years here at the lodge."

She thought he was trying to scare her. He just didn't know how tough she was.

"There's a first aid kit and an emergency roadside pack that you should put in your SUV. I also have chains for your tires, if you stay till winter you'll need those."

"That's it?" she asked between breaths.

"Yup."

"Again, thank you for your time." She headed back to the car.

"So the million-dollar maven has manners."

She darted him a quick glance, took three bags and hurried inside. When she returned he was sitting on the banister.

"How long you gonna be here, Ms. Money Bags?"

"Look Billy-Joe-Bob, I've got a lot of unpacking ahead of me, so if you're finished with the name-calling, then please be on your way." She stared into his granite eyes, ready if he said another nasty thing.

He leapt off the steps in one lithe movement. He snatched up her garment bag, train case and her overnight. "Anymore luggage, Iron Mike?"

Feeling dumbstruck again at his close proximity, she shook her head. He bounded into the house as she pulled out the Utopia boxes along with the super-market bags. He came back down the steps and re-lieved her of the items, flashing her an alarmingly delicious smile.

"Despite what you may think of me, my mama raised a gentleman. You just need to learn how to ask, Kitten. Kitchen?"

Jessica's tongue fumbled with some indignant sounds of protest when he took off into the cabin. She snatched the last remaining items in the car, slammed the door, hit the alarm and marched inside, ready to do battle. He blocked her path, startling her and ruining her momentum.

"This is God's country, no need for the alarm, no one here to hear it but me and you. It's like they say: if a tree falls in the forest and no one is around, does it make a sound?"

She looked into his gorgeous face and watched his pale gray eyes devour her. With each breath she took his body seemed to draw closer to her, trying to breathe her air, feel the pulse coming off of her body. Visually he drank his fill of her delectable breasts, following the curve of her neck down to the dark valley between them. She was both frightened and excited that he could do anything he wanted to her and no one would hear them.

"No need to lock it either, same reason. I'm gonna finish the wood and then go."

He started to leave when she stopped him with her wistfully childlike question, "What's your name?"

"Cloud Walker," he answered on a breath.

Chapter 9

Walker moved quickly back to the clearing. "Cloud Walker. What the hell is wrong with you, man? Since when did you start giving out your real name? I might as well have told her to call me 'Mighty Cloud Walker, grandson of Majestic Cloud Walker of the Cherokee Tribal Nation' and gotten it all over with. Tell her about my grandfather being the head of council, the tribal chief and regional director of the Rocky Mountain Offices of the Bureau of Indian Affairs, making decisions for nearly 30,000 souls for the last sixty years. Then confess I'm his successor and have been chief for the last six years."

Mike returned to the tree stump, his body thrummed with repressed energy. It wasn't due to the abrupt stopping of the work he had been doing or the work ahead of him but because of that woman who had gotten under his skin. She was as fiery and as impossible as the red color she dyed her hair but as hypnotizing and natural as the sway of her hips. Mike thought her huge, innocent doe eyes sparkled with rebellion. When he looked at her he wanted to run his calloused hands over the smooth, inviting skin, but her tongue would need some serious taming first. And so did his thoughts. He wasn't about to invest his time dealing with that hellion wildcat.

When he left Chicago, Mike Walker abandoned all those city ideals, especially the high-profile, high-maintenance girlfriend. Trisha Marie Carelli had taken more than her fair share of his soul, leaving him cold. No amount of sass or vulnerability was going to lure him into another bad relationship. Mike could see Miss Jessica Bishop standing outside on the portico over the woodshed and gravitated toward her.

When he first saw her trampling all over his wildflowers he thought she was lost. She looked too refined for his woods, and her rigid posture, frigid tone and perfect crease in her jeans confirmed this. Yeah, she looked like a Jessica all right, not a Jess or a Jesse but a Jessica. But now, seeing her jeans casually rumpled and her skin flushed against the backdrop of nature, she looked like a Jesse. Already she was blending in with her surroundings and if he wasn't careful, she would get the best of him. He wouldn't let that happen, he was determined to knock her off her pedestal and he planned on starting with her name.

She held a glass and sipped a clear liquid. "Probably bottled water for the spoiled princess," he grumbled. But he did not go back to work, instead he inspected her closely and, from where he stood, he could see her even, moderately short nails with their clear polish. He appreciated her choice. When he lived with Trisha she always had long talons done in very lavish colors to match her clothes. It seemed he worked just to pay for her grooming. The rest of the time he would work like a dog to prove to his mostly white colleagues that he was equal to, if not better than, them. He'd burn through paralegals like a brush fire, he'd win his cases and bring in the most revenue.

Now those times just seemed like a waste of energy and money. Trisha spent her entire salary and half of his on frivolities. Even her perfume was pricey as hell, stuff that made him sneeze for a good five minutes when he got near her and later managed to cling to his silk ties even after they were laundered. When he was close to Jesse, just now, she smelled of a subtly sweet aroma. He thought it was light and distinctly pretty. If he had to say she smelled like anything, he would say she smelled "yellow."

He bent down and picked up a twig, flicked it at her to get her attention. She didn't hesitate to smile, a smile that made his knees weak. He could see her blending into all his worlds, especially this one, even with all her Gucci luggage. He started to turn but looked back one more time and caught her pushing her short curls out of her face. Her profile softened as she looked dreamily at the landscape that he wished was his to give her.

She looked into his eyes and gave another quirky smile; he couldn't help but wink back. He looked around and saw there was enough wood for a month even if she made a fire every day. He collected the logs and put them under the portico in the shed off the back of the house.

Mike covered the wood with a plastic tarp, closed the shed door and walked back out. He noticed the cool lavender sky made a halo around her entire body. She wasn't the thin kind of dieting woman that Trisha was. No, this girl ate well and carried it even better. Now he could see where comparing women to hourglasses fit in. She appeared as tall as Trisha, her shoulders broad and back straight. Jesse was womanly where Trisha seemed girlish . . . He hadn't much worried about women since his relocation. He knew he could get company whenever he wanted but it was not a priority. His friend's little sister was not going to be that kind of company.

Chapter 10

"Hey, City, I'm heading back up to the lodge, when you go back inside, bar the shed door."

"I thought you said I needn't lock any doors."

"The bears sometimes sniff out the food, smartass. If they face some resistance they tend to move on to easier pastures. Everything here is done, but if you need help just call and someone can either instruct you over the phone or come out and give you a hand. There's a large staff."

"Okay, thank you. See you around," she said.

"Not unless you come to the lodge or something goes wrong. I keep a room at the lodge. I've got summer prep. Big money to be made. I'm not working for you, babe. I did promise Gideon I'd check up on you but since you're a big girl . . ." he quoted.

"Yes, I remember saying that," she said in a low voice that barely carried to him. "But you did say there's a large staff," she quoted. "I don't imagine you do it all alone."

He didn't like the idea of anyone being paid to do anything for her. "I'll be around."

"That's fine," she said. "I came here to be alone. I promised my family I'd take some time to relax. I'm on vacation." Her speech sounded practiced.

Mike pulled the leather thong from his hair before crossing his arms over his chest and putting his weight on his back leg as if he might be standing there a while. He watched her holding her glass of water, savoring the fluid as if she had a rare, lost vintage of wine.

Although she was distracted by the sexy cascade of his hair she did notice him eyeballing the bottle she used to refill her glass, sitting on the ledge. "I'm sorry, would you like some water? It's cold right out of the tap," she offered.

"No thanks, I'm good." He kept trying to compare her with Trisha. So far there was the fact that Jesse had been doing business as Jessica for years and Trisha had legally changed her name from Theresa Marie to Trisha because Theresa Marie was "a typical Italian name" and Trisha was "much more fun and playful" sounding. But Mighty became Mike when he left the mountain so in that they were all the same, creating a shell persona to give to the public.

He imagined Jesse's public persona was as full of bullshit as his and Trisha's. However, she was probably exquisite no matter where she was. She couldn't shed or hide that kind of beauty. Trisha was vulgar, with short skirts on long, ivory legs and low-cut shirts with push-up bras. Her long, bottle-blonde hair and Pearl Vision blue eyes enhanced her otherwise plain features. Trisha was cosmetically model-beautiful but shallow as a dry riverbed. She was a smart woman who played stupid to her advantage.

Jesse spoke with cool detachment. He suspected it

was part of her businesswoman veneer. He'd been the same when he worked as a lawyer for the Montgomery Group in their Mergers and Acquisitions division. They teamed his low-key, dramatic, intimidating negotiation tactics with Trisha's dynamic, sexually charged antics. Together they negotiated the merging, buying and selling of companies with the largest profit margin. But the days of Trisha busting into his office waving a bejeweled hand, clutching a new merger proposal, poking pouty, glossy red lips at him and in general creating a scene were behind him.

Jesse was a far cry from Trisha's cursing, tossing her hair, stomping around and throwing tantrums, but potentially just as much trouble. Trisha's behaviors spilled into their predictable sex life. Sometimes months went by filled with excuses and missed opportunities and when they did manage some time together, she was constantly worried about her dress, or hair or nails. Then there was the fact that the sex was without much touching, with few kisses, little fondling and no foreplay. Cuddling was as foreign to Trisha as McDonalds was.

Looking at Jesse, he imagined hours of touching to find her secret spots, massaging her neck and back, caresses exploring her arms and hips, and kisses for her legs and feet—each time stopping to look into her captivating eyes. He loved the small, pert nose, the permanent pucker of her lips, the baby-doll cheeks, the slight dimple in her chin, the arch of her eyebrows, and the lashes that were too long to be real but outlined her eyes in a flattering charcoal, making her brown eyes sparkle in her cherubic face. He would worship her slowly, making love to her over and over . . .

"Are you okay, mountain man? You sure you don't want some water? You look like you could use some. You're probably losing a lot of nutrients from all that sweat."

If he was honest with himself, he'd have to admit she reminded him of his big-business tactics, his extravagant expenditures, his city mentality, his rushed lifestyle and his superiority complex—the things that brought him back to this place four years ago, when it all fell apart and there was nothing of the old Mike Walker worth holding on to. "Trying to find yourself?" he asked.

"What?"

He saw her veneer waver slightly at the question.

She looked wistful again and gave another smile. He looked just as thoughtful when seeing his first sunset on the mountain after so many years away. He'd felt as relaxed as she looked now standing amidst the forest. He locked his car doors the first month, city toughness and distrust ingrained in him. The man he had been wasn't someone he would have liked to have been friends with, even Gideon said he was intimidating. Mike was ruthless, rude, pushy, bossy, and insensitive. Trisha had loved those qualities if it helped them seal a deal. His work with Trisha had merit and value at the firm, it was an easy progression to pursue more personal contact and then try to convince himself he was in love with her.

But being in this place helped him clear his mind. He learned how to let go of so many of the bad habits he had embraced while being Mike Walker, sadistic fuck. He let go of Trisha and her manipulative lust and was able to find some pieces of the Cloud Walker he was as a child. He was able to find the peace of mind that Jessica seemed to be in search of. He needed to get his soul back, his inner spirit. Michael Walker, Esquire, was Midas in the workplace but a bastard of an individual. The new Mike, well, there was still more of him out there to find. He sensed that Jesse was on the same spiritual journey.

"Hope you find what you're looking for. This is a good place to be alone, forget some stuff, maybe even solve a heavy problem or two."

"Thanks."

"See ya, City."

He moved slowly through the trees, He looked back and she was still watching him.

Chapter 11

Jessica felt the chill of the forest once the sun had gone down. She watched Walker move through the darkness with surefooted agility. She thought her attraction to him was completely physical yet she'd experienced his intelligence and quick wit. He spoke slowly but his formal education and common sense came through, loud and clear. Talking to him made her think. Too bad he already had a problem with her. She figured he was in the Eric camp, that it was her money and position he had a problem with. Most men couldn't deal with a powerful woman and she was more powerful than most.

She roamed through the front of the peaceful cabin, trying to settle her thoughts. She was surrounded by her brother's positive aura. A cozy feeling settled her troubled mind. She moved her bags toward the back of the house, looking at the two bedroom doors, a bathroom and a den at the far end of the hall. She looked into the smaller of the two rooms. It was neat and orderly, the theme looked mostly Southwestern. The rug, blanket and throw pillows looked all hand-loomed using natural colors and dyes. She took her smallest bag in first. When she checked the bureau, dresser, closet, night tables and even the cedar chest she found they were full of clothes and other personal items. So she went into the master suite and found it empty. "Oh, Gideon, you didn't have to take the guestroom on my account," she thought, but was warmed by the gesture.

She liked the guestroom with the hand-carved rocker, the linen curtains, the heavy, decorative wood of the headboard and footboard of the bed and the small fireplace mantel covered in hand-carved animals. Little crows, eagles, bears, mountain cats, wolves and turtles cluttered the space. The whole room looked as if someone had carved, finished and polished everything with care. The larger room gave off a distinct feel as well. It had a more modern feel to it. The furnishings were of a cream lacquer, which also matched the mantel of the fireplace that was filled with candles and flowers. A note card was sticking out and Jessica plucked it out and read:

> *Lil' Sis,*
>
> *I hope you arrived safely and in good spirits. You can take my room for the time being, I don't keep many clothes around the house, as a rule. I just don't have too many personal possessions, as you know. I made room for your collectibles, please put them out. Call me after a day or two of decompression, tell me what you think of the place. Feel free to make the place feel more like home. Don't forget to call Yusef at the* Sayetteville Sound. *He's expecting you.*
>
> Mi casa es su casa.
> *Gideon*

Jessica smiled at the sentiment. The perfume of the flowers tickled her nose and made her spirits rise. When she stood she saw framed photos of her and Gideon as kids, and the one at the Utopia opening-night reception. He had an old one of her parents when they were dating and two family photos: one was from a past Christmas a few years ago. Ma Bishop made the holiday picture happen, come hell or high water, and it was the least the family could do for her. Gideon had no pictures of Naomi and only one of Joshua. She assumed that was because Josh hardly stood still long enough for someone to take a picture and Naomi probably retained every picture of her in existence.

Jessica finished her basic unpacking. When she went to place her toothbrush in the small green room off the bedroom she discovered a well-lit, albeit tiny, laundry area. She then decided to check out the other rooms before dinner. The bath in the hall had the basics: throne, shower, sink and a linen closet. "I guess men never want to take bubble baths. How unromantic." Jessica loved the den. It was completely rustic, from the wooden walls to the throw rugs on dusty floorboards. The stone hearth of the fireplace was rough and unfinished. The couch was a type of redwood with an intricate diamond pattern that the craftsman followed and preserved. There was a blanket draped over the couch that looked well worn. She felt herself shiver and realized that it probably could get very cold in a room set lower than the rest of the cabin. She moved farther into the den, down five or so steps, and began looking for a light switch but found none. All she could see was the gleam of highly polished lanterns on the end tables, walls and mantel. Each appeared to be full so she went to find some matches. In the kitchen she located long, old-fashioned wood matches. She found herself skipping back to the den, waving the match like a wand. She lit all the lanterns in no time and found that the room had a wonderful glow. She then saw the five full bookcases and her heart flipped again. She ran her hand over the ten or so different dictionaries in heavy red, green and brown covers. She noted at least three types of Bibles and several other religious tomes. She saw books on culture, philosophy, economics, science, sci-fi, fantasy, travel and mythology. There was one bookshelf that completely mesmerized her. She saw everything from slave narratives to contemporary fiction by some of the most revered African-American writers. It was a festival of countless famous black authors, both contemporary and historical, standing tall and majestic. She pulled down a small book of poetry by Sonia Sanchez and *The Temple of My Familiar* by Alice Walker. Both were books she had not had time to settle into, but now her mind was ready to be filled with someone else's thoughts.

She lay on the comfortable couch, reading in the flickering lights until her eyes were straining to stay open. She placed the book on the floor and noticed the heavy wood door in front of her. With a light push the damn thing refused to move but with weight and willpower she managed to get it open on protesting hinges. She felt around on the walls but found no light switch. She went back to the den and got a lantern and scanned the room. It was bare and dank, the smell of mud and mildew permeating her senses. She took the creaking, rotting steps and moved into the room.

She saw the chain above her and gave it a tug. A naked light bulb flicked on precariously and she was able to see the wooden planks she stood on. A rusted sink sat in one corner and shelves that were falling down in another. A foot from where she stood, old pipes stuck out of the ground with a makeshift water pump. Next to that was a hole or a shallow pit. At one time the room probably had had a noble purpose as a storm shelter or root cellar, but now it was a piteous reminder of days before industrialization. High windows were black with dust and dirt. The walls looked to be made of tightly packed mud. Across from her was a rickety-looking bench that she guessed could collapse with a strong gust. She imagined that the room could serve as an office for Gideon, maybe as a darkroom so he could develop his own pictures, but she knew that Gideon would never work while here. It was his place to go to get away from work. He had continually badgered her about keeping her work in the office but she never did. Her work was her life and she had needed it to survive.

Suddenly the world seemed far away and her breath came in short gasps. She felt as if she couldn't get enough air in this rancid little room so she slowly backed up the stairs and into the den. Once she got there, the claustrophobia didn't cease. She sat down with her head between her legs, thinking it was just a panic attack. When it didn't subside, she moved into the spacious living room, throwing open doors and windows as she went. When she felt the cool night air on her face she realized she had stumbled right outside onto the porch. She held on for dear life. *Oh, my God, I'm going to die out here in God's country,* her mind screamed. This isn't how it was supposed to end. At thirty-four, she was considered a business mogul, and moguls died at seventy-nine in the plush comforts of a yacht or mansion or on an island somewhere.

"And I'm gonna die the left of nowhere all alone. Over what? One lost business? One piss-poor excuse of a relationship? My future? I'm fine. I have the skills and ability to do anything I want." She jerked herself upright sharply, only to nearly fall to the ground in a puddle instead of a graceful swoon like in the movies, but she held fast to the belief that she was fine.

"You're not dying. It isn't even a panic attack. It's the air. We're a little higher in elevation and at night the air gets pretty thin. Pant like you're delivering a baby."

She heard the voice before she saw the man. But she knew that it was him. A pleasant, woodsy cherry smell was coming from just beyond the circle of light that the front door gave off. "Where are you and what are you doing . . . ?" Her question died in her chest as she heaved deeply, trying unsuccessfully to fill her lungs. He moved up the stairs like a thief in the night, catching her just before she lost her balance as the dizziness swept her toward oblivion.

"Hang in there, City, let's go inside for a minute. And pant, damn it. Like you're in labor, not like a dog!"

"I've never been in labor," she choked out.

"Like this." He demonstrated but she was too hysterical to catch on. "Try harder, you'll need this for Lamaze when you do decide to have kids."

"I can't have kids, so figure out another way to help me," she wheezed.

He was stunned by such a personal admission. He stood immobile for a few seconds while she heaved in great gulps of air. He bent over so that his face was directly in front of hers and he started panting again so she would copy him.

With his arms going around her waist she felt secure, allowing herself to be propelled along. As he sat her on one of the stools his entire body came in contact with her left side. Walker's long, thick hair brushing the side of Jesse's neck sent tiny shivers through her. She arched involuntarily as she felt tiny sparks of excitement when he went in search of something in the drawers and he rubbed the back of her neck with a firm hand. She felt an unmistakable chill steal over her when he took a small step away.

He was dressed in clean, straight-legged jeans that did amazing things for his thighs and derrière. He wore soft-soled moccasins that she had seen in the windows of many of the Indian trading post shops, on her trip down. She imagined that she wouldn't mind seeing that sight eight hours a day. He leaned forward and shuffled around some stuff in the drawer and she leaned back to see the perfect roundness of his butt in his jeans. His button-down workman's shirt fit just as well as his jeans did.

He returned, handing her a brown paper bag, again his arm stealing around her. "Just breathe into that. I should have warned you about this, it's part of the welcoming speech, but I forgot."

The glint in his eyes told her different. He wet a towel for her forehead.

"How would you know to come now?" she huffed. He gently pushed the bag back to her lips. "And what if I didn't come outside!" His hand was softly stroking the back of her neck and she wasn't sure if her breath was coming in puffs because of the air or him.

"I knew to come sometime after dark, that's when I get the calls that someone is having a heart attack or stroke or some other serious affliction when it's really just city people getting adjusted to the higher altitude. You'll be fine in a second."

She knew what he was saying to be true. Gideon and she had gone climbing together once and he warned her about it. She was already starting to feel regular again.

"You seem better. If the cough comes back, don't lie down, call the lodge, ask for Tak in medical, or me."

"Thanks," she said, moving away from him.

"Not a problem, City."

"Stop calling me that, you hick." His rumbling laughter radiated through her and she wanted to punch him and make him swallow his gaiety. But she was still too weak and way too attracted to him.

"I know a lot more than you give me credit for, lady."

"I give you plenty of credit for knowing stuff. I'm sure you can handle a club and spear pretty well. And maybe do a good rain dance," she said in a mocking tone. "You can probably find the way home by the stars and which side of the tree moss grows on, and you probably know which berries are good to eat."

Her little joke had gone too far and Mike relit his cigar, standing in the cozy living room. "Do you not see me over here dying a slow death because I can't breathe? Take that thing outside. That's just damn rude and that thing is disgusting." She spoke the words into the bag despite the fact that she liked the woody, sweet cherry smell.

"Tough, babe."

"Get out," she ordered.

He looked her up and down past his flame. He clicked the torchlight shut and took a deep pull, methodically blowing out all the smoke in his body.

"Next time you think you're dying, put a little more effort into it and a lot less drama, okay, City?"

"No one asked for your critique."

"Yeah, well, it seems like you could use some sound advice."

"Not from someone who lives among some trees and old cabins. You probably only talk to people during vacation season. And I don't believe for a sec you 'forgot' to tell me about the air."

He was very shocked that she could hit so close to home. He was accustomed to the woods and less comfortable talking to people. He liked the isolation of his existence. And he did forget that part of the speech on some level so he would have an excuse to come to her rescue. But the rain-dance remark was thoughtless. He walked out of the cabin with a trail of heavy smoke in his wake.

"You're wrong, City," he said from outside the doorway. "I just know how to pick my battles better'n you."

She slammed the door and stomped into the kitchen. She tossed one of the prepared meals into the oven and went into the bedroom, trying to dismiss all thoughts of Mr. Walker from her mind. He was such a compelling creature. Something about the way he spoke to her put fire in her veins, making her feel alive, like when she first opened Utopia. But her mind insisted it had to be merely a physical attraction. Walker was her complete opposite, rugged and outdoorsy while she was sleek and refined. He was a domineering person, just like herself and she could imagine giving up control to him. Letting him ravage her body and make sexual demands of her. Giving up a certain amount of control could be fun, she thought, considering it would be only temporary and on her terms. There was no harm in casual dating. So perhaps dawdling with the man could have some benefits. She would enjoy her little adventure and then move on. But her life had been Utopia and she had no clue as to what her lifestyle was without it.

Chapter 12

Mike stood just a few feet away from the cabin. He told himself he was going to wait and make sure she was all right, and that this was as good a place as any to finish his cigar. When he first left on his evening walk it was to check on the few occupied cabins. He thought a shower and a fresh change of clothes was in order in case any of the guests wished to talk to him. Except that wasn't part of his regular routine. He usually shied away from contact after the occupants' initial arrival. The entire staff was trained to handle any crisis that might arise. But when he headed to Jesse's cabin, he secretly hoped she might be out.

He'd just been lazing against a tree smoking his cheroot when she came stumbling out the front door clutching her chest. He realized immediately that her lungs were not yet adjusted to the air and that a panic attack was in the making. When he put out the cheroot and went to her side he was secretly thrilled when her body molded so perfectly to his. He liked that she allowed him to be close without flinching and fighting. He found the skin at the nape of her neck to be soft and the muscles yielding as he trailed his fingers back and forth.

With her hair tangled around her face she looked like a scared little girl, making him want to take her in his arms. He'd wanted to rush her to the clinic but the venom in her voice made him feel stupid for even showing mild concern. As long as she was quiet, she was like a beautiful wood nymph—silky cinnamon skin, thick, firm legs, defined arms, round ass, cute curls and those slightly parted lips—but her mouth possessed a forked tongue. If only he could kiss that tongue to still it. He pulled the leather thong out of his hair with one savage tug and shook out his long black mane.

Through the window Jessica saw the wind lift his hair as if it was a living, breathing thing. It swirled about in a magnificent tempest until he blended into the darkness, so naturally and completely that he finally disappeared. She looked at the clock and saw that it had been forty-five minutes since she tossed him out. She didn't know why he had stayed out there for so long except that maybe he figured she'd come running out after him begging for his assistance if she felt dizzy again. But after her deluxe Utopia meal, she felt fine. She felt strong and independent as she turned from the window, after checking for him a second time. "Neanderthal," she said.

She prepared for bed, anxiety-free. She picked up her brush to do her hair when she realized she no longer possessed the high-maintenance hair she had had for the better part of her life.

"A foot of hair just gone," Charisse, her hairdresser, had said, spinning her around to get her first look in the mirror, three days before Jessica's departure from the city. "Now it will be doing someone else some good." It was going to be turned into a wig for someone who needed it after chemotherapy. The idea came to her when watching *Waiting to Exhale*. Angela Bassett's character sells all her ex's clothes, burns some stuff and cuts off her hair.

She placed the brush back on the bathroom counter and leaned closer to the mirror. "God, I love this hair." She vigorously shook her ear-length ringlets, laughing like a schoolgirl. The unusual color of red that she had dyed her hair enhanced her natural brown skin tone. She scooped the curls on top of her head into a rubber band, turned off the bathroom light. She tossed herself high into the air like a kid onto the king-size mattress and found herself dozing off in a matter of minutes.

The first images in her mind were those of Walker coming up the steps of the cabin, his hair blowing wildly in the wind and her opening her arms to him. He didn't speak and she was glad that his words couldn't ruin the moment. She slid her body into his and he was open and receptive. His head tilted toward her and she closed her eyes to receive whatever he was willing to give.

When Jessica awoke early the next morning she felt as content as a cat. She stretched beneath the pale shafts of sunlight peeking through the window and rolled over to find ruffled empty covers. Her dream had been so real, she expected to find Walker's beautiful body dozing next to her.

Her breakfast was simple: toast with scrambled eggs and coffee, the first meal she'd cooked on her own in a long time. While attending restaurant school she had acquired all the necessary skills to cook, she just never had the patience to make it cuisine. As a teenager she helped her mother prepare holiday meals and her father barbecue. She would create appetizers with sauces and dips that were raved about by her family and friends but nothing that could qualify as restaurant quality. She assumed she'd lost those basic skills after spending so many years eating the cuisine from Utopia and going to tastings and restaurants. But now she figured it was just like riding a bike.

Jessica also decided that instead of sitting around she could go out and exercise and take off some of the pounds that managed to settle happily around her middle and her thighs. She threw on some comfortable sweats, grabbed a bottle of water, tossed a towel around her neck and headed out the door into the woods toward the lodge. She decided to check out the workout room that was on the phone list. Although the sun wasn't fully in the sky Jessica soon felt hot and sweaty. The path twisted and turned so often, she quickly found herself just wandering around, with muscle cramps and aching feet. She had to struggle uphill and swat branches out of her way while going through dense patches of brush. "Who needs a gym when you can burn off the calories just getting there?"

Jessica stopped to have some water and wipe at the sweat on her brow while trying to decide which way to go, since she could no longer see her cabin or the lodge. She was grateful she had set out early because she had a sneaking suspicion it might take her all day to find her way to civilization, so she decided to slow her pace, relax and enjoy the splendors of her temporary home.

The tall trees glowed in several hues of green. The

different scents created enjoyably subtle fragrances. She admired several blossoming plants that she couldn't believe grew flowers in such shaded areas. She was about ready to sing a happy song when a snake slithered past her and sent her running until her heart was in her throat. She coughed until her lungs did a reenactment of the night before. She breathed as deeply and steadily as she could. She walked through a swarm of gnats and felt as though they were now nesting in her hair and ears, but tried not to let that get to her. She was scratched and smacked by branches that no one bothered to cut back out in the wild. Bees of all sizes and shapes flew directly at her face. Some of the plants made her itch and she began to worry that she had run through poison ivy while trying to get away from the snake. She managed to get pebbles in her sneakers and sand in her socks. At that moment, she desperately wanted her concrete jungle, with its rats, roaches, loud music and the smell of rotting garbage.

She heard voices faintly emanating from the trees and headed toward them, hoping to get some directions either to her cabin or the lodge. The closer she got, the more threatening the two gruff voices sounded.

"Young man, you should be reported to the manager for such insolence," a voice boomed.

Then a voice very familiar to Jessica retorted, "I'm not your personal valet and I'm not getting paid to coddle you. This is the wild, not the Ritz-Carlton, so don't expect that money is going to get you a whole hell of a lot of cooperation when a bear has broken down your door and is eating at your kitchen table." His nasty rhetoric was the same to everyone.

A woman's calm voice was then heard saying, "Gerald, dear, this is no way to start your vacation."

"This isn't a vacation, it's a step before they hoist *forced retirement* on me. They may have said, 'Here, go to the cabin for a few weeks and enjoy yourself,' but this is their way of telling me, 'Next stop, old folks' home, Gerry, old pal.'"

"Mr. Fitzbon, that isn't my concern. Your company sends plenty of business my way and as a favor I said I would contact them upon your safe arrival. Now, if you'll be quiet and let me do my spiel, each of us can spend the next few weeks carefully avoiding each other."

Jessica heard the telltale beep of a car alarm being activated. "No need for the car alarm, Gerry, old pal, no one to hear it but you and the pretty missus. No need to lock it either, no one around for a quarter of a mile or better, which is no morning stroll if you're trying to tote someone's belongings on your back. And if the animals want in they won't use the door . . ."

Walker's comment echoed in Jessica's ears. It would seem she'd wandered a quarter of a mile or more away from her cabin, considering she didn't walk in a straight line. And as much as she hated asking Walker for anything, he was currently the only one who could steer her back to her cabin with the least amount of walking. She started again toward the voices when she heard twigs breaking behind her. She turned in horror, thinking a bear or some other wild animal was about to attack, when she heard voices.

"I can't believe you expect me to do all this walking every morning."

"Zak, I didn't expect you to do anything. You offered to go fishing with me. But next time you stay home. You scared away all the fish with your constant talking . . ."

"I was singing."

" . . . And managed to complain nonstop since we left the lake. So do me a favor and don't volunteer to walk with me anywhere unless invited."

"I like fishing."

"I know, but you like fishing on the yacht, with a $250 rod, other guys cheering you on, with beer and chips and stories about how the big one got away. This is water-hole, Tom-and-Huck stick fishing."

"You're right, Lion, this isn't for me." Upon seeing Jessica, they stopped. "Lion, have we fallen down a hole somewhere and stumbled onto Alice in her wonderland?"

Jessica watched the two men as they came down her path, and had waited until they were in hearing distance before speaking. "I'm not Alice, but I am lost."

"Hello, Lost, I'm Zacharias Fallon and this is my fishing buddy, Lionel Randolph Prestwick the Twelfth," the thin, frazzled-looking, pale Caucasian man with white spiked hair said while bowing.

"Ignore him. I'm Lionel Prestwick."

"Cabin Five," Zak interjected.

"Friends call me Lion and so may you if you will tell me your name so we can get on with being friends." Lion extended a brawny, calloused hand toward her, which went with his Santa Claus–like frame that boasted of good living. He too was a white man, and he had slicked-back silver hair with a beard and mustache to match, his skin very tanned.

"I'm Jessica Bishop. Cabin Three, and still helplessly lost."

"Don't worry, we pass you on the way. In fact, I love

that cabin. There used to be a reservationist named Lila, I'd always ask if she could let us have it but she said it isn't a rental," Zak said, offering her his arm as if going to a cotillion, as opposed to a hazardous walk in the wilderness.

"My brother owns the cabin. I'll be staying in it for a few months."

"It'll be nice to have a neighbor we can both see and talk to," Zak said.

"We've been coming here for years," Lion explained further.

"Since our wives died, the kids keep trying to put us in retirement *communities*," Zak said. "So we run away here."

"And we've only seen Mike come and go from your cabin. We just assumed he must live there."

"Mike?" Jessica asked.

"Mike Walker, one-man welcome wagon. Sometimes you'll hear someone call him the Chief," Lion continued. "But I think I could get used to having a young beauty like yourself for a neighbor."

"Thank you," she said, blushing.

"Although Mike is very nice, he certainly isn't full of social grace, now is he?" Zak asked Jessica.

"Don't ask me because I damn sure didn't find Mr. Walker to be very nice, let alone possess graces of any sort."

Both Zak and Lion exchanged looks and then broke into a fit of laughter. "We try not to speak ill of anyone," Lion explained, after a few gulps of air. "We're both trying to be good so we can secure our place in heaven. But that boy is ornery."

"As a bull," Zak added.

"Did he give you the speech, 'No need for the

alarm out here, no one to hear it but me and you. Like they say, if a tree falls in the forest . . ." Lion began, with hands on knees, still laughing.

"Does it make a sound?" the three shouted in their best Michael timbre.

Delighted with her new friends' quirky sense of humor, Jessica allowed the two older gentlemen to escort her home. She laughed their infectious laughter and felt the contentedness of the morning steal over her once again.

talking and sharing an appetizer. He asked if he could get a few shots of her outdoors before he left.

Walker came by with attitude stamped across his brow, watching the two in the lovers' stance. "This looks cozy," he commented, as Yusef snapped shots of them posed against a tree.

"Good, that means it doesn't look contrived," Yusef answered.

Jessica threw back her head and laughed at something Sam said.

"Now *that* looked contrived," Mike said loud enough so that Jessica and Sam could hear him.

"Hey, Chief, didn't see you walk up. Long time no see. How're you doing? How's business?" Yusef asked.

"Fine and fine."

"Just fine?" Sam had offered his hand to Mike, who refused, showing dirt-stained hands. "Business could be booming. You've got a great story staying here at the lodge. This woman is walking publicity for this place."

"Stop with all the flattery." Jessica swatted at Sam flirtatiously.

"Great shot!" Yusef encouraged.

"It's not a big deal," Jessica said.

"Sure isn't. I've had plenty of folks more famous'n her stay here," Walker said.

"But none as charismatic," Sam informed him.

"Or photogenic," Yusef stated.

"The place does plenty of business. How 'bout you put that in your article," Walker said, turning to walk away.

"That's good for today, guys. I'd like to get some shots of you on one of the walks you mentioned, maybe meet some of the people you've made friends with. And, Chief, maybe you'd take a pix or two with Ms. Bishop," Yusef said, putting his equipment away.

"Not likely, Yusef," Jessica interjected, looking Walker hard in the eye, "unless you have something to barter."

"Yeah, free publicity. Chief? Can I interview you for the article? Maybe get a nice quote from you about having 'the famous' Ms. Bishop staying here?" Sam asked, flashing his winning smile.

Walker met her gaze although his words were directed at Yusef and Sam. "I told you she's not the most famous guest of the lodge. Check with Lila. She handles publicity. There are shots of the landscape you might want to use, and the names and photos of some really famous faces. 'Sides, she knows as much as I do about this place. I have more important things to do than stand around posing for pictures." Walker broke eye contact and started off again.

"That reminds me, I have a staff meeting in the morning, maybe you'd like to come to the *Sayetteville Sound* offices to finish the interview?" Sam asked, lightly draping an arm around Jessica's waist.

Mike swore he heard Sam's clothes brush up against Jessica, and turned around. The current in the air crackled as Jessica and Mike locked gazes for the second time in as many minutes. "Certainly, that sounds wonderful," she answered.

"I can have a car pick you up around ten. Meeting ends around ten thirty. I can finish with my questions, introduce you around, give you a tour, maybe meet my boss and we could have lunch together."

"Perfect," Jessica answered, not really paying Sam any attention. She was too busy watching Walker's face get harder.

"It's a date," Sam said, dropping a friendly peck on Jessica's cheek.

Walker's gaze narrowed as if he had laser vision.

"After your lunch I'll follow you up here, okay, Jessica? Sam, grab this for me," Yusef said, well aware of the growing tension between Jessica and Mike even if Sam was not. He was too old to break up any fights or save poor Sam's life. "I'll bring my wife and kids to play background guests and we'll get you doing some hiking and nature stuff," Yusef added, handing Sam the keys and a bag. "Hopefully this time it won't look like *posing*. Right, Chief?"

Mike's eyes finally released Jesse. "Like I said, talk to Lila, or you could try Sylvia. But stay out of restricted areas," he said, walking into the lodge. "I wouldn't want anything bad to happen to you guys while on my property."

Chapter 14

Jessica stood outside the lodge, dressed in business casual in order to be in sync with her companion. Jessica was picking imaginary lint from the front of her puffed-sleeve, shirt jacket, waiting for her ride to the *Sayetteville Sound*, when Walker rumbled past her like a locomotive, practically knocking her over, and leaving her in a wake of soot and dust that settled nicely on one side of her clothes.

Jessica followed him to the door, seething, "How dare you!"

Walker looked up, not certain she was talking to him. Then he saw the black dirt all over her outfit as if he had given her a hug instead of rushing past her. She was ranting and raving as she marched toward him. "You oaf. You . . . You . . ."

"Dirty old man?" he asked, raising an eyebrow for effect. It was incredibly funny to see her at a loss for words. He was working very hard not to laugh, which only made matters worse.

"This is not funny," she said with narrowed eyes. "Who do you think you're messing around with?"

"I'm not messing around with you yet, but when I am, you and the rest of the lodge will know it," Mike answered with a smirk.

"You'd need at least a week in the shower before I'd touch you."

"Ohhh, low blow," the desk clerk hissed from across the room.

Zak playfully slapped her hand and they went back to pretending to mind their own business.

Mike looked around the lobby and saw a small number of staff and patrons watching in horror. He imagined that they saw the little five-foot-six sexy spitfire shouting at the filthy giant, who had thrown dirt on her. He wanted to drag her out of earshot but she finished her tirade. The last he saw was her taut light blue-suited ass marching away from him in a huff.

"Chief, this isn't my place to say . . ."

"Sure isn't, Sylvia, but I know you're gonna say it anyways, so g'won, git it out of your system."

"That was the most boneheaded thing I have ever seen you do," Zak said. "She works for you, I don't," he added, flicking a thumb in Sylvia's direction, "but I'm pretty sure that's what she was going to say, right Sylvia?"

"Yep."

"You practically ran her over, Mike. We saw you through the door," Zak said, Sylvia nodding like a bobble-head doll.

"Very unprofessional, Chief," Sylvia tsked.

"I said I was sorry," Mike said, brushing off soot where he stood.

"Then you laughed at her . . ." Zak said.

"I wasn't trying to be funny, but it was funny," Mike grumbled.

"Not to mention the sexual innuendo . . ." Zak included, shaking his head.

"In front of witnesses to boot," Sylvia volleyed.

"That was some fight," Zak said.

"You need to go after her. Oh, yeah, and tell her we'll handle the dry cleaning. Have her drop the suit with the front desk," Sylvia added.

"Fine. Like I don't have enough to do."

"I'll take care of it myself," Sylvia offered. "You just go say sorry and make the offer."

"I was cleaning chimneys since six this morning, I'm going to take a shower."

"Uh-uh, has to be done now."

"You want me to walk down that hill to go kiss that princess's ass? I don't think so, no one gets special treatment here."

"Are you buggin'? You messed up. If you screwed up with any other guest you'd fix it, so fix this."

He gave Sylvia a look that said she was treading on thin ice. But as usual she ignored his warning. "And tell her not to worry about her meeting. I'll hold the car and call the paper and leave a message that she'll be late, because of *you.*"

"Oh, is that today? Is that why she was standing right in front of the door? I mean, who wears light-colored silk in the forest and then plants themselves in the line of foot traffic? Yeah, go ahead and call 'Squeaky Geeky Sam,' let him know his 'date' has been detained by me."

Sylvia and Zak watched Mike leave, not believing for a minute he had forgotten about Jessica's date with Sam. "I think he took way too much pleasure in passing along that order," Sylvia said.

The door was ajar when he went to knock, so he entered and gave it a hard nudge closed so Jesse would hear him.

"Zak? Is that you? Did you see what he did? And you know he did it on purpose. Five people could stand on those steps with luggage and not get touched. My favorite suit! It flatters my hips while hiding my stomach and slimming the waistline . . ." She walked into the living room buttoning her dress, slipping on ballerina-style shoes and holding a clutch under her arm. She looked up into Mike's smug face.

"You looked good in the suit and in that dress," Mike said honestly. "However, the clothes don't make the woman. I've seen you look just as good in T-shirts and fatigues." He didn't know much about fashion but almost everything she wore accented some part of her full figure. This particular dress had a June Cleaver housewife look. It brought the eye right to the deep V of the neckline, calling attention to the swell of inviting cleavage that cradled a delicate gold chain. The pale violet color was vivid against her cocoa-colored skin.

"How dare you just invite yourself in, and who gives a damn what you think of my clothes, and fu . . ."

Mike didn't want to hear anymore. In one motion he grabbed her by the wrist, gently twisted it behind her back, pulled her into his arms and kissed her soundly. She gave a tiny yelp when her feet left the floor, but his lips silenced her quickly, his body bracing hers. Jessica's head swam with the sensual heat she could feel in the deepest, most delicate parts of her. She felt his tongue running along her lips, his hand wrapped tightly around her waist holding her firmly against him like that first night. Mike felt her body thoroughly give in to him, the genuine passion igniting a flame within him that threatened to burn out of control. Her nipples had turned to stone beneath her dress and he could feel them through the flimsy fabric, his body unconsciously rubbing against them, keeping them taut.

Her hand gripped his back, silently pleading with him for more. Mike's tongue had coaxed Jesse's lips to part. Their tongues began mating in an ancient dance, causing even more electricity to pass between them. He imagined he could smell the scent of her female essence as his tongue plunged into her mouth, acting out what he wanted to do between her legs.

Her ardent response fanned at the fire consuming them both. He made slow love to her mouth, drinking in his fill; then his arm relinquished its desperate hold. Mike pulled away, letting her drift to her feet. He saw the wanting in her face and the thirst he'd awakened between them and he also saw the time and care she'd put into getting dressed for a date with another man.

"There's something for you to think about if you get bored at your meeting." When she didn't respond or move he added, "And I'm sorry about your clothes. Leave your suit and this dress at the front desk. I'll get 'em cleaned for you."

Finally, she blinked herself back to the here and now, she looked down at her dress and saw the black powder. "God damn you, Walker!" she screamed.

But he was already gone.

Chapter 15

Jessica was able to again get washed up and dressed in record time. Sam assured her the delay was of little consequence as long as she had arrived safe, sound and in good spirits. His interviewing technique was equally refreshing. Sam asked questions as he gave the tour, gathering information through informal communication. He wasn't concerned with gathering facts, figures or statistics. He wasn't a prisoner to research, notetaking or direct quotes.

"I can learn much more about you as a person by spending a few days with you than I could by reading a million articles. In fact, I'm supposed to be reviewing a restaurant in Waynesville this weekend, how about you go with?" When she hesitated he sweetened the deal. "I'm filling in for the food critic and I admit I love to eat but having you offer your critique would be more credible. And it also helps me to see your talented palate at work."

"I have plans to do some sightseeing with two friends of mine."

"The gentlemen you told me about? They sound

like fun. I'd love to meet them. Bring them along. I'll have Yusef bring his wife so you won't feel outnumbered. Is it a deal?"

"You don't make it easy for a girl to say no."

The restaurant gave them a semiprivate VIP room. Yusef told stories as interesting as Lion's, with Zak's flare. Sam and Yusef's wife, Fatima, seemed to add fun facts and historical filler to the evening. Jessica didn't answer any probing exposé-type questions or reveal much if anything about her private life.

Sam drove Jessica back to the cabin. He helped her out of the car casually, suggesting they have a seat inside. Although Jessica didn't see anyone she felt a change in the air, the singular cheroot scent wafting over her, the heat of him somewhere just beyond the gravel drive. Walker was out there watching them. Catching her unawares, Sam laid a gentle kiss on her cheek, placing a cautious hand on her waist. He leaned in and gave her a wholesome peck on the lips that most women would have considered sweetly romantic. For Jessica it was nice but little else. Jessica felt the wind whip the hem of her dress and cause the trees to do a dance. Nocturnal animals all seemed to be talking at once. Looking out into the woods she could have sworn a path was being cleared and Walker was on it.

She placed a placating hand to Sam's chest, giving him a firm good night. She didn't believe Walker was going to reveal himself, let alone intervene, but she was uncomfortable with Sam's advances. And bothered that Walker may have been a witness to them.

Jesse stood alone on the porch, the moonlight casting a flattering glow across her skin, bathing her in iridescent light. She was stunning in a simple black dress; the contrast of shadow and light emphasized each curve and dip of her delicious silhouette.

"Are you here to make sure I get inside safely, Mr. Walker?"

He stepped into the circle of moonlight. He was closer than she had expected, but he emerged from the spot she had been looking at. Mike hadn't been spying but happened upon them when going to check the cabin. His feet propelled him forward with the intent to hurt Sam. By the time he reached the edge of the clearing Sam was in his car, pulling off. "It's my job to check on the guests in the cabins. Make sure everything's all right for the night." His hair hung down below his belt. He looked freshly showered, the ends of his hair slightly damp and curled. He was wearing a stark-white shirt, crisp dark jeans and heavy work boots. "Did you have a good night, Jesse Ruth?" he asked, moving toward her, the smell of his cheroot engulfing her.

"Yes, I did. We went to the newly renovated Horizons." Her eyes never left his face, the dark shadows now being softened by the moon's illumination. He walked with a strong sense of self. It was impossible to turn away. Jesse was tempted to reach out and touch the firm jaw, run a finger across his thick brows, or sink her hands into his thick mass of waves. Instead she curled her hand into a fist, the nails biting into her palm, fighting the urges.

"Never heard of it." He walked up the steps without making a sound.

"Formal attire is a must, and half the staff speaks only French," she said haughtily.

Mike pulled on his cheroot, thinking he should have been annoyed with her pompous attitude but he wasn't. He blew smoke away from her and put out his cheroot. Jessica continued, trying to keep her nerves from jumping at his closeness. "We had appetizers of Bar-B-Que Rock Shrimp over Creamy Grits. The soup was Roasted Butternut Squash and the salad was Salmon Caesar with Meyer Lemon Truffle Anchovy Vinaigrette. The main course was Blackened Catfish with wild mushrooms . . ."

He wrapped his arm around her waist, closing the distance that separated them. "Pretentious," he said, letting his tongue lightly trace the outline of her lips. He leaned back and whispered in her ear, "Those are just uppity words for food I cook right here at home." His breath brushed her hairline and then he drew his tongue lightly around her earlobe, savoring the taste of her. "They use that hoity-toity language for the tourists so they can stick a high-falutin' price tag on stuff I grow in the yard." Mike widened his stance to lower himself to better reach her neck. His touch and tone were hypnotic and she found herself a willing hostage in his possessive grip. She fit perfectly between his powerful legs. Jessica felt his hardened manhood pressing up against her stomach. He nudged her head to one side, trying to identify her perfume, until he figured out the heady scent was natural fragrance coming from someplace lower. He needed to find out if it were as sweet as her skin. The air was sultry between them, her head spun with the sensations he was creating. Jessica felt the wetness pooling in the crotch of her panties. Walker was doing things not just to her body but to her mind as well. She could no longer recall what she had been saying or where she was standing. All she could think of was him. Not just the beauty of his face and body, but also the pull of his will. Jesse no longer wanted to resist, and something inside her just let go. It was as if he'd patiently waited for that one moment to touch her, to kiss her, to remind her of her power as a woman. His hands began roaming the hills and valleys of her body, and she gripped his arms to keep from falling because her knees were no longer capable of holding her up. His large, calloused hands continued following the outline of the delicate sheath from her hips to the dip of her waistline until he was touching the outside of her breasts, his thumbs running along the underside and brushing very close to peaks that puckered. Then he was raising her hands above her head and touching the sensitive skin along the inside of her arms, his face so close. Mike was luxuriating in the feel of her velvety skin, admiring her deep and even color that looked so good against his. He was watching his hands on her skin and she was watching him, his eyes studying her form with a mixture of pleasure and awe, as if he was cherishing every small piece of her. She felt the wall of the cabin at her back and his hand pulling up the hem of her skirt while his body slid down.

He swore she was wearing stockings but he was wrong. His hands came in contact with her satin flesh and his lips were forced to follow. Jessica felt his hands moving up her thighs while kissing and licking all the places the moon could not. He found a tiny spot at the bend of her knee that sent her swooning; he then nibbled on the supple flesh of her inner thigh and the small shockwaves were heightened as he dug his fingers into her rounded butt cheeks. She gasped when he removed her panties in one swift motion. Mike removed her shoe and massaged her instep while kissing her high arch. His lips found their way to her shapely calf and slowly, almost reverently, moved up to the spot that begged for attention. He had placed her leg over his shoulder, opening her to him for discovery. Jessica let out a low moan, seeing him poised before her like a man at worship.

"You're beautiful . . ." he whispered, as his tongue eagerly began tracing the folds, his large, calloused fingers spreading her wider for his mouth's sensuous exploration, sending shivers through her that reverberated back to him. Mike's tongue sought a liberal dose of the nectar that had previously teased his nostrils. Her body undulated, her moans grew louder as she pushed onto his face, nearly throwing them both off balance. He grabbed her hip with his other hand, pressing her back against the wall, raising her off of the ground. This also exposed the nub that had been tucked away. His mouth was immediately drawn to it. He lightly flicked his tongue over it and her body arched away from the wall as if she had just been struck by lightning. He then gently rubbed it with the pad of his thumb. The new sensation of the rough texture of his fingers against her tender flesh sent shocks of intense pleasure through her. He looked up to see the ecstasy on Jesse's face when he heard her panting uncontrollably. He buried his face between her legs capturing her clit between his lips, nibbling lightly while alternately sucking. Her body did a series of convulsive moves and her hands buried themselves in his hair as she pushed herself deeper into his mouth.

"Don't stop," she breathed, "oh, God. Oh, God." Mike wanted to watch her cum, and Jesse didn't feel the floorboards or hear them creak when he put her down with ease. He slowly stood up, his fingers still in her keeping pace, "Jesse, show me what I do to you," he whimpered and his mouth sought hers, his erection pressed against her, and then he felt her body grip his fingers, pulling them deeper within her heated wetness; she gripped his arms in desperation as she oozed her completion onto his hand, her whispering smothered in the kisses they shared. Reluctantly he pulled himself away from her He wasn't done with her, yet. In fact, he somehow felt that he'd probably never be done with her. She was his now, and what was his stayed his.

Mike helped her fix her dress, and set her down on the porch swing, and slipped her shoe back on. He jumped the rail, landing without a sound, and walked off back into the forest, the same way he came.

Chapter 16

Jesse didn't think she could ever face Mike again. She simply could not believe she'd allowed that to happen. For God's sake, she didn't even know the man—didn't even like him! Jesse groaned with shame at the thought of them outside in the open air, plainly visible to anyone walking by, and she having the longest, most intense orgasm of her life. Mike coerced, confused and annoyed her. He was bullheaded and a downright pain in her ass. And yet, she knew the moment they'd shared was so much more than she'd ever thought possible. He'd looked inside of her with those crystal gray eyes and broke down invisible barriers that let him into parts she'd thought long dead, parts she'd never even knew existed. It scared her. The solution was simple—she'd avoid him.

One evening, Sam suggested they have a nightcap at the lodge after attending a local News Media Awards Ceremony. It was very late and she expected Walker to be out in the woods checking cabins. But no sooner were they seated at the bar than Walker came in and, locking his gaze on Jesse, seemed to be on a straight path towards them. Luckily, a silky-haired woman intercepted him. Jessica felt a spike of envy when the woman laid a hand on his chest and he looked down into her eyes. The petite woman squared her shoulders and said a few words to Mike. She then walked off towards the kitchen. Jesse felt him draw breath and hold it. He stared directly at her, his gray eyes intense and stormy.

Jessica turned to Sam and said that she felt it prudent to turn in for the night. Sam tried another physical overture that she easily rebuffed. In the following days, the ever-attentive Sam Evers invited her to go sightseeing, out to the theater, and to the movies. When she tried to politely decline, he always added that he needed to spend time with her to get a better sense of who she was for his articles.

Sam stopped by Jessica's cabin early one morning to extend a personal invitation to a dinner party at his house. She told him she wouldn't make his private affair, explaining that she felt this was more than the articles and she wasn't ready to commit to the type of relationship she thought he was looking for.

"It's Mike, isn't it?" he asked.

"What?" she asked.

"Don't be embarrassed."

"Why would I be embarrassed?" she asked, wondering if maybe Sam had come back that night and seen them on the porch.

"For being attracted to the Chief. A lot of the women want him. His looks, his body, his money, his title, his hard persona, I don't know, but it's always something with women and the Chief."

"I don't know what you're talking about," she said, her indignation evident.

"The other night in the lodge bar, I saw the look on his face when he saw us together and you had the same look when you saw Lila try to stop him from ruining our night."

"That was Lila? The lodge manager, who just had the baby?"

"One in the same." Sam could see the relief on Jessica's face. "I was hoping you would give us a chance to build a solid foundation. But it wouldn't matter. The two of you are destined, like it's written in the clouds."

"I'm perfectly happy as I am. I don't need a man to complete me and certainly not a man as repugnant as him."

Without further argument, Sam chuckled and said, "Can't blame a man for trying," and left.

She took a long shower and changed into a peasant-boy shirt, cargo pants and her favorite beat-up sandals.

As she passed Walker on her way to the restaurant she heard him mutter, "Your boyfriend get tired of your overbearing ass? I saw the shrimp drive off with his smile a little crooked. You finally let that worm off the hook? Remind him what a big fish he is in a small pond and no way could he get a barracuda like you?" He handed her messages to her, effectively stopping her if his comments didn't.

"What's with the fish thing? And he's not my boyfriend. He's doing a series of articles for you and Gideon. You'd think you could be more gracious instead of always scowling at him." She arched a brow. "And how do you know him so well?"

"Raised round here just like me. Sam's homegrown as they come. Star athlete, Homecoming King, valedictorian, graduated from the local college in three years instead of four, found an apartment, got himself a car and fell in love with the prettiest girl in town. He moved into his parents' house when they died. Big ranch style, with the white picket fence, plenty of bedrooms for rug rats, and has been working on the paper since he started delivering them at the age of nine. His girlfriend left then, pastel dresses and flower gardens were not her forte."

Something in Walker's voice caught Jessica's attention. She looked at him closer. "You came between them?"

"You got it wrong, Red. He couldn't keep the prom queen then and I reckon you were more than that Boy Scout could handle now." Mike's gaze stroked over her as if he was touching her with his hands. She plucked at her shirt in an attempt to get the air-conditioned air to cool her, but his look created unfathomable walls of heat around them. It was as intense as the moment when he first kissed her, his body an impenetrable force pulling her to him, her body unable to resist what his was offering.

"Men can complicate one's life," Jessica said in a husky voice.

"That boy is like stopping to tie your shoelace. There's nothing complicated about it, and it don't take much real effort."

"It's business." Jessica laid down the messages she didn't need at the moment and turned to walk off.

"You read his articles? Journalism 101," Mike said, watching the snug fit of her pants, his temperature having risen ever since she started touching her clothes. She was as palpable now as she was the night on the porch and all he had to do was lick his lips to recall her feminine taste. Jessica heard triumph creep into his voice.

"How do you know about that, Mr. Walker?"

"Sam's been writing for one local paper or another including our high school *Gazette*. If'n you ask me, he hasn't improved much." Mike moved from behind the desk, standing as close as he dared, allowing them both to be engrossed by the heat of their banter without being swept away.

"Don't worry, Mr. Walker," Jessica said, stepping back from him. He was suddenly stealing the air from her lungs. "I enjoyed catering to your friend's strengths." She paused, feeling his gaze turn cold, the abrupt change wiping the smile from her face. This was not a battle she wanted to have. Unconsciously, she took another step back. "The stories are light-hearted, funny, entertaining pieces."

"Nothing like you." Mike's hand went to rub his chin.

"I, Mr. Walker, am like nothing you'll ever see."

"So, Jesse Ruth, you think of everything, do you?" Mike goaded.

"I try to. However, I can't seem to figure out a way to avoid you." Before she was able to get in that final barb, Michael Walker was moving at a brisk pace toward the doors. Somehow she always saw the back of him first and she was determined to soon be the first one to leave one of their exchanges.

Jessica made her way into the lodge dining room to meet up with Zak and Lion. They had a great breakfast and it seemed as if they touched on every imaginable subject.

Jessica gushed about her first antique purchase as she walked with Zak and Lion back to their cabin. "The porcelain tub I bought isn't scheduled to be delivered until tomorrow. I'll have to make this an early night so I can make room for it."

"Good, 'cause you've been putting a cramp on our bedroom time." Zak grabbed Lion's arm while giving Lion a lusty eye.

Jessica stiffened. "What?"

"Zak, why didn't you just slap her across the face? Might have been less of a shock."

Zak looked at Jessica's wide-eyed expression. "My goodness, didn't you have any idea?"

Jessica shook her head.

"And you didn't tell her?" Zak accused Lion.

"Sorry, precious," Lion offered while holding her hand, "I should have said something at one of our morning outings."

"Yeah, you should have. You've had more than enough time," Zak said.

"Not everyone needs to know," Lion said, directing his comment at Zak.

"I don't see the big secret."

"Does Gary know yet? You've had more than enough time, Giselle has been dead for fourteen years."

"He's my son, Lion, and a football player to boot. Lay off! I don't see you yelling from the rooftops," Zak said, in a real tizzy.

"What I do in my bedroom is my business," Lion huffed.

"I just didn't . . ." Jessica said.

"We're two elderly men, coming to the mountains together for the past eight years. Hint, hint," Zak said in a dramatic flurry of snapping wrist action. "Sometimes you act like Lois Lane. She works with the guy day in and day out and can't see that even with those stupid glasses on he's really Superman, c'mon."

"I'm supposed to assume your sexuality because you vacation together? I don't know how you spend the rest of the year."

"Didn't you assume we were straight?" Zak asked.

"Because you're both widowers. You've both had wives, and children. But I would never speculate about your sexuality beyond that because . . . I don't want to have a picture in my head of either of you having sex. It's kind of like catching my parents," Jessica said helplessly and shrugged her shoulders.

Lion gave a bark of laughter. "We've defiled a few trees and lakes, too."

Lion's mention of outside "activities" reminded Jessica of her own with Walker.

"Good, she's seen the error of her ways, she's changed, she's grown . . . Now, can we please talk about me?" Zak announced.

Chapter 17

Jessica half-listened to Zak and Lion's simple chatter that did remind her of her own parents' bickering: loving, considerate and light-hearted. She was glad to see them being free about who and what they were to each other.

"Pooh. I'm telling you if I had a shop we could do twice as much business."

"Maybe, or you'd find yourself with a lot more babies."

"What about babies?" Jessica asked.

"His flowers. He gives them names, calls them his babies, then won't sell the little bastards."

"But you buy all kinds of odds and ends, and never find rhyme or reason for it all," Jessica said.

"I do woodworking. Whatever I'm in the mood for making, I finish and glaze and sometimes airbrush or paint the items. Zak decorates with all the stuff we buy on the road. Shows people all the multiple uses, and we can drive up the price," Lion said. "And Zak's flowers. The man can raise cactus in Alaska. Some of the prettiest stuff you ever saw."

"For sixteen years my wife and I owned and ran a flower shop. My garden is the only one with exotic foliage," Zak gushed.

Jessica couldn't deny that. She often wondered how they managed to keep their garden in full bloom in the middle of the rough woodlands. When they arrived at Cabin Five, Zak was running on about the garden, explaining planting techniques and special care provided so the plants could thrive with one another despite the different climates they were accustomed to. "Let's go in so you can see where we work."

Jessica had never gone past the kitchen. She stole a glimpse into the master bedroom as Zak propelled her to the back of the house. She could see the massive dark furnishings that reminded her of Lion, each piece a cranberry-red shellacked to a glossy, mirror-like shine. The accents were done in beiges, golds and creams while roses subtly graced the odds and ends in the room. The comforter, sheets and curtains combined all the colors in thin stripes or paisleys and yet the minor contrasts all harmonized.

"Fabulous," she said.

Zak beamed. "Lion did all the woodworking himself. I decorate, of course, but I figured this was so manly that the flowers wouldn't appear too feminine."

"You know, it's a refreshing use of patterns. I always thought patterns were just too busy for my tastes but after seeing how you pulled it all together, I might steal a few of your ideas."

"Just ask and we can decorate together." Zak led her into his exclusive room. "This is my paradise." The room held decorative, hand-painted, one-of-a-kind pots of flowers in various stages of growth. The pots were wood, ceramic and metal, each perfectly suited to a particular plant style or flower color. Suddenly Jessica wanted her secret room to be a greenhouse. "My God, does Lion do pottery too?"

"Every meticulous piece is handcrafted. If not by him, then by someone. Lion complains that pottery takes too much time. It doesn't speak to him the way wood does. There's a girl downtown who does most of the stuff."

The view of the forest was an incredible backdrop for the plants, just like the greenhouses she'd seen on television. The temperature was warmer in some areas than others, she noted as she moved around. The scents that assaulted her ranged from the delicate smell of spices mingled with flowers to the pungent odors of earth and wood.

"Lion did this room with all of my fondest wishes in mind," Zak added, following her gaze up and down the room.

"More like his incessant whining," Lion said, giving Jessica a gentle nudge from behind in order to get her moving from the spot she had suddenly become glued to. "Mike was kind enough to have the greenhouse put on. Said it would only increase the value of the property. As much as I tease Michael, he's a good guy."

"That is totally a subjective statement," Jessica flatly stated.

"He may keep to himself but he isn't the ogre people seem to think he is. He's kind of like a knight without all the hoopla. He knew we couldn't afford to buy this place because our pensions barely cover the cost of rental, so he gives us a break. He even lets us renovate whenever we like."

"We don't even bother with paperwork. We keep

our key, come and go as we like," Zak said while snipping at plants. "I wish the man were more friendly, but Mike doesn't do friendly."

"I like him. He's just being himself," Lion went on.

"It's true," Zak agreed when he saw Jessica's skeptical look. "He's too comfortable with himself to be a false person, which is to be commended, but he doesn't make fast friends with that thinking."

"Not hardly," Jessica added.

"He had to have worked nights and paid Zak's ramblings at least an iota of attention to get it all just right," Lion said. "So secretly, he'd have to care."

"You cared. He was just along for the ride." Zak threw his arms around Lion, who shrugged him off.

Jessica smiled lovingly at the two men, not feeling the least bit uncomfortable spying on this affectionate moment. She started thinking of herself and how Eric viewed her. To him, she was a means to an end. She had just enough contacts to cement his position in the high society world. He also thought she was cold. Her friends might disagree. But either way, she shouldn't be criticized for being herself. Maybe Lion was right, Walker wasn't rude, just matter-of-fact. He could look at you or through you, but he always heard you. He always got you your end result. And hadn't she been that way? For the first time in days images of Walker flew into her mind uninhibitedly. His confident stance, his self-assured walk, his dominant posturing, and the way he tucked long runaway strands of dark hair behind his ears right before making some snide remark. Even now her body was starting to warm as the distracting images rolled over her. She couldn't remember Eric affecting her in such a way and Sam, as cordial and well-intentioned as he was, did nothing to make her feel like a woman. Walker was an enigma that drew her in and if she wasn't careful she would drown just in the thought of him.

Zak was still talking nonstop and Jessica was trying to pick up the thread that caught her attention. " . . . Oh, yeah, don't look at me like that, the man is fine and women notice. You know, come to think of it, you and your *Mr. Walker* make quite a headline."

"I can see it now: 'Woman kills lodge caretaker and caretaker uses final breath to kill woman,'" Jessica said in her best newscaster voice.

"I was a cop for thirty years. It would have been nice to see a crime with no one left standing, and both murderers accounted for. Less red tape," Lion responded.

"So you prefer Sam's company?" Zak asked.

"No."

"Seems like a nice enough fellow. Steady job, clean-cut, okay in the looks department. Good guy," Lion noted.

"Very, very nice. I'm tired of 'nice.' Neat hair, nice skin, clean shaven, smells pretty, perfectly nice clothes, with all these 'nice' little candy-coated, rose-colored, 'Life is like a box of chocolates' sayings. If I was looking, and I'm not, I guess you could say I'd want a dependable, big city gritty man."

"Well, Mike did spend some time in the Windy City," Zak offered.

"Really? I guess that's why he's hard-headed and self-centered. This is his world and we're just squirrels trying to get a nut." Jessica sucked her teeth. "He's awful."

"Two completely different men and you dislike them both," Lion remarked.

"I don't dislike Sam, I just don't want to date him. Walker I don't 'like,' but I can respect."

"I guess that's something," Lion said.

"Sam is boring but not Mike," Zak added. "I'd much rather talk to Mike."

"It's really more like Zak talks at him than to him. Zak talks, Mike nods and grunts to signal the end of the conversation."

"You like talking to him too," Zak defended.

"Heck yeah, the man's a straight shooter, never pretends to be anything but himself," Lion said. "Talks to everyone like he'd rather be eating a handful of nails than stand there with you . . ."

The two men continued their bantering as Jessica plotted ways to try and cross Walker's path.

Chapter 18

Jesse was waiting at the front desk of the lodge, repeating her given name over and over in her head, trying to adjust to the sound. She had plans to meet Zak and Lion for a game of pool and then brunch. She opted to skip her morning breakfast walk with Lion for the downy softness of her bed. For old guys they stayed up late and drank like fishes, something Jessica Bishop managed to master in order to fit into the "old boys' network," a skill she no longer appreciated or needed.

Jesse managed to acquire a membership to a very old, exclusive men's club. She would have been rejected if it hadn't been for a charter created in 1967, stating that in order for a club to sustain operations within New York City, membership must be open to anyone who qualifies. The charter was never held up for scrutiny until Jessica Bishop.

Jessica had given lavish gifts of robust cognacs, rare wines and aged whiskeys. The club began ordering the exclusive vintages through her company, and her reputation grew as well as her clientele. Utopia became known as a company that could get anything from anywhere in the world for the best price. Eventually the wives of said men began asking after her and her catering firm. Word of mouth caused history to be made. The club made it painfully clear, however, that she was accepted, but not welcome, until, of course, they began benefiting from the publicity.

The idea of being a member of the exclusive club had come from a vague comment that Eric had thrown on the table while trying to create an image for Douglas. It had not been a suggestion for her public persona, but Jessica decided to try. At the time she took pride in being the first African-American woman allowed into the club, as well as being able to drink with the best of them, but no longer. Now, *Jesse Ruth Bishop* preferred the nonalcoholic beverages, with funky umbrellas and neon colors that Zak was so fond of making.

"How can I help you?" the receptionist's sharp voice asked. Jesse noticed her glossy, airbrushed nails flipping through mail quickly, looking annoyed but unhurried. She wore a tight red shirt over round, pert breasts, her jeans fitting like a second skin.

"Hello, I'm Jessica Bishop from Cabin Three."

"Uh-huh," the receptionist grunted without looking up.

"I'm trying to find Mr. Walker."

"Uh-huh."

"You wouldn't happen to know where he is?"

The young woman looked up, pushing straight hair off her creamy-white face. "Nope." She leapt off her perch and with swift hands tossed the mail into each little cubbyhole.

Jesse felt as if this woman was deliberately snubbing her.

"Well, then maybe you could help me," Jesse forged on. "I've been here for over two months and have yet to receive any utility bills. I get letters and junk mailings but no bills."

The girl spun lightly on her feet with a buoyancy that wasn't there before. "Here it is!" she shouted, holding up a pink slip of telephone message paper. "Sorry, I wasn't ignoring you, I was trying to focus. I misplaced an important message for Mr. Humphries and I just got chewed out, but I knew I handed it over to his wife, who now wants to have a 'private word' with *Mr. Walker* about my attitude, which really means she's looking for a reason to talk to Mike alone, while her husband is away handlin' 'business.' You know: shake her breasts, toss her hair, casual touches, anything to get a rise out of him. All the wives do it at some point. Not you, you're not a groupie. If you ask me, he's never paid any woman as much attention as he has you. Sorry, Jesse, Jessica, uh, Ms. Bishop, I should shut up now. What was your question?"

"Groupie?"

"Oh, that. 'Groupies' is how the staff talks about them. Would you believe it? Women get one look at him and all it takes after that is a pleasant word or a nice gesture and they come up here every day trying to lure him to their room or cabin. Especially when the husbands have business to take care of. So the Chief . . ."

"The Chief? Cute nickname."

"No, he's the real deal."

"He mentioned something about Clouds to me?" Jesse was fishing for information without arousing suspicions or fueling gossip.

"Really? That's cool. He doesn't usually tell too many people that he runs the whole shebang. He tries to keep a low profile, but anyone who is born and raised on the mountain has heard of Chief Mighty Cloud Walker."

"And all the guests know him just as Mike?"

"Yup. Mike Walker is his alias, his alter ego, his Clark Kent. It followed him from Chicago. When he first opened the lodge almost all the guests were his old business associates. So what was I saying?" The receptionist flipped subjects like people flipped the remote, but Jessica had gotten an earful already. ". . . Oh, right, so the Chief is constantly being called by these women to change a lightbulb, move a box, find a tool, open a window. It's ridiculous, as if he doesn't have 'real' work to do. It's shameless. And he's so cool. He manages to leave them happy without ever touching them or embarrassing them. Then he stomps back here, and gets pissed at me for sending him on fools' errands. Stuff I should have known that anyone can do. He tells me, 'Lila would've handled it for me.' I say, 'She ain't here, you're stuck with me.' But I know he's just frustrated, he gets pretty busy running this place. But things are so much better when Lila is running the show. But she's preparing for some conference and she just had a baby. She's amazing, you and her will hit it off great, she's like a really cool business chick like you. I can't wait for the summer crowd to pick up. By then they'll hire extra help, and the Chief will go to his cabin and I'll get to waitress more. You don't get tips over here."

Jesse nodded and hoped that the receptionist never found out that she was really looking for a face-to-face with Walker. The last thing she wanted to be was a

Walker groupie. But, Jesse rationalized, her visit was for a legitimate purpose.

"Your question, about the bills, I can answer. All the bills for Cabin Three are taken care of via an account. Everything is paid directly, that was the easiest way for Gideon and the Chief to divvy it up."

"Even the phone bill?"

"It would make sense, but I'm not sure," the girl said slowly. "Look, there's the Chief now, go on over and ask."

Jesse's shoes clicked on the floor as she took ground-eating strides in order to catch up to him without yelling his name. She also didn't want to give herself the chance to back out. "Excuse me, Mike," Jesse said, "could I speak to you a moment?"

He turned, faced her and planted his feet firmly on the ground. His arms were folded across his chest in an unfriendly manner. He held this stance for a long moment, and she was afraid he wasn't going to make this easy. "Speak," he said, throwing down the gauntlet in order to start the first round of battle.

She decided honey would catch this bee. "I've not received any bills since my arrival and Sylvia just informed me . . . that there's an account set up to cover the bills for the cabin. Does that include the telephone bill?"

"Yup." He turned to walk off, concluding round one.

But she shuffled along next to him. "I'd like to deposit money into the account to help cover my expenses while I'm here."

"Not necessary."

He continued moving like water flowing into the

ocean. She couldn't help being physically attracted to the easy way he carried himself.

"I realize that it's not necessary but I would still like to contribute. I'm used to paying my own way."

"Talk to your brother."

"You know he won't let me."

His narrowed eyes pinned her. "He won't let you talk to him?"

"He won't let me pay."

He stopped walking and glared at her. He pushed long strands of his dark hair behind his ears. He spoke in forceful tones like a parent does when constantly repeating themselves to a headstrong child. "Have you asked him already?"

"Well, no, I'm just . . . finding . . . uh . . . out from you," she sputtered uncharacteristically. "But I know he's going to protest." She rushed on, trying to defend her actions. "He'll tell me it's taken care of and not to worry."

"That's because it's taken care of and you don't have to worry." He watched a tempest of emotions play havoc with her features, each more attractive than the last. He had tried his damnedest to keep moving, not to be caught in the onslaught of heat that infused him every time he thought about her. But her determined nature forced him to look into her fathomless brown eyes. Without a thought he went to push a wayward tendril away from her flushed face.

She slapped his hand away before he touched a wisp. "Don't you dare patronize me. I'm not a puppy who needs a reassuring pat on the head."

"You are so wrong." He started to walk off again,

trying to get away from her while the spell was temporarily broken.

"You like being condescending?"

"You like fighting just for the sake of fighting, don't you, Hellcat?"

"If I did I would have gone with my first inclination to punch you in the face."

His laughter was a low rumble bubbling from his chest. She saw his body shake as the laughter picked up momentum and gained in volume. His arms dropped to his knees to help hold himself upright, and people at the far end of the lobby began to gawk in their direction. She was mortified by the spectacle of this giant man laughing at her. He sobered slowly, his laughter dying in his throat, as she suddenly looked like a more formidable opponent. She looked taller, stronger and sleeker than when she had first arrived. He thought she derived power from the words of the threat. The menace in her was palpable. Mike decided to rise to the bait. He dropped his shoulders and moved his face closer to hers. She didn't blink or flinch, most people would have taken a step back, just to get away from his shadow. "You wanna fight me, cool, but I'm not holdin' back," he said, admiring her bravado while looking her up and down.

Jesse pushed out her chest. "I wouldn't hear of it. But don't expect to drop me like bricks, either," she said.

An unbidden image of their bodies hot, naked and sweaty popped into his mind as if she put it there. His body and mind shifted direction. "When you do hit the ground I'll be on you like white on rice."

Jesse leaned forward, exposing rounded cleavage cradled in a peach-colored, spiderweb-thin lace bra. The move ignited a pulsating intensity throughout Mike's entire body. The sound of his blood pounding through his veins was resounding in his ears. His eyelids fluttered shut like butterfly wings.

"Don't play games with me, Mr. Walker, I don't lose well and I win even worse."

His eyes snapped open while she spoke, her face mere inches from his. He saw the flecks of gold in her red curls, skin so flawless no makeup was needed, the way one perfectly arched eyebrow raised up. Those heart-shaped lips that he wanted to still with a kiss; he wanted to hold her close and turn her angry heat into passionate lust. Instead he said, "Don't come looking for me and no one has to win or lose."

Everything about her persona transformed. She went from vicious to gracious, a vibrant smile on her lips, triumph in her voice. "Good. So we have an understanding.

Her smile never wavered, her voice now pleasant, but her eyes were a dark, mysterious brown that gave away no secrets. In business he'd never encountered anyone with his own sincere, forthright approach. It was unnerving and uncanny, especially to find it in a woman. He had to admire her for it, but not right now. Right now he was angry that she had created another public scene, one that he had clearly lost. She put out a hand in truce. "Just walk away, Jesse Ruth. I'm not in the mood for this." Her eyes turned an alluring amber, her stance softening and her smile prettier.

"I'll be on my way now, I have two gentlemen waiting for me. Tah."

She walked off with a spring in her step and left him feeling disturbed and dismissed. Jesse had gotten the better of him, yet he couldn't help but sneak a peek at her gorgeous ass and shapely legs. He finally headed to the front desk after she was gone. Sylvia eyed him suspiciously. "What?" he asked in a hostile tone.

"Nothing," Sylvia sang as she tried to look occupied. "It's just that I haven't seen sparks like that since the Fourth of July. She looks nice, like she's been working out. I like her style, she dresses with flair, without looking like she's trying. She's workin' them jeans . . ."

"I haven't noticed."

"You know she makes a great Ali to your Foreman. You two are really perfectly matched."

"I'm not looking for a sparring partner."

"Well, you could just ask her out." He gave Sylvia such a hard look that she remained quiet as they continued to work side by side. "Oh, darn," she said.

"What now?"

"I forgot to give Ms. Bishop her messages. There's some from New York, lawyer stuff, lots of Mr. So and So's."

"And . . . ?"

". . . And four from Sam."

"What's he want?"

"That's her business," Sylvia answered, watching Mike become agitated.

"They back on?"

"Again, her business."

"Not if I find his ass trespassing on my property."

"Then that would be going way outside of your character to put yourself in her business," Sylvia said, hiding a grin. "Might even land you in jail."

Mike snatched the small pile and began reading.

"You shouldn't be doing that," Sylvia said.

"As proprietor, it's my job to make sure you're doing your job and these look important. Look, Ryan 'expects her at 10 sharp,' that's a local number. Wouldn't want Ms. Bishop to think I'm keeping her from dating."

"A doctor, originally from New York, hoping they could get together for dinner."

"Who are you to be taking down such detailed messages like her personal assistant?" He slammed the stack of pink papers on the counter.

"I have to take detailed messages because we cater to a business clientele, they can't afford to get screwy messages. She's no different."

"She's not here on a working vacation and she doesn't need a matchmaker. Let her follow her path. Alone," Mike remarked.

"Don't start that Indian Sky talk with me, *Ulo gidv*, give it to Lila. You want Sam to stop calling, then go put in your bid. Let it be known you're interested."

"She ain't ready to fly with the Eagles yet."

"You keep walking like a slug and even that guppy Sam will have a shot."

"I told you I'm not into that woman. Too city for me."

"Sam is small town and they seem to have a good time together," Sylvia said matter-of-factly.

"She said she's not dating Sam. Besides, I'm not interested in her like that, now drop it."

The edge had returned to his voice at the mention of Sam's name. He didn't mind old, passive Sam, he just hated the idea that he and Jesse had been spending time together. Sam might get it in his head to fall in love and try something. Jesse might be lonely enough to take him up on it. Mike wanted to be the one she turned to, not just in a brief moment of weakness, but out of a desperate need to be with him. He wanted to possess Jesse, to take her in his arms and make love to her. The moments they shared had only made him long for her more, her body answering his call, her lips pliant. Jesse's stack of messages stared at him, a silent reminder that she was a woman that men noticed and that if he wasn't careful someone else might take her away.

Chapter 19

Jesse ran to the lodge bathroom, splashing cold water on her face. She had woken up every day with a purpose. If she was honest with herself she had different ones each morning that made her feel complete again. She embraced the solitude that had once frightened her, and found friendships, new interests and contentment. But now, because of her encounters with Walker, she felt her newly constructed life unraveling, yet she didn't understand why. Jesse was used to dealing with men. She learned early on that sex was a dangerous weapon. A woman in business should not exploit her sexuality, nor let it make her a victim, and should always wield it with decorum. Being a woman had only once been a weakness. And that one time had been hard to forget.

But this was a different level of play. She was totally out of her element in trying to match her meticulously crafted facade against Walker's raw sexuality. She was attracted to him in ways she couldn't define. His eyes were a maelstrom of metallic-gray anger or liquid silver when he laughed and smiled. Either way, she had dived into elements unknown to her when arguing with Walker just now. When she was near him electric sparks threatened to incinerate her senses. Although she hadn't planned on being that close to him she wanted to feel his breath on her skin, she wanted to see the slightest shift of color in his eyes, she wanted to be close enough to kiss him, a fantasy she could no longer effectively suppress. Her self-control slipped and she could no more stop herself from being drawn to him than she could prevent rain from falling.

Walker was creating havoc in her otherwise organized-and-orderly existence. But wasn't that existence already ruptured? Hadn't she barely been holding it together when she ultimately needed to escape Utopia? Didn't she treat Douglas and Fred as if they were the enemy, when her problems weren't clear-cut and her world was collapsing around her? It was frightening to look into Walker's eyes and see so much of herself there.

He was like a caged animal protecting himself by lashing out at anyone who got too close. It was painful to watch him burn within what she thought was his own manmade hell. She wanted to reach inside him and extinguish the fire. In her dreams, Jessica had seen herself trying to ease his suffering with her entire being focused in one touch. He would become as compliant as a trusting child who had lost his way and fell asleep but awoke in a familiar place. She would hold him close, giving comforting kisses where he was injured and bruised. But the encounter in the lobby was far from a dream. Normally, she would have been elated to turn the tables on a man in a duel of wits, but instead she felt that hollow, empty feeling she had that had driven her out of New York. His pain was raw, like her own, and she managed to expose it. And neither of them was able to soothe it, to put it back in its carefully constructed container, and it threatened to engulf them both. How long had he been alone?

She dried her face and made her way to the recreation room.

Just walk away from this, Jesse Ruth. I'm not in the mood.

A cheery voice beckoned to her. "Ahh, look, Zak, I told you our young, gorgeous companion wouldn't let us down. Hello, *Jesse*. Hello, *Mr.* Walker."

"Actually, it's Jesse Ruth, but Jesse is fine," she said with a smile.

"Didn't know that. Very nice," Lion said.

Mike tossed a head nod in the general direction of the trio. "Zak, I have the power to move you to Cabin Six, you call me that again."

"Lion, Zak, sorry I'm late. I had something to take care of," Jesse said. She could hear Walker harrumph under his breath from across the room.

"We have lived 120 years between us, what's a few minutes more," Lion offered.

"Speak for yourself, old man. I need every precious moment I can steal so let's move it."

"You boys can't convince me you aren't getting younger every day. I attribute that to a healthy dose of me."

"I'm going to the bathroom, get the good table," Zak said.

Lion and Jesse chose their regular pool table in back. "I caught part of that scene of you in the lobby," he said.

"I swear that man can be incorrigible. I had one

thing I wanted straightened out and, bang, we're at each other's throats."

"I know you're not a Walker fan, but let me tell you something he said to me after Zak and I told him about our life. He explained that this is considered God's country. And you really can't hide from God here. It's almost like your thoughts are picked up directly by his network 'cause there's less static. So I'm thinking maybe Mike has found a kindred spirit when he met you. Even if it takes a bit of arguing to prove it to you."

"There's somethin' high-test between you two," Zak said as he came over and set down his drink. "Sylvia's having a hell of a time putting a collar on that bulldog since you arrived," Zak said. All three peered across the room when he stormed out.

"You planning on fighting with the man again?" Lion asked while racking the balls.

"Every chance I get." Zak and Lion smiled knowingly while choosing cue sticks. "And please, call me Jesse from now on. God knows it's time everyone called me by my real name." She winked at Lion. Jesse looked at her reflection and asked, "Do I look like I'm losing weight?"

Jesse spent the rest of her afternoon back in the cabin getting in touch with friends and family. She called Phaedra to tell her about the gourmet café she found in Asheville that carried Utopia frozen meals. Jesse was never certain Utopia meals were as healthy as advertised. But she was seeing the results for herself. The meals and her daily eight-mile walks were melting the pounds off her.

She also called her mother to arrange a visit and tell her about the work she was doing in the back room of the cabin and her weight loss. "I suppose with all that work I was bound to muscle up a bit . . ."

"*Jesse Ruth?*"

"Yes, Mother?" Jesse answered, loving the sound of her name, while flexing her arms in the mirror.

"Are you happy?"

"Yes, Mother."

"Good. When I see you next month I'll tell you if you're losing too much weight," her mother said with a wink in her voice.

Her mother was always direct, succinct and right as rain. Jesse hung up feeling very self-satisfied.

She tried on outfit after outfit, only to find that nothing fit properly. She had never been unhappy with her extra weight but now that it was gone she felt exceptionally good. Another thing she noticed was that the weight had previously masked the proportions of her breasts, hips and backside. She was visibly as curvy as an hourglass, like a pinup girl from the fifties. She was also impressed by the muscle tone she'd developed. Her newly acquired shape was unintentional, considering she was trying to work on her inner self. But it was an appealing side effect. She looked at the giveaway pile and her eyes rested on an original, custom-tailored, suit. It was several shades of blue, in a wonderfully soft velvet, the jacket navy, the blouse neon, the tie a silver blue, the skirt a slate blue, total: $2,200. The suit, hat, scarf, sandals, purse, lingerie, stockings were like new. She held it up against herself one last time and tossed it into the giveaway pile. "Some nice woman will look fab going to church in that thing." Jesse's desire to have her clothes define her was more or less gone.

Jesse also managed to kick her television-news habit, her coffee addiction and her obsession with the stock market, although she was sure she'd gotten Lion hooked. After dinner she had just sat down on the living room couch with a bowl of peaches and whipped cream and a John Saul novel when the phone rang.

"Yup."

"Hello, Sistur," the familiar voice singsonged in her ear.

"Hi, Naomi. What's doing?" Jesse answered.

"Calling to see how your 'sabbatical' is going."

"It's a vacation and it's going well. In fact I've lost some weight," Jesse bragged.

"That's good. You were a very unhealthy size," Naomi replied.

"I was never unhealthy."

"Does that mean you're trying to impress someone? Is there a special someone?"

"Naomi, I came here to be alone." Jesse was getting exasperated.

"'You won't be alone forever, there's a pot for every kettle,' Ma says. I suppose meditating helps with the lack of sex. So, guess who I ran into the other day when I was leaving my meeting at Utopia?"

"Why were you at Utopia?" The question was out of her mouth before she could call it back. Jesse had kept this flaky sibling out of her business. But Utopia was no longer her castle, so what did it matter?

"Umm . . . Faye hasn't told you?" Naomi asked, feigning innocence.

"*Phaedra* doesn't call me to gossip."

"Oh, no, not even about me and Eric? Or about me

designing the new uniforms for the wait staff? Isn't that fabulous?" Naomi enthused.

Jesse ignored the first comment, and instead addressed the uniform statement. "The green, burgundy, gold and white not so stylish anymore?" she asked.

"Just drab. I've spiced them up with gold braided trim, epaulets and signature Utopia buttons. It matches the new image of Utopia as an upscale catering hall. It will be all socialite, corporate and entertainment accounts."

Jesse wasn't exactly up on what was going on, but that was in line with Fred's ideas. "If you'd like I can fax you some photos. I'm also trying to get the contract to redesign the ballrooms and shops. I've never done interior design before but it should be a piece of cake. If you did it, then I should be fabulous at it."

Jesse and Doug had had a hard time designing the original Utopia and all the stores because they both had lots of ideas that weren't practical in application. Jesse took limitless classes in home design, decorating, drafting and every how-to class in construction she could find. Each night she would check over the work done on the warehouse and revise the plans. Jesse had no doubt Naomi didn't have the qualifications to land the job. But if by some twist of fate she did get it, Jesse didn't care because she was living harmoniously in the woods.

She smiled broadly at herself, grateful to have had the opportunity to learn from her mistakes, but she was glad to be away from it all. She was also certain Naomi would not accept any advice from her. "Just e-mail me," Jesse said, thinking about her never-used laptop sitting out in the seldom-used SUV.

This sibling rivalry was a brick wall between them that Naomi refused to stop building and that Jesse no longer bothered to climb, let alone understand. Naomi was a typical statuesque beauty. Tall and thin, long tresses, big, wide-set brown eyes framed by thick curling lashes and perfect cheekbones. A shapely mouth gave her a Lolita quality that caused all types of men to fall at her feet. Her breasts were antigravity devices, she had a milk-and-coffee complexion, and she was a size seven "when I'm bloated." Everything on Naomi seemed perfect, right down to her feet.

Jesse knew Naomi had a distorted way of viewing situations, especially involving those with men. It must have all started the day Naomi was born and the sun rose for the first time. Although Jesse couldn't change her sister, maybe she could change the way they interacted with each other. It was past time she tried.

"Naomi?"

"Yes?"

"Do you remember that summer we spent in Georgia?"

"Yeah."

"And we got caught in that field in the lightning?" Jesse asked.

"Yeah. You were so scared you started crying," Naomi taunted.

But Jesse kept going. "I also remember you and me lying down trying to be small, so the lightning wouldn't get us."

"Yeah, I learned something about that in science class," Naomi explained.

Jesse could practically hear her sister nodding into the phone. "You held me tight, kept telling me stories. One was about how the Clouds were arguing and fighting so much that they created thunder and lightning."

"That was a good one, wasn't it?"

"And then you explained how we needed rain so God could cleanse the earth and we could have a fresh start."

"I was deep even then, wasn't I?" Naomi asked in a nostalgic voice.

"I wrote a paper about how my big sister saved my life . . ."

"You're kidding me." For the first time in a long time Jesse heard her sister laugh a genuine laugh.

"I told anyone who would listen how my beautiful sister was so smart and brave. I was so proud and grateful."

"I guess it can't be any worse than me showing my portfolio. Almost every picture is you and clients you've sent me. I have to admit I love picking out clothes for a woman with an unlimited budget."

This time they both laughed. Jesse could feel another part of her lonely, empty shell fill up with hope.

Chapter 20

Jesse was elated. Her conversation with her sister ended better than she had imagined. They made plans to go shopping in New York and then return to North Carolina together for a visit with their parents. Jesse was so wired she went to the back room to release some energy. Her sanctuary. She started work on installing the toilet and was thrilled when the first flush went off without a flood. She was halfway through with the vanity when the phone rang, yet again.

"Three calls in one evening is excessive for me," she answered in lieu of a traditional greeting.

"Well, if you checked your e-mail more often I wouldn't have to call and disrupt your vacation."

"Douglas!" Jesse shouted. "How are you?" she asked, genuinely glad to hear his voice. Slowly they had begun rebuilding their friendship. And over the past few weeks she'd come to look forward to hearing from him.

"Everything is good."

"We just spoke a couple of weeks ago, didn't we? What's up?" she asked, a frown furrowing her brow.

"Utopia stuff. Can I cry on your shoulder for a minute, not as a partner but as a friend?"

"Go!" she said, shutting down her project for the night.

"Fred is making progress but he's lousy at being you, business is starting to pick up, a majority of the staff stayed, I only closed one store and our stock is viable. You hurt us by taking a break, you know."

Jesse took the cordless and wandered outside. A light, cool rain was beginning just beyond the steps.

"I know what I'm . . ." Jesse stopped abruptly, she was getting sucked back in, in less than a minute, the cold feeling creeping over her, making her joints ache and muscles stiffen. "Doug, you said you needed to vent. I don't want to fight with you." Just that easily she was carried on a dark current into a once-familiar place that was now ripe with foreign dangers.

"This isn't an argument, or a business call or even a 'help, help, help, Underdog.'"

"Whew, I had hoped I wouldn't have to fly back and bail your ass out."

"I think he's trying to do too much at one time. He wants people to see the Fred Tyler touch and not just the Jessica Bishop stamp."

"Yeah, Naomi told me about the redesign."

"Yeah, you would know that if you read your e-mail," he accused.

"Who has time for that when one is communing with nature?"

"I don't know how he advertised but Naomi applied, just like anyone else. He moved her to the top of the pile, because she's your sister."

"I don't subscribe to nepotism but I have faith that you and Fred will make the right decisions where

Utopia is concerned. 'Sides, my sister's good, isn't she?"

"What do I know about fashion? I'm a chef, he's a chef and together we're less than half the business-woman you were. Are."

In the form of jokes and general chatter Jessica outlined some business strategies, in particular utilizing Phaedra's expertise. "So that it?"

"The baby is due soon and Katherine wants to make sure you'll be here for the birth. Her family is giving her grief for insisting you be the godmother."

"Aren't kids supposed to have four godparents?"

"To your good fortune, you're it. We couldn't imagine someone telling you what to do so we decided to spare the other poor saps. Unless you find the perfect person to help you out."

"Right," Jesse answered sarcastically. "I'm just learning how to play nice with others."

"Can't wait to see that."

"I'll make arrangements to be in town at least two weeks before and three weeks after the birth. That will give us plenty of time to talk."

"You said you'd make it to the baby shower. I don't want to have to feed Katherine your empty promises."

"My heart wants me to be there but my body isn't ready to go back to the real world. I've got almost three months to sync them up." Jesse shivered at the thought of leaving this secluded spot. She shivered again against the wind that was now throwing rain at her.

"Katherine and I want to fly down to see you."

"What, you planning on her having the baby here?"

"No, but she swears you don't treat her *special.* Her words, not mine. I think pregnant women deserve special treatment. So she wants to see you, I want to see you, we see you." His voice was no longer accusatory. He was Doug again. "You got room for us?"

"*Mi casa es su casa,*" she answered with a smile.

"And please check your e-mail."

Jesse noticed the driving rain only after she hung up with Doug. The trees swayed forcefully in the darkness that was closing in on the cabin. She located and flicked on the radio. She tugged off her dirty duds while listening to the weather report. She took a brisk shower and threw on a large sleep shirt, fresh out of the dryer. There was no mention of a storm front so she assumed it was speeding through the area undetected. She closed all the windows and carried out all the instructions on the storm list as a precaution. It was just after ten and she was bone weary. She placed the radio back in the cabinet next to the walkie-talkie and looked out at the rain pelting the SUV. It seemed so far away to deal with tonight so she dragged herself to the bedroom muttering, "Damn laptop, I hate e-mail."

Mike Walker was prepared for the flash storm. The eleven o'clock news had predicted 25- to 30-mph winds and at least five inches of rain after the storm was already in "batten down the hatches" mode. far surpassing the predictions. The well-dressed, dry man on the screen standing in a studio pointing at swirling white blotches promised it wouldn't last long as it was moving quickly. He even said damage would be minimal. How Mike wished he could send him a bill. Mike hadn't actually watched the weather report, he instead had watched the sky all day. He watched the efficient flight of the birds leaving the area. He noted a similar migration in the land animals. Smaller animals had begun to collect food and burrow. At about eight, the wind changed direction and speed. He knew then that the storm was going to be a driving one and that it would probably stall in the area since lightning loved his mountain as much as he did. The man on TV was just a putz with a pointer. Computers and radars be damned.

Mike and his specially trained staff were out at various locales after answering several calls from cabin dwellers. Guests had either contacted the lodge at the outset of the storm or soon after, waking to ground-shaking claps of thunder and electrifying cracks of lightning. The staff was trained to check water and acid levels in the creeks, lakes and other bodies of water on the property. They also maintained the emergency roadways and attempted to prevent possible river overflows, flooding or mud slides on the hilly terrain. Each outdoor staffer had specific duties to carry out including rescuing and protecting wildlife. Other staff had been dispatched to fill generators, check window shutters, and bring radios, batteries, food, water and other miscellaneous supplies overlooked by the vacationers. Even the empty cabins were checked and closed up against the storm. Mike had verified that all the guests were checked in. All except one.

He was marching up a particularly muddy slope, muttering a string of curses. He had no real reason to be upset. He had to go to the cabin even if no one was there, since it was part of his assigned rotation. It just pissed him off that he had no idea if she was safe inside or stuck somewhere in the storm. It was his responsibility to account for the lives of any persons in danger on lodge property and he had more than enough capable bodies to find and rescue anyone in any dangerous scenario. He had ex-park rangers, retired sheriffs, environmentalists, botanists, zoologists, medics, EMTs, three veterinarians, and two family doctors on payroll. He even had mechanics, lumberjacks, volunteer firefighters and construction workers for impossible situations. And not once had he been unprepared for an emergency since he took over on the mountain. He was breathing hard and trying to rush head-on into the driving rain. He needed to get to her so he could kill her if she were okay. It was making him careless. He would never make progress this way and Mike knew better than to fight the elements.

He stood stock-still and breathed deeply. He stopped to center himself. For a moment the rain lifted and the wind ceased and the trees told him which path to take. This was the way he was taught as a boy when he was first brought to the mountain. A picture of beautiful gray mists began to form in his mind. Clear, glasslike crystals began to dance against heavy base rhythms while lights flashed to the music of the rustling *shk, shk* that he heard. His inner eyes had been opened. He slipped up the hill with the wind at his back, his eyes closed the entire time. He walked over the ground as if it was solid concrete under his feet as opposed to cascading mud. The rain felt like tiny kisses instead of beads of ice. He was able to see far into the night and focus on the cabin. He was communing with the mountain, gliding on the brisk winds, listening to the thunder, respecting the lightning and moving between raindrops. "Cloud walking" is what the Native Americans had called it, and it was a gift his grandfather had given to him. His grandfather had said, "Like the Cherokee Spirit People released from the sky-vault, it is ever important to remember where you are in relation to everything else . . . Be aware of what is around you, hear what is inside of you and you will always know where you are . . . This is cloud walking." The toboggan moved steadily behind him, no longer bumping along as an encumbrance threatening to tip over. Despite the unwieldy cargo he maneuvered as if he was a part of the storm.

Each makeshift toboggan was filled with supplies and enclosed in plastic. Anything from a first aid kit to heavy woolen socks could be found inside. Food, batteries, extra radios, blankets, and an assortment of games, flashlights, candles, books and magazines were just some of the basics. Stuff that any of his guests might need or want.

With his anger in check and his cargo in tow, he pulled his hood forward and walked up the front stairs to her cabin. He pushed on the locked front door and his composure completely snapped. "Goddamn her!" He stood beating against the unforgiving wood. His hand would protest later the punishment he was giving it now. "I know you're in there! You just want me to yell like a banshee, don't you? You're doing this deliberately, aren't you? You must know by now I don't carry spare keys? LET ME IN!!"

He tilted his head back and let fly a shout any wild animal would be proud of. Lightning broke the sky in two and thunder rolled and rumbled over his head. He almost expected her to come to the window and scream, "Not by the hair of my chinny chin chin." He laughed at himself despite the rain soaking into his clothes. He left the toboggan and walked around, checking the other entrances but, as he assumed, the cellar, shed and windows were all locked. Totally drenched, pissed off, cold to the bone and covered in mud, he recalled that he never fixed the busted lock on Gideon's bedroom window.

He walked under the window and found it wasn't as close to the ground as he had remembered. He began to stack logs, figuring they wouldn't sink into the ground as quickly as the legs of one of the porch chairs. He climbed up, pried open the shutters with his knife and rattled the window until the lock fell back. The room was darker than it was outside and appeared undisturbed. Maybe she was sleeping in the den with the large fireplace. He hefted himself over the edge with a stealth only he imagined. He managed to catch his raincoat on something and went tumbling wildly to the floor, face-first. A flash of light and throbbing pain seeped through his adrenaline rush, when a second bolt of lightning and thunder rattled him. Either the storm had followed him inside or a large man had just laid waste to him. He struggled to pull one eye open but when it refused to cooperate, he tried the other. He saw a pair of legs, and from the pain now reverberating down his neck, no doubt he'd been kicked in the face. "What the fu? . . . *ump.*"

The leg launched into his midsection, sprawling him onto his back and knocking most of the wind out of him, nearly causing him to completely black out. He moaned aloud as his head rolled to one side. The hood of the raincoat brushed back and sounded like a rock slide in his ears. He heard what might have been his name and again attempted to open his eyes and get a fix on his surroundings. Jesse towered above him like Paul Bunyan. She wore a short T-shirt that barely concealed shiny satin panties. Her thighs looked incredibly powerful and sumptuous from his prone position. The gun in her hand was steady as he heard the click of the safety going back on. He realized he was staring at the business end of his own shotgun.

"Why the hell are you pointing my gun at me? Do you know you could kill someone with that? Do you even know how to fire one of those things?"

"It would only be a club if I didn't. And, yes, my intention was to hurt someone sneaking through my bedroom window at two in the morning."

"Do you know you could have hurt yourself too? There's a considerable kick to that thing."

"I'm not stupid. I had Lion teach me about it. He said each cabin had one, just had to know where to look. So I looked and found this one. We practiced on some trees . . ."

"You do know trees are living things too."

She stared at him, trying to decide if she should just shoot him where he lay.

"Help me up and onto the bed, please."

"Not on my bed. You're gross." She helped heft him from the floor. His legs were unsteady but holding. He felt hard beneath the wet clothes that were pasted to his frame. Every flex of his muscles sent a warm flush through a new part of her body.

She stumbled and nearly dropped him twice and he ground out, "Could ya be careful? I'm a little injured." She was moving him into the guestroom across the hall.

"Shut up," she snapped, "if I did any real damage you would be unconscious."

"Don't sound so disappointed."

"If you were a real intruder, flying on adrenaline, my kicks would have been worthless."

"Oh, they did about a thousand bucks worth of damage on my face and ribs, babe."

"They were meant to incapacitate."

He couldn't believe what he was hearing. "Are you berating yourself over a less-than-stellar 'kicking my ass' performance? 'Cause if that's the issue, then get me on the bed and I'll pass right out for you and your ego," he spat.

"Oh, no you don't. You'll go into shock."

Her take-charge bossy voice was back. Despite the gentle way she handled him he still felt as if he had just been in a sparring match.

"You're cold, wet, dirty, hurt and bleeding."

"Yeah, I only had three out of five before I came in here. The other two are on you."

"No one told you to come crawling through my bedroom window. Hmmm, I wonder what the law says about B & E's out here?" She shoved him down onto the bed with more force than he would have liked. But he did like seeing her standing over him with her hands on her hips ready for battle, in the white T-shirt that was see-through in spots because of the rain that had soaked into it from his jacket. Only he couldn't appreciate it because she was pissing him off with her stinking attitude.

"I would have come through the door except it was LOCKED!" he bellowed like a bear with a thorn in his foot.

"Knock."

Now he laughed.

"Now wait . . ." She pointed a finger in his face to reprimand him and he lunged at her and pulled her back onto the bed. "What is your goddamn problem?" Cloud said.

"Don't you start that laughing again or I swear I'll blacken the other eye," she said, pulling free of him and getting back on her feet. "I repeat, you could have knocked."

"In a forest, during a thunderstorm, how much knocking you 'spectin' ta hear? But don't think I didn't try." He showed her the raw knuckles on his left hand.

"You scared me to death!" Jessica said.

"I thought I made myself clear, no one is even close to this place and animals don't use doors."

"Neither do you. And I've seen you out there more than once roaming around, smoking cigars in the forest—which has got to be a fire hazard, as well as detrimental to your health—looking at this cabin. Do you know how freaky that is?"

"It's my job." Exasperated, he let himself fall back onto the bed. "And I don't inhale." He was nearly asleep when she returned from closing the window in her room, getting a washrag and a bowl of warm water to clean his abrasions. The more he thought about it the more he realized she had almost shot him. He remembered her unchambering the bullets and putting the safety back on before she helped him to his feet. "You really were gonna fuckin' shoot me. Goddamn you, woman. Did you ever once think maybe it was me?"

She ignored his ramblings while she tried to focus on her ministrations. Touching the deep bruising next to one eye and on his cheek, her mind kept straying to the body that she had seen chopping wood, the lips that had kissed her off her feet and the tongue that had made her cum on her front porch. She knew what was under the ragged and dirty rain slicker and even felt the muscles beneath her hands. She knew what he could do to her. She tried to turn him over to help get the grubby clothes off, but his massive size was now dead weight. She dumped the water and washed out the rags. She let him rest to restore some of his energy and put some physical distance between them. Even asleep he was a dominating presence. She rummaged around for one of the sets of clean flannel pajamas she'd previously worn on the cooler nights of her stay. She always returned them to the top drawer of the old bureau on the left-hand side. She found wool socks and flannel boxers in the dryer where she had left them after their last use. She also thought it would be smart to slip into some jeans and a bra, so she ran the dryer to warm the clothes and went to change. Then she remembered she ought to check his ribs. She grabbed the first aid kit in the kitchen before getting the clothes and heading to the guestroom.

When she walked in the room he had thrown most of the tattered items to the floor. Walker had a small towel that only half-covered his genital area. The way he was reclined he reminded her of the Calvin Klein ads with the buff men in their tight boxers. Her eyes took in the smooth skin and even lines that made up his legs and she gawked with an open mouth at the rippling muscles of his stomach. She was hypnotized once again by the straight dark hair that formed an image of a rising bird up the middle of his chest. She had forgotten all about his ribs when she saw that on each nipple was a circular metal ring. "Oh, my God."

"You say His name entirely too much."

"I'm very religious," she answered, tearing her gaze away.

He knew exactly what she was looking at, but he opened his eyes to see the look on her face.

"I hadn't noticed, um, that first day when you were chopping wood."

"I didn't have them on in case some beautiful woman happened upon me in the forest. And I really don't want to catch them on anything while I'm working."

"What made you . . . ?"

"Peer pressure." He explained, "I took Sylvia to get her belly button pierced and walked out with these." He flicked them and Jesse flinched involuntarily.

"That seems a bit extreme." *To impress a girl,* she thought.

Mike started drying himself off and Jesse felt herself blush neon red, her eyes glued to the precariously balanced towel. Walker moved with such fluid grace that her mouth went dry.

"Jesse."

"Jessica," she responded by rote.

"Jesse, hon, you're not gonna do me much good standing way over there, staring."

She gave herself a good mental shake and sat down on the edge of the bed, handing him the warmed clothes. He started to put on the shirt, winced and decided to wait.

"I already poked around and I don't think anything is broken, but let me check you more thoroughly."

"If you're gonna touch me the way you were and look at me with those whiskey-brown eyes you need to give me time to relax."

She turned her head for a minute to give him a chance to dress but when she looked again he had pulled the pajama bottoms across his lap. "Give me that towel, I got a nose bleed too. I think from falling on my face."

Jesse slowly ran her hands up his sides. She lightly massaged his neck and back. Her lips were only inches from his when his tongue moistened his dry lips as he removed the towel from his face. But when he felt the hard peaks of her breasts brush against him he grabbed her arms and stopped her exploration.

"Nothing is broken," he said in a husky voice.

She looked into his eyes and saw their stormy-gray color. She was pinned by the simmering heat she saw there. "Just pass the first aid kit and help lightly wrap me up." He slowly released her arms and by the time she turned around from placing the kit on the dresser he had gotten on the pajama bottoms.

She worked as quickly as possible. His powerful grip and startling reflexes made her realize just what a volatile situation they were in. It didn't escape her notice that his body was responsive to her ministrations. Walker was a large man with a solid physique. Not overly buff like those weightlifters she'd seen at Gold's Gym, but wonderfully firm with gorgeous definition. He let out a long moan that was somewhere between pain and pleasure. His eyes had flitted closed when she first started working on him but now his eyes were translucent and bore right into her, appraising her from head to toe. A look that men give women when they want them, that hungry, determined look. She was offended by the implication since he had just admitted to defacing himself for a girl—how dare he strip her with his eyes?

"You don't need my help in dressing so I'll go heat up something for you to eat and start a fire in the front room. You can come and tell me why you're out here."

"What?"

"It's obvious you're checking up on me. But for the life of me I can't figure out why. I followed all your instructions before the storm hit. I covered the wood, checked the generator, brought in a full gas container, closed up the shed, cellar and windows, checked the supplies, got the matches and kindling, found the batteries and listened to the radio, locked the door, then went to bed. Like normal people."

He stared at her as if she had two heads and a horn, then he spoke in a cold and distant voice. "You forgot to turn on the two-way."

"Oh," she said simply.

"And I don't appreciate you going through all my clothes."

"These are my brother's clothes. I musta kicked you pretty damn hard if you think these are your clothes."

A grim smile of Cheshire Cat satisfaction spread across his face.

"I may not ever wear these but, yes, these are my clothes. And to further answer your question, I'm here because I live here."

Chapter 21

She put on a pot of tea, heated up some of her left-over dinner and stoked the fire. She was stunned and furious by his declaration. She swore Walker was trying to purposely sabotage her peace of mind. She had left an urgent message with Gideon's answering service that he get back to her and straighten this mess out, pronto. She was entering the kitchen when his gray eyes met her fiery brown ones.

"I helped myself and I also put on some soup I brought with me."

She looked at the toboggan leaving a puddle in the front entranceway that she had just buffed and waxed earlier in the day. "Your house, make yourself at home," she muttered in his general direction as she made mugs of tea for them both.

"Mine and Gideon's. Didn't really feel right having him fork over so much cash for a place he barely lives in, especially when it needed a whole heap a work. And it never felt right taking the best cabin for myself so we agreed on this arrangement. Don't look so deer-caught-in-the-headlights, I keep a room in the lodge, too."

Jesse made a small plate for herself and sat across from Walker. He dipped his head in what looked like the shortest prayer and he ate with zeal, shoveling one forkful after another into his mouth without pause. She half-expected him to choke to death.

He pushed away the empty plate, wiped the corners of his mouth, and sat back.

"A man sated," she commented.

"That wasn't half-bad. Not half-good either. I suppose I expected more from an ex-caterer."

"I didn't actually prepare the meals, we have a knowledgeable staff for that." Jesse wasn't defensive.

His stomach was full and he didn't get food poisoning. He had noticed most of her meals were prepackaged Utopia meals that she could mix and match and heat up.

He moved in slow motion over to the pot of soup, filling up two bowls, and breaking flaky bits of bread over a plate. He had somehow managed to put on a T-shirt and she saw the soft, straight black hairs on his arms like the ones that feathered his chest. Again she was taken aback at the sheer mass of him as he filled out the T-shirt in a flattering manner.

"Here, try this," he said. He placed the bowl of fragrant, steaming soup in front of her and then took his seat with a bowl of his own cradled in his giant hands, remembering the feel of those hands on her. He ate with vigor as if he hadn't just eaten a plateful of food. "You like?" came the cavemanlike question.

"Yes. I like."

He looked pleased with himself. "I cooked."

"Did you?" Jesse was reluctant to admit that the

hearty soup was filling without being heavy. The mire-poix tasted as if it had been sautéed in a butter-and-garlic sauce to bring about perfect harmony. The herbs and spices mingled to perfection, creating a unique blend as opposed to startling the tastebuds. There was little meat but it was melt-in-your-mouth good. There were plenty of thick mushrooms and an assortment of legumes. And he used some kind of stock that was rich and robust while still remaining true and clear. It was the best soup she'd ever had. But she'd be damned before she admitted it to him.

He could sense she wasn't going to give him more on the topic of his soup, she seemed to still be brood-ing over the issue of losing to a man. This woman seemed hell-bent on killing him with her own hands. He figured he needed to smooth over the situation. "I'm here at the cabin for the next few weeks. Summer-season prep and we took on some more staff. I've got three guys bunking in my room at the lodge right now, so I'm here for a while. I'll stay out of your way, mind my own business and be gone most of the time. And if you tolerate my intrusion, I'll cook all the meals."

"It's not as though you need my permission." She crossed her arms over her ample bosom. "And if you hadn't noticed I can feed myself."

"You're probably grumpy from being forced to eat those little frozen foods."

"I could still shoot you."

The swelling under his eye was starting to change colors. Pale sunrise yellow to a plum purple and in some places a vibrant red.

"Why didn't you just shoot me earlier? Most people would have put two bullets in an intruder, before trying to find out who it was."

"If I fired the rifle there wouldn't have been any-thing, of either of us, left to identify. Besides, I spent nine hundred and fifty dollars on self-defense classes and I'll be damned if I never get to use them."

"You kicked me," he said, pulling out a cheroot, with a sarcastic smirk across his sexy lips.

"I suppose," she answered wistfully, staring at him and into him. "I had formulated a plan and executed said plan. If you hadn't stayed down, then I would have shot you. Simple."

As she cleared the dishes off the table he watched her buttocks, all rounded and cute in the too-big jeans. He lit the cheroot.

"Don't smoke at the table, or I may have to shoot you anyway."

"For smoking at my own table?" he asked, leaning back to open the sliding doors for ventilation. The wind and rain immediately swept into the room and he shoved it closed to a small crack.

"Listen, I know you said you'd be staying here this week . . ."

"A few weeks."

"Okay, but I've got my friend Douglas coming and we need the spare room." At the mention of a man's name, Mike's spine went rigid. Her brother said she had a bad breakup, but nothing prevented her from seeing the jerk again if she wanted. All women changed their minds and she was, after all the pomp and circumstance, a woman he wanted to love and kill all at the same time.

"Why can't he sleep with you? You know what? He can sleep on the futon in the damn den. I'm not giving up my room. And don't worry, I won't be underfoot much. I'll have a lot of work to do after this storm. I'll be out before either of you wakes and I'll be back late."

Jesse could practically feel the anger jumping off Walker.

"I would also ask that you don't smoke those in the house while my company is here."

"No, we wouldn't want that. How about I just go outside in the storm?"

"Don't be silly." She closed the sliding door. "The den would be fine."

He stomped out as loud as his stockinged feet would allow. Maybe he needed some time in the sweat lodge at the back of the house, he thought. It was an extension from the old root cellar that he and Gideon agreed could be used for the old Native American ritual that Mike had grown up with. They would heat rocks in a huge cast iron pot in the fireplace and then place them in the sink off to the side of the room. Then they would make a traditional fire in the mud hole at the center of the room, pour water on the rocks to let off steam and, finally, burn and smoke special herbs in order to induce visions.

Mike opened the door and slipped down the steps. He never needed the light to enter the room before but he suspected something was awry just by the smell and that the woman was involved. He groped for the string light and met with tons of air, he twisted about in a strange aerial dance that he was glad no one could see. He kicked and slipped when his leg came in contact with a heavy object. "Damn it."

Suddenly bright lights shined on him as if he had just escaped from Alcatraz. Jesse stood, calmly wiping her hands on the apron she wore, his apron, looking very domesticated and normal in his home. "You okay? I thought you might have hurt yourself."

"I did. What the hell is this?" He glared at the tub as if it had bit him, and she couldn't stifle her giggle.

"It's an old-fashioned porcelain tub. I did a bit of redecorating back here," she said cheerfully.

A bit? he thought. He stared at the water cascading in intricate rainbows and patterns on a state-of-the-art skylight in the high, cathedral-like ceiling. With the lights dim around him the storm seemed harmless from this perspective as lightning pierced the sky. Mike heard a gurgling brook and looked over at a manmade rock fountain. He saw the incense and herbs that he burned in sturdy, yet delicately designed, hand-pounded metal containers. Some were perched on the rock ledges while others hung with votive candles. The old sink remained although it had been sanded and reglazed. Where the fire pit had once been there now stood a stoic, gray ceramic clawfoot tub with shiny new brass piping. The matching sink stood lazily against the left wall. The tub was filled with tools, assorted building supplies, wall hangings, dried flowers and other feminine decorative stuff. He wandered over to an old-fashioned free-standing medical cabinet of all white wood and glass. It was now a makeshift herb cabinet. The bench had been sanded and a gray plush carpet cut and fitted to the seat. A small table on wheels held a radio. The walls were a remarkable combination of the original mud and unfinished, broken marble tiles, juxtaposing starkness and the decorative, bringing about the marvelous sensitivity of the architect by utilizing only natural elements. He turned and glared at Jesse.

"What the hell did you do to my sweat lodge?"

"Sweat lodge? I didn't know that it had a purpose. It was just a cellar. A very unused, unloved, pathetic little cellar, at that. So I fixed it up. My brother's note said make myself at home. At home, I have a tub."

"How much did you pay for this to be done?"

"What?" Her breath was leaving her quickly as she thought she knew what was coming next.

"How much did you pay? I'll give you your money because I'm going to change it all back."

Jesse was just too deflated to argue with him, it was the only thing she had in her life now to give her purpose. "Your house. I paid around three thousand."

"Bullshit. Any crew pays each man hourly scale, minimum. This looks like union labor because it all looks better than city code. This was easily a five-man job for about two-and-a-half to three weeks of labor at six hours a day. We're talking a quick ten thou, twenty with an architect, designer and inspection. The floor and walls should have run you five grand easy."

"Inspection? You need one-way out here in the woods?" Jesse asked, biting her lower lip, looking like an impish elf. Mike breathed an exasperated sigh. Even though the room was less than half-finished, Mike was impressed by the craftsmanship. He also liked how cute she looked when she bit her lower lip. He could almost see her mind working. He could have done a better job but not by much. There was no doubt everything would pass code.

Jesse's eyes moved across the floor and up the one mosaic wall she had constructed with Zak. "Well, it took me about two months. Me, one licensed electrician (Jonathan), two skinny kids and Lion. Zak and I went and got the supplies at different wholesalers, in Asheville and Winston-Salem. Cash-and-carry to avoid taxes and delivery charges." Jesse was feeling a bit proud of herself, and very superior since Walker mistook her work for that of a professional. Walker was touching surfaces, shaking the exposed plumbing and kicking the walls as he listened to her detail her experience—almost as if he was buying a car. She folded her arms across her chest and, despite his disgusted façade, she could tell he was impressed.

"I could finish the tub and sink for you in a few hours."

"I like doing the work myself, at night, when it's quiet."

"I'll get the inspection done before it's finished in case something needs to be redone."

"I thought you were going to rip the room apart."

"Changed my mind. It has potential. Do the windows open?"

"No," she admitted begrudgingly. Then defensively added, "I don't really think you need them to open."

"Yeah, you do. This place is a breeding ground for mold and mildew since the walls are still mainly mud, but I can fix that."

"Won't they let water in when it rains and just compound the problem?"

"Let me worry about that."

"You didn't have any damn windows before," she said, her anger kicking into overdrive.

"No, just a trap door to release smoke."

She was starting to resent his helpful intrusion when his eyes went to some exposed wires. "Jonathan showed me how to put in a dimmer on the lights and hook them all up to a universal remote that I'm gonna bolt to the table, which will have the radio, towels, and soap. I was also thinking that maybe I could make the big sink into some sort of counter, and stack the towels on that instead."

"If you'll let me, I could do that in no time," he said, a little harshly for a man who was trying to apologize without apologizing.

"No, I don't want any help. I don't want this to go quickly. Right now, it's one of the few things to occupy my time. But, I was talking to Lion and Zak and I might need your help on a project for them."

"I used it for the hot rocks to steam the room."

"What?"

"The sink. I would heat the rocks on the fire in the mud pit"—he pointed to where the tub was currently positioned—"and put the rocks in the sink, pour water over them and create the steam. But I could put a removable countertop and get new rocks since you used all of mine."

"I'm sorry. But there are plenty left. I put them in the old-fashioned washbasin by the bench. It looks kind of pretty, right?" She looked at him worriedly as if this would cause him to suddenly disregard all her work and undo all she'd done. To distract herself Jesse started talking. "As I was starting to tell you before, I bought the old bakery in town for them." He barely looked at her over his shoulder as he inspected his rocks. "I need to convert one room into a woodworking area and the other into a nursery. They wanted a store. So I want to get it ready so they'll feel too obliged to say no."

"No problem."

She was so ready with more of an argument that she had to stop herself from running into the room to convince him of the plan.

"I said, no problem," he said closer to her stunned face. "You're supposed to say 'thank you.'"

"Yes. Thank you."

"Are you gonna help?"

"I'd like to. And I'm sorry about the room, it's just that Gideon told me to make myself . . ."

"Stop worrying. I like it, it's coming along fine."

"Thank you," she said again in a small voice. At this rate her panties would be wet just from the soft, sensitive look that he kept tossing at her with those words. His mouth went dry from the vulnerable look she was giving him, but he was finally able to cough out the question.

"Can I ask you for a favor? I'd like to drain this fountain so I can still practice my Native American rituals."

"Indian?"

Poof, spell broken, and all she did was speak. She watched his face go from soft to hard. His features suddenly tightened. His cold silver eyes burned into her. She wasn't sure what she had done to set him off, but she was ready to fight fire with fire. Her back straightened and her head came up. She stared at him stonily.

He couldn't believe her ignorance. He looked from one of her eyes to the other so he could make sure she was paying attention as he schooled her. "Not Indian, *Native*. You know, the people who were here before this was called America, before Chris Columbus showed up and renamed the land and the people who already had names. Those nations of people were the Natives, sweetheart, and there were at least eight million of us here. And, yes, I'm a Native, a Native of

Nantahala, Stone Mountain, this mountain that you're standing on."

"You were born here?"

"Yes, and so was my grandfather and his grandfather and practically every Native you see around here."

"Native sounds barbaric," she said, hoping to diffuse his anger and learn more about him in the process.

"Negative connotation, like Negro."

"Don't you mean *nigger?*"

"Nigger is an insult. Negro is just harsh sounding because of the connotation. But calling Natives *Indians* when India is east or west of here is just stupid." Her eyes made his skin tingle as if Tinkerbell had sprinkled fairy dust on him. With her head tilted at that quirky little angle she looked as if she was about to ask the infinite "Why" question that kids always ask of adults. "It isn't about semantics, it's about how those words have been suppressing cultures for years. How labels and categories come with stigmas. Categories made up by men who are not of my ethnicity."

"Sometimes you gotta forget the words and what they mean and just live your life to the best of your individual ability. My parents told me once, 'It isn't what they call you that's important but what you answer to.'" Jesse said.

He was ready to fight to the death. How could she be so blasé and he so passionate when her people have long suffered from hurtful, derogatory terms?

"If I believed in stereotypes I might have been held hostage by my own. If I did that, I'd never have opened my own business."

He took a deep breath—at least she had given it

some thought and formed an opinion. Trisha believed that the world was a perfectly rosy place and that "it's really about the beautiful people and the not-so-beautiful people—black, white, Oriental, Chinese, Indian or Spanish, anyone with good looks can do whatever they want." He'd argued with Trish: "Oriental is a rug, Chinese only covers one culture, and Spanish is a language, not a people."

How women made his brain hurt. "Look. For a minute we had a nice little truce. I leave the room if I can have this one section and access to my sink a few times a month."

"Actually you can steam the rocks in here." Jesse flicked a switch on the wall and the water stopped gurgling and slid down a hidden drain. "I didn't want to maintain an indoor fishpond, and standing water isn't good under the mold and mildew conditions." When she flicked the switch again the fountain came to life. Another turn of the dial and little discrete lights came on under the water, tucked into some of the rocks. "It's all recycled, it won't attract fungi and it'll be much easier to clean. If you want you could use the rice paper and bamboo screen I picked up to block yourself off from the rest of the room."

Jesse gave Mike a wholesome smile that held him spellbound. Mike's eyes languished over her body, sending flutters through her. She needed space so she led the way into the den. She tried to speak around the thickness in her throat. "Listen, maybe you could do me a favor and keep Doug busy while he's here."

He became solemn and angry as he ground out his cheroot. "I don't consider myself close enough to you to be entertaining your boyfriend." He'd forgotten about what had driven him out of the kitchen in the first place.

"Doug isn't my boyfriend, he's my *best* friend. He was my partner and chef at Utopia. We're not involved sexually."

"Is he gay?"

"No." Jesse took a second cigar out of the box next to the futon, cut it, lit it, took a pull and passed it to Mike.

"You're telling me you're not sharing his bed *and* he's a chef. He has to be gay." He checked the cheroot and was impressed with the perfect cut and light of it. He nodded and took a deep inhalation.

"You cook pretty well, with two nipple rings to boot, are you gay?"

"Touché." They both blew smoke up into the exposed wooden rafters of the ceiling.

"After reaming me about the Indian comment I was sure you weren't into stereotyping."

He wasn't into stereotypes, and he really didn't believe what he was arguing, it was just that he liked to watch her face become all flushed and animated when she felt insulted. He liked the spark that would flash in her eyes when she drove her point home. And the way her body vibrated with suppressed energy. But he mainly couldn't believe that all men didn't find Jesse attractive for one reason or another. Her mind was sharp, her body voluptuous, her smile innocent and her eyes captivating. She was in control of her life, she could stand on her own two feet in every situation thrown at her; any man would be more than a little tempted.

"Doug and I have been platonic friends forever. My

COME WITH ME   163

parents 'unofficially' adopted him when we were in our junior year of high school."

Jesse could almost see the lightbulb go on over Mike's head. He might not have remembered the name but she knew at some point Gideon would have mentioned his "other brother from another mother" to his friend. "The trip isn't for Doug, it's to help his wife get her mind off the baby."

"The baby?" he inquired, raising a very sexy eyebrow with a flash of straight white teeth. She kicked him lightly and he passed her back the cigar.

"Their baby. I'm to be godmother extraordinaire and I'm getting a jump on things, by reminding Kat that she's equally as important as the baby is. So I was thinking you and Doug can spend time cooking, smoking cigars and just being guys. Only I don't think chopping wood is something within Douglas's capabilities."

Walker took back the cigar, looked sagely at the tip and nodded. "Gay, definitely gay."

Chapter 22

The storm had let up so the only sound to break up the silence was the musical sound of the rain that was still coming down off the trees. "I think I'm coming down off my high. I'm about ready for bed," Jesse said, barely suppressing a yawn.

"Yeah, me too." He followed her closely down the hall until she stopped at the door to the master bedroom. She turned stiffly and like an idiot, stuck out her hand to shake. In a small voice she said good night and pumped his hand vigorously. She closed the bedroom door and once inside she began to softly bang her head against it. When she stopped she distinctly heard the clearing of his throat and a knock on the door.

"Yes?" she asked, opening the door a crack. Walker lifted a chin toward his room across the hall, moving slightly so she could see past his broad shoulder. Mud was now dried and clinging to the bedspread, with gleaming puddles of water around the boots he had discarded. The leaves that had been on his clothes had left several damp areas on the carpet and bed where he had been lying. And the remnants of torn clothes covered every surface. She looked at him lounging against the doorjamb, then looked back at his room, and again at him, to find Mike looking intently at her bed. Her mind screamed '*No no no!* as she improvised a plan. "How about we set you up in the den? I just washed all the sheets for Doug's visit, I'll pad the futon since you must be sore." The words made her flinch as she just gave him his argument.

"Not good enough. Remember, my body is how I make my living. I have to be comfortable." He stood unmoving, enjoying her panic at the possibility of sharing a bed with him. He could almost see the wheels turning in her head.

"How about the couch? It's soft. You'll be comfortable. Or, better yet, give me a few minutes and I'll have the mess in the other room cleaned up."

"You can take the futon or the couch, or the other room, I'll take this bed. I should have my choice after what I've been through tonight just doing my job." She flushed deeply and it enhanced her nymphlike beauty. He walked past her with his self-assured, patented swagger and it nearly drove her insane with anger.

"Are you sure your girlfriend won't take issue with you and I sharing a cabin and a bed all in one night?"

"Girlfriend? You're taking me back with that one. I haven't had a *girl*friend since I was a boy and I haven't been a boy in quite a few years."

"Well what do you call *Sylvia?*" she asked as she watched him climb into *her* bed. This man had some gall.

"She had a crush on me when she first started, but she grew out of it once she got to know me."

"Smart girl, learned the error of her ways quickly."

Ignoring her, he finished his thought. "She has a really nice fiancé who lives near her parents' home. That's one of the reasons she doesn't take a room at the lodge or in Ulo gidv Village. She'd rather take the hour-and-a-half drive to and from work each day and be near him. Tak or Lila play concierge nights and weekends."

Jesse couldn't believe she had felt a moment of jealousy over this man. The arrogant bastard was removing his T-shirt and socks. And she was getting hot just watching him. Why did he have the power to turn her into a lovestruck adolescent? It was because she had never been with a man who caused her to feel.

He was not just a perfect body, he had strong opinions and his own ideals. It made him more of a man in her estimation. And that, she reasoned, was why she could not think rationally in his company. But she was a grown woman, who should be able to share a bed with Walker without feeling like one big hormone.

She closed the door and flopped on the bed on top of the covers next to him. "'Sides, what makes you think we could have done what we did when I already got someone? I know you don't think that badly of me. You gonna get the lights?"

He had a point, she really didn't believe he was the playboy type but that didn't mean she wasn't jealous. Even when she saw him look at Lila in the bar she felt her eyes turning green. Jesse glared at his prone figure draped under the covers. His skin was a deep, honey-gold and he made a dynamic picture with his arms behind his head and a lackadaisical smile on his perfect lips.

She dimly recalled turning off the light and lying

stiffly next to him. She was acutely aware of his hard thigh pressing against hers through the heavy cover. Her mind swirled at the sexual tension snaking through her body. His hair, curling at the ends where it had not yet dried, flirtatiously touched her shoulder. Her breath was practically coming in gasps.

"Aren't you cold?" he asked.

"I'm sleepy. Move over," she replied tartly, and used her body to push his. The subtle rumble in his chest was all too familiar and she knew he was laughing at her, yet again, but this time she wasn't annoyed. She found the sexy, uninhibited sound doing incredible things to her nether region. She had to get a grip, she was completely losing control when it came to this man.

Walker was fighting his baser instincts every time she wiggled and twisted her supple body against his. The smallest brush of her fingers against his leg, or when her arm rubbed against his already-sensitive ribs, sent blood thundering through his veins. But the final straw was when her round butt in the rough jeans pushed right up against his hip when she turned away from him. He was relieved she couldn't see his arousal in the darkened room. In order to get his mind off of the image of her breasts rising and falling so enticingly beneath the thin cotton top, he tried to think of the several confrontations they had had, but that wasn't working. The one taste of her had him wanting more. He felt like a ridiculous, infatuated schoolboy. He tried a deep-breathing exercise to help calm himself, but then he would catch the faintest scent of autumn coming from her smooth neck and his manhood would become even more responsive. Even her feet held a sleek beauty that he'd never quite imagined one woman could possess, which was especially distressing since he had no intention of giving in to this desire to kiss her feet again. Reigning in his raging hard-on was a task that was keeping him from sleep.

As Jesse regarded what she thought were the even and light snores from Walker, she quietly got out of bed to remove her jeans and bra and then slipped under the covers. His presence in her bed was cozy. Her senses were reeling from the smell of the rain mingling with his natural masculine scent. His massive body dipped the mattress so that she slid right up against him. She imagined her body entwined with his, his firm arm wrapped around her waist, his thick, muscled legs pinning her to the bed. A low moan erupted from somewhere deep in the back of her throat. She was mortified at herself for succumbing to the thought. She shifted around, attempting to find the perfect position away from him.

"City, I'm not asleep enough to take too much more of your wriggling around. I'm a man with normal urges. Add to that, that I know how good it feels to kiss and hold you, and love you with my mouth and you're asking for trouble."

The rasp in his deep voice made her all the more aware of her equally tentative state.

"I'm sorry . . ." came out as a strangled sound that she despised. When she stopped moving she was again pressed against his side.

"Mmmmm."

His moan sent another flash of heat coursing through her. She was finding it very hard to maintain her cool façade when she felt him look at her with eyes dark with passion. The swelling black and blue mark enhanced his air of danger but did nothing to reduce the wanting she could detect just beyond the dusting of his dark lashes. Her common sense abandoned her as she was swept up in a current of sultry sensations as she tried to move again.

"Oh, God, Jesse." She was aroused by the sound of her name off his lips. He had hardly moved but Walker was responsive to every blink and blush that Jesse made. All he wanted to do was take her face in his hand and kiss those tantalizing lips. "Keep moving like that, I don't need much more incentive." Jesse's body helplessly and shamelessly writhed against him. "I'm not going to be able to stay a gentleman," Mike whispered.

"Good." She smoothed a small hand across his bare chest. Jesse moved her body so that her leg gently massaged his. She found a warm spot on his neck that she kissed.

She then kissed his lips with a depth of passion that had him clinging to the last strands of decorum as if he was a man adrift on the ocean holding a life preserver. She moved lithely over him like a warm breeze. He was so caught up in the urgency of the blissful touch of her soft lips to his that he ignored the short-lived complaint from his ribs as she lowered her pliant body to fit on top of him. One of his arms moved around her waist while the other pressed against the back of her neck to bury his fingers in her hair. The sweet scent of her was so pervasive that his mind was becoming a whirlwind of sensation. He could feel her body molding to his.

She was so lost in his lush lips that her body was responding of its own accord, raw heat consuming her. His hands moved over her in a familiar way, as if he touched her like this every day. It all felt so right that when her tongue slid into his mouth she didn't want to stop. She kissed him with uncharacteristic abandon, her self-control slipping as her tongue met with a honeyed sweetness. She drew back her head, her eyes full of accusation. "You expected this to happen. Didn't you? You prepared for it. You slipped some candy or something in your mouth after the cigars."

"It's no secret, I'm considerate. I would have gargled but I noticed that my mouthwash has mysteriously disappeared."

"Listerine is too strong. It burns my gums . . . and stop changing the subject. You assumed we were going to be intimate."

"I *assumed* no such thing. I figured if something did happen I wanted to be ready. 'Sides, I don't like waking up with cigar breath. We can stop if you like." He massaged the tense muscles at the base of her neck and was running his other hand over the curve of her back, placing little fluttering kisses against her shoulder. Her eyes closed at the tingling sensations. Her body arched like a cat against his and just as he suspected she fit perfectly in the V of his legs. "You were nice enough to share your bed with me and I'm willing to be the perfect gentleman. I'm not inclined to take advantage of you. But you did make the first move."

He flipped her onto her back, burying his hand more forcefully into her hair, tilting her head back, exposing her delicious neck for tender exploration.

Suddenly, he felt her stiffen. Jesse had been giving to him and taking from him, he felt it in her touch, tasted it in her kiss and saw it in her eyes. But not anymore.

She looked back at him and said, "Cloud, I can't." In silence, he accepted and she carefully left the bed, tucked him in, kissed his forehead and quietly left the room. He was left feeling frustrated that he wasn't holding Jesse's body next to him anymore, that somehow things had gotten way off course. He wanted to go back to that moment where everything seemed perfect and he could have just gone to sleep with her in his arms. The kiss was such a sweet gesture that he smiled himself into a deep sleep anyway.

Chapter 23

Jesse purposely rose extra early and accompanied Mike to the medic. He was okay, but she insisted he get his face checked. The Wooden Lodge medic was a medium-sized man named Tak the Texan. Between his old Texas accent and his new Southern drawl, it took Jesse a while to understand him.

"Mike, I dunno how ya 'stained two bruised ribs, a strained shoulder and a black eye all from landing wrong *into* the cabin. I could see falling out a window and landin' wrong in the storm, rollin' down the slope, bumpin' a tree. Or falling debris swiping atcha, trying ta walk out inna storm and slammin' inta trees, or catchin' a mini mud slide could tumble ya good, but fallin' inna window, I never knowed ya to be *that* careless."

"I done tole you what happened, I'm not in the mind of repeating myself," Walker answered from the bed behind gritted teeth.

Jesse knew Walker didn't tell the whole truth, but Tak wasn't all that dense.

"Mike, do you need me to call Digg up the mountain

or get Fish and Wildlife up here? If'n 'twas a bear, dat needs reportin', report it, you know they won't hurt 'im. If'n it's something else, you might want a restraining order. It's more common than you think for women to be the abuser these days." Tak and Jesse laughed while Walker threw them dirty looks.

"I don't need the sheriff and I don't need you two standing over me makin' a bigger deal of this than it is."

Tak had given Walker painkillers, but they remained untouched. He was adamant that they often did more harm than good because of all the chemical processing and additives. He showed Jesse how to brew several homeopathic remedies that had properties similar to the painkillers prescribed but with no real side effects. She was glad she hadn't thrown anything away when she cleaned the back room because among the old dried spices, tree barks and other natural elements were the ingredients he instructed her to use. Her told her each of the organic names and scientific names of the herbs. He told her their properties and which medications they were used in.

"Don't go mixing anything without my help. It can be very dangerous for a city person to be messing around in God's medicine cabinet. Most plants have powerful poisons that can be transformed into the most dangerous chemicals the world has ever seen."

"I'm not an idiot."

"'The American Native is of the soil, he fits into the landscape, for the hand that fashioned the continent also fashioned man for his surroundings.'"

"Who said that?"

Mike stopped labeling bottles and looked over at her. She wasn't being antagonistic, she was asking a plain question. It took him a minute to remember the answer. "Umm . . . Standing Bear, Ogala Sioux, a distant relation of your photographer friend."

"Yusef is Native American? He looks like an African-American."

"Os Rouge, black and Indian. Man is only one tiny part of the world and all the tiny parts make up the world just like a tiny part could remove man from it."

Jesse smiled while she worked. "I'm listening."

"The, uh, the Anishnabeg people and Ojibwe people tended to make very complex mixtures with different parts of plants, which were tended different times of the year, mixed in specific proportions and administered in varying doses and dilutions. You can always buy this stuff but you don't always know what you're getting, so I get it here on the reservation. I keep the medicinal stuff here and the herbs in the kitchen."

"This smells and looks like oregano, shouldn't it be in the kitchen?"

"*Origanum vulgare* . . ."

"Spotted bee balm . . ."

"That's *Monarda punctata* . . ."

"Catnip?" Jesse asked, holding up another jar she just labeled.

"Yes. *Nepeta cataria* or *Gajugensibu*; when brewed in a tea it brings down high fevers and tastes okay."

"There's sassafras, goldenrod, pine needles, I've seen those in gourmet groceries."

"Most of those you can cook with but ground-up pinches are added to other roots and a brew is made, sometimes dried and stored. Some are complete remedies, others you make into creams and pastes for

burns and stings. There is a science but also an art.
These remedies aren't even from one nation. And I'm
constantly learning more. These are secrets that are
mostly handed down verbally and kept within a family.
That also helps to keep locations of useful wild herbs
bountiful. I was taught to only pick from every third
plant to ensure propagation. And most importantly, it
is required to ask permission of the plant to pick it."

"You must look crazy out there talking to yourself,"
she said with a smile.

"I'm not talking to myself, I'm talking to the plant.
I also leave gifts."

"Like what?" She sat back on her heels, satisfied that
everything was properly labeled.

"Small hand tools, a basket or a bundle. Something
to show someone was there so the next guy who
comes upon it will take care. It's tradition. I've found
notes, beads, hair combs, mulched leaves and fresh
mounds of dirt. Come on in the kitchen, I'll show you
some of the stuff you've been drinking."

She didn't recognize any of the herbs. She learned
that blackberry could be used as an expectorant when
prepared the right way, yarrow juice aided in digestion,
wild ginger helped with gas, wild rose had a rich source
of vitamin C and was used in the fight against the
common cold, and that sumac was known to reduce
fevers, soothe poison ivy and alleviate sore throats.
Mullein, a very old herb, is used to ease asthma attacks
and can be boiled for tea and used as a mild sedative.
It is also used to reduce the swelling of joints as well as
soothe irritated tissues. Jesse made a mental note to find
out how to prepare it.

* * *

Determined not to let her mind turn to mush, Jesse continued educating herself by going online to do more research. She recognized many of the tastes and textures once they hit her tongue and realized that Utopia had used many of these same ingredients in their organic health food divisions. *My God,* she thought, she spent so much time in her office she had forgotten how much fun she used to have identifying food types and dissecting recipes.

Sylvia answered many of her questions about Native American history when she revealed to Jesse that she too was Indian—Lakota.

"I don't really live that way. I wasn't brought up on the reservation, my father is a white dentist from Greensboro. He married my mom and then he went to school for dentistry. They have a very profitable business. But Mom is more upper-class snooty now. She can't be bothered with her Indian family. And for a long time I acted that way too."

"But you seem to know a lot about your culture."

"Grandmother. She still lives up on the mountain. Don't get the wrong impression. My gran is way cool. She taught me about being a modern Indian. I didn't have to give up Saturday-morning cartoons, or food out of a box. But there are plenty of full Indians who don't like mixed bloods and definitely want to preserve the old ways. She couldn't be so bothered, even now she'd rather be at work than chanting at the sky."

"She works?"

"Heck, yeah. She's a dealer over at Harrah's. She's always worried about losing her eyesight and getting fired, but I bet she can see straight through that mountain to us." Sylvia waved and so did Jesse.

* * *

Jesse found out that Lila was a homemaker, in addition to working at the lodge, which was why she seldom caught her around. She worked mainly weekends as of late but was slowly making her way back. She, it turned out, was full Seminole Indian, a warrior tribe mixed with Africans before the Europeans enslaved them all. The Seminoles had managed to maintain a strong foothold in the swamps of Florida. Lila was the color of wheat, with straight hair that was turning prematurely gray, but still plenty of shiny blue-black mixed in. She had six kids, from ages eight months to nineteen years. All of them were the color of blackberry molasses with a variation of Lila's smile duplicated on each face. Lila went by the cabin to say hi to Walker right after his "accident." However, it gave Jesse the opportunity to tap into Lila's cooking and herb skills.

Over the course of the following week Mike continued to do light duty at the lodge and Lila brought several traditional Native dishes to the cabin for them to have for dinner. Jesse loved Kanuchi, a delicacy that can be served as a soup or a spread, so it was the first she tackled. Next came Fry-Bread, which, to Jesse, was like Italian Zeppoli and, finally, deer-meat, which Lila taught her to make in a casserole cooked with wild rice, chopped, fried onions and gravy.

Jesse had just finished setting the table when Walker walked in the door, ramrod straight. By the time he got to the kitchen he seemed slightly hunched and moving slower. "Are you all right?" she asked, putting out the food.

"Yeah. I might have overdone it a bit today."

Jesse had seen Walker playing catch with Lila's kids earlier in the day. In fact he seemed to limp or be under the weather only when she was around. "Hmm . . . I thought you were feeling better," she said while getting seated.

They bowed their heads and Walker said grace. Jesse didn't understand the words, but he spoke with power and conviction, two traits the Cherokee Nation was known for. Over dinner Walker opened up and talked about his job at the lodge and his love of the mountain, which he spoke about as if it was a living creature. It was an intricate part of his Native American background and childhood. "In a constantly changing world you have to change too. So I adapted. I could cook a meal on a fire I built on the ground and then have dinner at the most expensive French restaurant in town and never once confuse a fork. I can order an Italian meal in Italian and speak a dying dialect of the Tsalagi Nation."

"I thought this was Cherokee territory?"

"Yes. Tsalagi is Cherokee in . . ." he said, rolling his hand to get her to join him.

"Cherokee . . ." they both said together on a light laugh.

"You're like a modern sort of renaissance man. I'm impressed. I lived in the same house all my life. I attended the same neighborhood schools that my siblings attended, my parents knew all my friends' parents, my friends were the kids who lived around me, and almost all my clothes were hand-me-downs or hand-me-overs. We always ate at least one meal a day together, we always went on the same stupid vacation every year to see relatives in North Carolina, we all did chores on Saturday and went to church on Sunday. My parents gave me just enough survival skills so I wouldn't cut off a finger in the kitchen, could sew buttons and properly do laundry so all my whites wouldn't be pink."

"Sounds kinda nice to me. I didn't have many close friends."

"I thought you grew up here?" Jesse asked while clearing the table and bringing out slices of cherry pie for dessert.

"I was born here to teenage parents. I lived with my grandfather while they finished college. They got jobs in Chicago, set up a beautiful home and eventually sent for me when I was two. Dad was a lawyer, Mom a secretary. But with working as much as they did, trying to stay on the career fast track, they thought it was better for me to live with my grandfather. You know, have family raise me instead of some babysitter."

"I spent summers over in Charlotte," Jesse said. "My parents finally settled there. I think most of my teen years I wanted to get away from my parents, but my parents are cool. Most kids want to get away from their parents."

"Maybe, but it always felt like I didn't have real parents to get away from. And as a kid I was mad because I felt like they didn't give it a chance. Three years I was back with Majestic, my grandfather."

"Oh," was all Jesse could say.

"Don't get me wrong, I loved them as much as any kid loves their parents. They visited, called frequently, sent money and presents. I saw them every holiday and spent one month every summer vacation with them. They died in a plane crash when I was seven. And they never had more children. So it was always just me."

"I'm so sorry."

"It was a long time ago and they did what they thought was right by me. They also left me rolling in dough. I never wanted for anything. And yet somewhere deep down I know I would have traded being well off with my grandfather in order to be poor with my parents."

"The grass is always greener," Jesse said, understanding all people seemed to want what they didn't have. "As a kid me and my friends sat around comparin' spankings and siblings, especially the siblings part. For example," she said, hoping to lighten the mood, "if you had siblings you would never have gotten to eat a cherry pie all by yourself."

Mike looked down at the pie tin that now sat where his plate had been. While talking he must have switched their places in order to get at the pie. "I'm so sorry."

"No, don't be, it's good to see you still have an appetite. For a while I was worried I'd never get you to eat my cooking."

"You made this?" he asked around a mouthful of pie.

"Yup."

"This is decent." He nodded while scraping the last of the crust from the tin. "It was a perfect finish to Lila's casserole."

Jesse had just started running the water to wash dishes and tried to correct him over the noise, but he was already outside on the balcony having his cigar.

By the end of the week Jesse prepared Walker's delectable soup on her own, following Lila's directions.

Walker had spent the day supposedly resting. Tak came by with the sheriff for a visit.

"Where is that boy? Don't tell me he ain't got out of bed all day?"

Tak and Sheriff Diggs dragged Walker, none too gently, from his room.

"Get away from me, you brutes. I'm not feeling well!" Walker yelled.

"I seen ya out there all week working around the lodge. Now all of a sudden you wanna rest round the house?" Tak asked, flopping down on the couch next to Walker. Sheriff Diggs started the fire before sitting down unceremoniously on the other side of Walker, who let out a low moan.

"You two are brutal," he mumbled.

"Anyone hungry yet?" Jesse asked.

"Yeah," Walker ground out between the two fidgeting men.

"Would you like some soup, Tak?" Jesse asked.

"Sure. I've got some time 'for' I have to man the desk."

"Digg?"

"Do cows make good shoes?"

"I'll take that as a yes." Jesse pranced out of the room jubilantly. She expected Walker to be the only one here to criticize her cooking, but now she had two unprejudiced palates she might impress.

"Who's there now?" Walker asked.

"There where?" Digg asked.

"At the desk. Stop talking, Digg, you're like the lost stooge sometimes."

"I started that new girl 'bout round the time you fell in dat dere winda. Figured I'd let her alone while I check you. Just little ova an hour and my pager hasn't gone off yet."

Jesse placed bowls before all three men along with plates of warm bread that she baked herself.

Tak took a big, Texas-sized spoonful of soup. "You know this has always been a dang good soup but if'n I didn't know I'd swear it's gotten better."

Digg looked behind them at the quickly retreating back of one Ms. Jesse Bishop. "You didn't make this, boy?"

"Lila probably brought it by. She's been bringing us her leftovers."

"Can't be Lila's, she ain't been back," Tak said between bites.

"So who made it? It sure wasn't one of you clowns," Walker answered, reaching for the steaming warm bread.

"I cook 'bout as well as you fake being sick," Tak said, poking Walker in his rib cage.

Digg took a piece of bread for himself. "Dat dere Jesse looks pleased as punch. Looks to me she fooled you."

"I wasn't fooled."

"Yeah, you were," Tak said on a guffaw.

"I swear that woman couldn't microwave popcorn without messing it up when she first got here."

"I guess her nestin' instinct done woke up takin' care of yo' butt," Tak said.

"More like she just wants to prove she's better than me."

"Maybe, but either way, I don't see you losing in this here scenario. In fact you look like one fat happy bastard," Tak said.

"At least now we know why he goes to work every day and comes home and plays sick," Digg added.

"You two done?"

"Yeah, just about," Digg answered for them both.

"Good, shut up and get out. Drop your bowls in the kitchen on your way to the door. Sorry, but I'm too sick to throw you out myself."

"Naw, you don't move, wouldn't want for you to exert any energy."

Tak laughed his way down the hall as a spoon came flying after him. "You keep him on that couch by feeding him that good and he might quit his job," he said to Jesse.

"I guess I'll go back to burning stuff, then, I can't take too many more days with him."

"Jesse! I'm done. Bring me a napkin!" Walker yelled from his throne.

"I see he done ate his manners too," Digg said, stuffing more warmed bread into his mouth.

"Yep, a little more every day."

"Good luck to ya'," Tak said.

"Thanks, guys."

"You ignore him, heah? He knows you in heah puttin' yur foot in it."

"I don't know what you said, but thanks," Jesse said, leading the two men to the door.

Chapter 24

The close proximity was driving them both crazy.

Walker was up and about every day and night. He fixed the broken latch on the window, cleaned the chimney, scrubbed the potbellied stove and swept the fireplaces. If she put down a cup he swooped in, washed it, dried it and had it back on the shelf before she could decide if she wanted more.

One evening, in order to irritate Walker by giving him a taste of his own medicine, she went about the house mopping everywhere he stepped, and sweeping imaginary crumbs as he finished lunch. She would wipe down the phone every time he hung it up. Before dinner she even found some nails that she had hammered into the wall in the back bathroom, removed them and hammered them in again while he tried to read in the den.

When they sat down to dinner things were tense. He seasoned his plate of food and she removed the items one by one. If his napkin was dirty she would crumble it up, and toss it out, never staying put. He knew the game she was playing but he wasn't going to cooperate. He wasn't leaving. And he wasn't going to let her get to him. Being locked up with a beautiful, vibrant vixen of a woman makes all kinds of thoughts pop into a man's head, and when his patience grew thin, he would show her just what she was doing to him. Her scent made his blood thunder through his veins. Walker had found himself waking with painful erections, taking ice-cold showers by lunchtime and ready to fling her onto a counter by dinner.

One late night, Jesse got out of bed and went to check on Walker but instead found his empty bed. In a panic she opened the door to the back room just a crack, praying she wouldn't find him there laid out on the floor. He was fine. Statuesquely fine. He sat stone still and beautiful in the flickering light. The smoke did not hinder her vision and he was also very, very naked and, although she couldn't see the X-rated parts of him, the exposed parts made her flush furiously. How could she be thinking these lustful thoughts when he was performing a sacred ritual?

She went to close the door and leave him to his ceremony when she felt the heat of the room intensify. Steam began to hiss from some unseen source and she thought she heard him invite her in. She sat on the steps, her lids growing heavy, the sweat soaking her clothes. It was dark, and she recalled reading how this ritual represented the ignorance of humans; the steam, the creative force of the universe; the hot stones, dormant life. She felt light as if carried on air, and all around her she saw wonders she had never noticed. The vibrant green of the grass, the strength of hundred-year-old trees, the short lives of insects, the smell of the earth and the freshness of water. Feeling around her, she felt sand and rocks and saw the night sky with its winking stars looking down at her.

All of a sudden, her head was being held down under the coldest water she had ever felt. She kicked and fought but could do nothing against the large hand that held her down. At one point she thought she would die just from the sheer cold. Finally, her head popped up and she sat very unladylike in the tub. She looked around and up into Walker's cold, unforgiving eyes.

"Women and men should not share this ritual, the spirits are fickle and we are especially vulnerable to them," was all he said by way of explanation for trying to drown her. She pushed his hands away and refused his help in getting out of the tub.

Later, in his room, he thought about what he had seen. It had started in the normal way, feeling the tensions leave his body, watching the evil in him manifest outside of him and him pushing it away. He felt stronger, his body unyielding to the impish spirits trying to distract him from his quest. But in the midst of his sweat he saw her calling to him, in a sweet and sensual voice. She was as naked as he and she was standing in a clearing, laughing and dancing. At first he told his mind to move on, that it was just another spirit feeding itself from the images in him, but she didn't fly, or try to lead him. It was like having a neighbor who simply waved and went on their way.

He followed her to the river and watched her reach up to the sky, but he couldn't look away from her beauty to see the stars. She turned and welcomed him and together they went into the river. He could feel her trusting eyes on him and he took her in his arms, held her close and felt himself becoming lost in the wonders and textures around him. She was real. Her skin was silky, her eyes so loving, her touch tentative, her lips moving to meet his. He felt their softness, tasted her breath, smelled her hair. They moved as one, with the passion mounting between them, the water bringing them closer. He held her tighter and they touched every inch of skin that could be and revealed those secrets each shared; and when he entered her he felt like he was drowning.

The world shattered around him, his eyes blinded by the power of the moment, his ears pierced by the sound of his own voice, his body convulsing until he awoke with fire burning in his throat and into his chest. It was long moments before he could shut out the panic.

The room, however, was not completely dark, the fire not out, as it often was when he came out of meditation. He looked around and saw Jesse laying facedown on the cold tiles. He turned over her unconscious body and found her pulse slow and erratic, her temperature high. He lifted her to the tub, turned on the ice-cold tap, hoping that she wasn't yet close to the end of the vision. It wasn't that he meant to deny her, but it was very intense and even more real than any he had ever experienced. He worried that her earthbound body could have a stroke or a heart attack. The worst she would suffer from the water was shock, which would shut her body down long enough for him to get her to the hospital. At best, she would fight for her life.

He held her down for two or three seconds, then let her up. He waited twenty seconds, then dunked her again. When she flinched a tiny bit he held on to the side of the tub for dear life. He was so happy to see that sign of life that he made plans never to be so irresponsible again. He would never make such a strong and potent mixture when others were in the house. He didn't know how she came to be in the room with him, but he would not be that careless. He was stupid in attempting to dispel the intense sexual feelings he was having for Jesse all in one night. He had lit every herb he could find to possibly induce a coma, and give himself and his spirit guide plenty of time to sort it all out.

She looked angry when she tilted her head up to look at him, but relief was so strong in that second, he wanted to grab her by her curly red locks. He let out a bellow that Jesse was sure they heard even at the lodge.

The next day Walker went with Digg back to the station, and hid out with Tak for a few hours. Over the course of the week, he tried to find ways to keep his mind busy. He would read and then look down the hall in enough time to glimpse the smooth small of her back and toned midriff before being engulfed by his oversized Northwestern shirt. He'd have to cease reading and go masturbate just to regain some semblance of control over his mind and body. He'd be going into the bathroom when she would be coming into the house in her spandex workout clothes, her body covered in a soft sheen, her hair pulled up into a curly poof on the top of her head. He'd go straight into the shower for a cold one.

One afternoon Jesse had come in to collect laundry and help change linens. She was singing along with her CD Walkman. She stopped and spoke to him in civil tones. He barely heard her as he was trying to shut her out of his mind. She told him an interesting and funny story about her morning. As she spoke all he cared about was how she looked in her outfit. She was wearing a Jimi Hendrix concert shirt and cutoff jeans making her legs look thick and scrumptious. She didn't seem to notice at all that he was so attracted to her. She had the audacity to walk around with no bra, the round globes jumping with her movements, her ass cheeks fully covered but looking so inviting as she danced around. As soon as she left the room, he jumped and refixed the window. When she left the house he went to the back room to meditate. He wanted to be free of the sexual image of her. He tried another potion, one that he had not tampered with, but that was not as potent as the last.

He had an intense sweat. Nothing like the Jesse vision but definitely a complete body cleansing and revitalization. He could stretch without the tightness and he was able to eat dinner with her without picturing her naked. He even slept a dreamless sleep. But when she came in sucking on a lollipop, he puffed his cheroot with lightning speed, popped out of the rocking chair and headed to the shower.

The day she came in from the shed hauling logs, she was laughingly telling him about a deer who was standing sentry over the woodpile that she tried to shoo away like a dog, only to be chased around the cabin. The minute she finished he got on the roof, cleaned the gutters, then had two shots of tequila. His cold shower lasted for twenty minutes and he still was forced to relieve the tension while under the frosty blast. He only hoped she hadn't heard him call out her name.

Although it would probably be easier on him to just leave, he wasn't about to let her win this battle. He had started the obsessive cleaning to get under her skin. But in the end, he simply ended up with diligently prepared meals; a home that sparkled with a polished military shine; friends who wanted to hang around; a beautiful, if unbearable, female companion; and restless nights. So far, he'd kept his silent promise. She wasn't ready and he wouldn't push her.

He stayed up late one night after all the stress of work and cleaning. He glanced up and saw her nude silhouette going past his door. She came back and paused, peeling back the crinkly paper of a Twinkie. When she took the first bite, it was his undoing. Every image—from giving her flowers to fucking her while sweaty—came into his mind, and now he was about to confront this issue before she drove him crazy.

Walker padded across the carpet and into the hall. Jesse was polishing off the last of her midnight snack. He grabbed her around the waist, spun her around and placed her palms on the wall. He knew her words were about to be colorful.

"I don't want to fight, Jesse, I want to make peace, maybe more."

She wasn't nude like Walker had first assumed, she was wearing some sort of flesh-colored mesh camisole and matching panties. His heart beat in staccato. Her body was thick and firm, pressed flush against his.

"Deal."

His response to her was immediate and Walker could feel the slight arch in her back that brought her ass in perfect contact with his dick. It wasn't so much his pulling her as their gravitating toward each other. Even though her back was to him, he could feel her breath coming in gasps as if she had just finished one of her kick boxing classes. He could hear his name on her lips like a prayer and the soft protests being swallowed by the moment. His muscled arm went gently around Jesse's neck, brushing with an open palm, touching all the skin from one shoulder to the other. One of her hands shot from the wall to his arm, her nails digging in his skin.

He did not let that deter him. He set out to show this woman that there was no urgency in their time together. That they had all night and day, and hopefully more nights to come. Walker did not just want her bodily, he wanted to move her heaven and earth. He wanted and needed to believe in love. He was determined that when his body and her body came together, it was going to be something that neither of them would ever want to live without.

Jesse's breathing was shallow, she held his arm so tight, she may have drawn blood. But her eyes were closed and all she could think of was how she wanted to give herself to this man. To let him be the man. She had finally grown tired of fighting the good fight alone and being alone. She was tired of being in control and she hadn't felt this safe since leaving her parents' home so many moons ago. She'd always been her own safe haven, always protecting her heart and keeping her feet squarely on the ground and, for all she had, living with Walker, watching him happy in this godforsaken little plot of dirt made her feel wonderful and needed. She felt herself sway and yet she never fell. His arms were around her, holding her, protecting her just like on that first night.

Whenever she had nightmares she could find him smoking his cigar in the rocker next to her. It was odd that first night, waking up startled, and stifling her screams and seeing him in the chair. He explained that the only way he could relax was to see for himself that she was just dreaming. Since that night he often sat vigil when the nightmares engulfed her; his presence quickly became a comfort, and he never mentioned it the next day. Up until now, the nightmares had been hers and hers alone. She took heavy sedatives whenever she was at her parents, or when she traveled with Gideon or Doug. She tried to bring herself to confide in her friends and family, they would talk to her, understand and accept her, just like this man . . .

Jesse woke from her thoughts with a jolt, immediately trying to struggle out of his arms. "Walker, no, no, no, Walker, don't . . ."

"Slow down, Tiger. I'm not gonna hurt you," he said as he petted her arms. "You've built a wall around your heart. You're not the first person to do that and you won't be the last."

"Don't go psychoanalyzing me."

"There's nothing psycho about it. Your wall is so nonpsychological and real that I can see it. It's so tall no one can scale it, it's so thick no one can crash through, it has no doors and no windows. I don't even know how you get air."

"It's not that serious."

"Yeah, it is, because the problem with keeping everyone out is that you get stuck inside."

He was right on the mark. Her body went pliant beneath him and she closed her eyes and felt his warm breath on her neck. She leaned farther into him until she felt the heavy beat of his heart and they drifted together to the far wall so that his back was up against it and she cradled in his arms.

"Cloud," she said, weary in defeat, "having lived in my tower for so long, I don't know how to give of myself. I just know it's kept me from getting hurt. It's as if my emotions were all raw. And one day I just sorta removed myself. I could still see and hear the people, but they were no longer rubbing me raw. You should be worried that I may hurt you."

"I'm not afraid of you, I'm afraid for you. You're like a zoo tiger trying to claw his way out of steel and cement. Whenever you see people you cringe because you've trusted them and been hurt or you lash out trying to take everything down with you. I know you, Tiger, I was the bear across from you. The one with the loudest growl and the saddest eyes. You're here to find yourself, you have that freedom to walk on the outside of the cage."

His words sort of blew across her ear in an imagined whisper. His right hand brushed lightly over her full lashes as he spoke so her eyes fluttered closed again. His left hand splayed seductively across her abdomen. His warmth infused her and her head lolled back against him. He moved her curls with gently coaxing fingers, then turned her face so a blank canvas of wet, sandy-brown skin displayed itself to him. One kiss after another, one light, one deep, one long, one short. Each one something different from the last, her senses heightened to an intensity that was maddening.

"Is this the skin you call tough? I bet I couldn't find a rough spot on your whole body, Jesse Ruth. Even your combat scars are smooth and soft." He had seen the small marks on her legs and forearms. He figured they were the root of her nightmares. Walker was rubbing the deep indent on her back with the pad of his thumb while he followed the line of Jesse's neck with his tongue where he now placed what seemed to be the one hundredth kiss. "Your skin is beautiful."

"What if *I'm* afraid?" she asked.

"Then I'll hold you until you're ready to handle it on your own, your own way, and you ask me to let you go." With that he dropped one last, lingering kiss on the back of her neck. He extricated himself from her presence. Feeling a profound cold at the loss of his body heat, she opened her eyes to see him standing before her, holding out his hand to her. She tentatively placed her hand in his and he slowly led her into the master bedroom.

Mike left her standing by the door as he built a fire and lit the oil lamps in the room. She shivered but not from the cold. The flickering light reflected the quivering she felt in the pit of her stomach. He returned to her and led her to the bed. Jesse's mind was a jumbled mass of confusion as he communicated his need of her without words. Mike stood before her and undressed himself slowly, peeling the white shirt over his head, revealing toned golden muscles to her. He was bigger than Jesse remembered. His chest was a solid expanse of untainted flesh leading to broad shoulders and his stomach was ridged like an old-fashioned washboard. From a distance Jesse thought he had been ruggedly handsome but now up close she saw how smooth the planes and angles of his face were. His eyes were clear pools of limpid gray framed by a firm brow and a stern jaw, but it was his succulent lips that caused her to dream. She remembered how those lips felt and saw how moist and inviting they were now.

Mike allowed his shorts to fall to the floor so that they both wore only their undergarments. He felt vulnerable as her eyes raked over his physique, but he wanted her to see that he was willing to lay himself bare for her. When he laid a heartfelt kiss on her neck she shamelessly exhaled all the fear, tension and loneliness she had been holding on to for so long. He was exposing not just his body but also his soul, he wanted her prepared for the same. He slowly removed his underwear, and watched her eyes' blatant perusal of his maleness. She looked surprised and a bit daunted. The steady thrum of his blood increased and so did his heavy erection. He put a finger under her chin to focus her attention on him, her face flushed, she was shorter than he first deduced because of the fact that she carried herself with such assured confidence. Without the pretense he could see the fragile creature that stood before him. Jesse started to remove her undershirt and Mike's breath caught.

Watching the round swells pop free of the flimsy cloth sent his pulse racing. The mounds lowered enough so that their sumptuous weight rested in the palms of his uplifted hands. He took a step back and in one seamless motion she removed her underwear. He looked upon her precious nudity in the soft golden light, and his breath rushed from him. But he was determined to take it slow, to make it more than just this night, to show her love.

He took her hand and placed it on his chest. Her eyes widened when she felt his pulse racing beneath her fingers. His voice was heavy with passion, his eyes lidded. "Touch me anywhere, any way you want." He closed his eyes and trusted her. He didn't expect to feel her mouth in the center of his back up between his shoulder blades. The feel of her mouth added to the ache in his groin.

Jesse felt his body vibrate with energy. It was as if he was charging the air in the room with sexual heat. She lowered herself and sank her teeth into the plump cheeks of his ass. First one, then the other, making sure to lick and kiss after each bite, she slid her hand around to test the stiffness of his cock and almost fell on her butt. She moved in front of him, wide-eyed, and knew it must have grown another inch.

"I promise to take it slow with you," he whispered.

Cloud let his tongue roam a spot on the underside of her breast, causing her to inhale and hold her breath. Next he kissed her left hip, while his hand snuck around to cup the juiciness of her ass. He felt her breathing become labored and looked up to see the glorious rise and fall of her chest. He sucked on the delicate flesh behind her knee, and massaged her mound.

He could hear little tortured sounds escape her, and Mike felt his body responding with a fierceness he could no longer hold at bay when she said, "Cloud, please."

From there Jesse's knees gave in to the desire she felt. He caught her in the perfect position, his face between the fleshy heat of her thighs. Wrapping his arms around her hips, he slowly licked and suckled. She was panting and writhing on the bed—pleading and begging him for anything and everything. Mike thought she tasted of the sea and he wanted to drown in it. He felt her body tremble and she tried to bring her legs around his head but he held the inside of her thighs firmly, keeping her open, drinking in as much of her as he could. He watched as her hands cupped her breasts and she moaned long and loud when she came. The sound and the taste of her nearly undid him. Carefully, he gave her one last kiss and moved up beside her.

Jesse waited until her breaths slowed and came over him, nuzzling his neck, his jaw, kissing his lips and forehead. She stroked his broad chest and gently touched the silver rings. Mike stared intently at her, loving the flushed look on her face. She moved down and grabbed his large member, slowly lowering her mouth on him. Mike nearly came off the bed when he felt himself secured within the confines of her hot, wet mouth. He wanted to push himself all the way in, but he barely restrained himself and allowed her the agonizingly slow ministrations. She took as much of him as she could, flicking the underside of his head with the flat of her tongue, using her hand to stroke his length while gently cupping his balls. She was astonished at his hardness sheathed in soft delicate skin. When she gently began licking his balls, he gripped a fistful of crumpled sheets with one hand and grabbed her hair with the other.

"Jesse. . . . Jess . . . please stop . . . stop." Mike could barely get the words through his clenched teeth.

Jesse loved the sheen on his body, his earthen scent. She felt a woman's pride knowing that she could make this strong man lose control. She alternately licked and sucked her way back up the swollen shaft, drinking in the hot, sweet and salty juice. Mike made a hoarse, strangled sound and pulled her up and moved on top of her and dipped his head to lick the valley between her breasts. He took a breast in each hand gently kneading and massaging them until the peaks had further hardened. He laved each one and moved down to kiss her stomach. Sensing that she was ready for him, he leaned back and rolled the condom over himself and then came down, placing an arm on either side of her head. He fitted himself between her legs, hovering, waiting, and somehow fearing that this was just a dream. He leaned down and kissed her forehead, her nose, her lips, her cheeks. He ran his eyes over her face, giving her all the time she needed to turn away, change her mind, push him off. He couldn't control the trembling of his body and the few seconds it took to finally see the slight nod of acquiescence from Jesse almost killed him.

He cradled her head and neck, adjusted himself and began to push inside of her. He felt her body stiffen, felt the inner resistance and saw what he thought was slight discomfort in the crease of her forehead.

"I don't want to hurt you, sweetheart," Mike whispered while testing her and pushing in a bit more. "I just want to be inside of you. Let me in, Jesse."

Jesse flexed her hips and Mike glided deeper inside of her. She'd been nervous at the feel of him, his size and his hardness, but she knew that he'd never intentionally cause her pain. She saw the way he so carefully watched the responses of her body. Her tension eased and slowly her clenched insides began to relax. He pushed deeper and she accepted him, feeling herself almost painfully stretched to the limit. Moaning low, she desperately clung to his arms, biting her lower lip, not daring to move, overcome by emotion and the insistent pressure.

Mike stilled himself once he was completely buried

inside her. He wanted to give her time to adjust, to prepare herself for him. He grappled with the instinct to slam into her warm sheath, to take and claim her in a fury of love and lust. In his mind he saw himself without a condom, riding her hard and spilling his warm seed deep inside of her. Sweat broke out all over his powerful body. He shut his eyes to will the image away, but he could feel Jesse's eyes upon him. She saw the vulnerability and desperation on his face and it made her want to weep.

He loved the way she hugged him, the contours of her body seemed to be made just for him. He felt her wetness, the way her inner muscles clung to his shaft and knew her body was welcoming him, so he began thrusting slowly.

Jesse loudly sobbed at the feel of him moving back and forth within her. He was so big and male that he could have easily overpowered her, but didn't. He held much of his weight off of her, allowing her the freedom to move unfettered. She tried to match him stroke for slow stroke, the delicious feeling of fullness becoming more intensely pleasurable with each thrust. She nibbled at the taut flesh of his collarbone, buried her hands in his silken hair, and gently kissed his tensed jaw. She massaged his muscled back, telling him that she was fine, that he could just let go. Jesse felt some of the tension leave his body as he lowered and settled more fully on top of her. He moved his lips to a spot behind her ear that caused her to whimper and hold her breath.

His thrusts became heavier and went deeper. He firmly gripped the back of her thigh, lifted one leg and wrapped it around his waist, and settled his hand back on her taut buttocks. Jesse's head lolled back and she felt as if the world was falling away. He placed a trail of fiery kisses along her neck, flitting across her collarbone and ending at her shoulder.

"Stay with me, baby . . . it's all right," he cooed, while moving his hips this way and that, trying to give her the most pleasure and hold back his own. He listened as her body yielded its secrets, heard her grateful moans. She placed her hands on his massive chest, trying to do his bidding, to stay with him, to stop hiding. She knew that she'd never been made love to so completely, not in the truest sense. Mike was inside her body and touching her soul. He was marking her for eternity.

He reveled in the look of pleasure and hunger in her face. He couldn't keep the slow pace anymore and sunk even deeper inside her, loving the feel of her pliant and sweaty body beneath him. Fully adjusted to his length and girth, Jesse's hips moved with the natural ease of the ocean waves and he fought desperately to stay ashore. Her hands began to dig into his back. She made plaintive sounds and wrapped her other leg around him, begging him to go deeper, harder, faster. He held back, knowing it'd be over soon if she continued that sensual rocking motion. He removed her arms from his back and held them above her head with one of his. He used the other to hold one side of her hips steady while he continued to deeply plunder her innermost parts. He leaned down and kissed and suckled her breasts, wiping away the moisture that had pooled between them and smoothing her moist hair away from her face. He could barely control his breathing.

"I want you to see the way we fit together, Jesse."

He leaned back, half pulled out of her and willed

Jesse to look down at where their bodies joined. Watching his thick staff inside her was almost too much for her to bear. She felt feverish at the sight, she looked in wonder and almost disbelief that he could fit, that he could bring that much pleasure. Her legs were shaking uncontrollably. In a raspy voice that she didn't recognize as hers, Jesse said, "Please . . . I can't . . . I want you to . . ."

He heard her loud and clear. He drove all the way inside of her ferociously, and for a slight second feared that he'd hurt her, but Jesse's body told him differently. She was wetter than before, alternately opening and tightening around him. His face was of intense painful concentration as he repeatedly buried himself to the hilt, adjusting so that he'd make contact with her clitoris on every heavy downward thrust. The only sounds were those of the night, their bodies coming together, his heavy strangled breaths, and her long moans. He gripped her around the waist to keep her steady and Jesse twined an arm around his neck. Together they instinctively sought each other's free hand and held it. He couldn't hold back any longer, his sac drew up close to his body and with his lips drawn over his teeth, Mike growled low in Jesse's ear, his pace becoming frantic, giving in to his need, slamming into her over and over. Her legs drew up around his waist.

They moved together in perfect synchronization, with Jesse's body coaxing, goading him on. She was letting him know she could take whatever he was offering. He'd never met a woman who could. It was a painfully erotic dance and Mike didn't think he'd ever be the same afterwards. Jesse's eyes glazed over, her mouth opened as if to speak but there was no way she could. Her heart slammed into her chest, she could feel the blood rushing through her veins. Mike seemed to be everywhere at once—in, over, beside and underneath her. She was helpless in his maelstrom. Her spine arched and she buried her face in his neck as her orgasm overpowered her with brutal strength. Her inner walls clammed rhythmically on his member, drawing him in. Mike drove on, keeping pace, preventing her from cresting. Jesse managed a hoarse scream and bit into his powerfully corded neck. She heard Cloud call her name, felt his entire body shudder, heard his strangled sounds as he filled her even more. He was drowning in her wet heat, his senses completely in tune with hers, his member throbbing. He felt his soul fly out of his body. For several seconds Mike was nowhere and everywhere, floating on a cloud of intense pleasure, his seed flowing from him in long, hot spurts. They kissed deeply and looked into each other's eyes, speaking without words, breathing heavily, coming down from their high together. After a while, Mike managed to disentangle their sweaty bodies, although he instantly missed being inside of her. He drew her close, running his hands over her arms, kissing the top of her head and the back of her neck. He let his arm come to rest around her and palmed her breast, drawing her even closer, marveling at the way her body curved and fit perfectly into him.

"Did I hurt you?" Cloud asked cautiously.

"No," she answered, barely able to restrain the tears. She'd never felt this way, never knew she could.

He lowered his hand and let it come to rest on the soft down of her mound, marveling at its secrets, feeling her swollen labia, hoping that she wasn't sore because he was already feeling the stirrings of desire.

Despite the magic of that night, being vulnerable didn't come naturally, and Jesse viewed it as a weakness in herself. Jesse was uncomfortable that Walker dragged that side of her out of her murky depths and cleaned it up just so he could dissect her in the light. He needn't have bothered, she knew who she was and what she was, she had no problem with herself. She knew the exact date she had made Utopia her marble tower.

The stroll down tragedy lane and the barely repressed sexual tension between them finally drove Jesse out of the cabin. One day she drove three hours to Kent to shop for exotic ingredients for Doug and Katherine's welcome dinner. She window-shopped at every antique store, looking for the perfect antique cradle for Katherine. She'd been on boats and in barns near Lake Lure, to the beach and, most recently, she had taken a trip to boredom and back. It was liberating but also at times frightening to have no particular purpose when she woke. In fact she had no one in particular to worry about, talk to or visit. She met some interesting people, she rented jet skis with a group of women from the Cancer Awareness Foundation, North Carolina chapter, making a sizable contribution on their behalf to cancer research. She volunteered at the community center and took a pottery class from a girl of about sixteen, named Viona, with purple and blue hair. At night Jesse would put finishing touches on the bathroom until recently, when she went in and there was nothing left to do. She spent some days jotting down business plans for

Lion and Zak's store. She couldn't wait to include Katherine in her escapades.

Jessica made the mandatory calls to her family, accountant, attorney, financial adviser and publicist. She met with Sam to complete the articles and took photos with Yusef. When she wanted company, Zak and Lion always invited her along somewhere or she made plans with Sylvia or Lila. Jesse ventured farther and farther; she drove all the way to the other end of North Carolina just to spend an evening with her parents. They were thrilled to see her, her mother assuring her she wasn't losing too much weight and her father impressed to have her help in the garden and see her in the kitchen. She even managed to get her brother Josh on the phone while she was there. On the way back she realized that talking to her family was really just listening intently with a sprinkling of "uh-huhs," "reallys" and a few "okay, I wills" for good mea-sure. She would do exactly as she promised them and take care of anything they asked her to take care of. They weren't demanding or ungrateful, it was just the way of things. It didn't change the fact that she loved being with them, her mother was always her rock and her father was comic relief.

She had had no real social life to speak of when living in the city, but she had always had her latest client event to fill the void. She did make it a point to speak to Phaedra, who had kids to watch, feed, chase, yell at or help . . . So the calls could drag on a bit with Jesse on indefinite hold or they could end abruptly with a crash in the background. The only reason Jesse bothered Phaedra, was that she had her nose in the papers and her finger on the pulse of everybody in the Utopia structure.

She had become such a different person. Now it was her quiet moments with Lion, her comedy sessions with Zak, her chats with Lila, irrelevant stories from Tak, the gossip from Sylvia and time with Walker that kept her going. Apparently, she needed people.

At Utopia someone had called every three minutes or needed to see her every five and had wanted ten minutes and always wasted fifteen. She saw clients, consumers, competitors, staff, and crowds and crowds of people on the streets hustling from one place to the next. Tourists asking for directions, strangers striking up conversations about the weather, in order to distract you while they steal your cab, maitre d's kissing your ass when they see the Platinum card.

"Oh, man," she lamented, "I'm losing my mind. I need to get out."

Jesse ate at every restaurant on the map. Spoke to anyone who remotely looked in her direction and smiled until her face hurt. No one knew her from the holes in the walls at the places she chose to eat, but people found her easygoing, helpful, witty and informative.

Jesse took a break from running all over North Carolina to work the Southern Highland Handicraft Guild Fair with Lion and Zak, and for the entire day the men teased her mercilessly about sharing a cabin with Walker. The men used very X-rated dialogue, painting incredibly detailed images. Jesse's marketing skills managed to sell out the stand except for a few magazine racks. "You guys might want to consider opening a mail-order business. I bet it would help you buy that cabin full out. And you'd only have to make stuff you already have orders for. You get the names of the out-of-town customers who buy from you at the fair. Hit them at the autumn holidays, make a killing through the end of the year and close up shop till June."

Suddenly, both men noticed the empty booth. "Lion?"

"Yeah, Zak."

"She did it. She sold those ugly little wood duck bobby things you make."

"Yeah, and she got rid of those two nasty batches of messed-up cookies you baked."

"We'll be busy all night restocking from the storage shed, baking and loading up the plants." They stood wide-eyed. "Imagine the money. You think it'll be this way tomorrow?"

"Only if Jesse Jane comes," Zak quipped.

"Not I, said the blind man to the deaf dog. I'm going to the Newton Day Spa tomorrow at 10 AM. Got a facial and massage scheduled. You two really should consider a seasonal business, I can draw up a really simple plan, get you two or three investors, a distributor, help you get out a small catalogue," she said, moving away. Jesse hadn't had the time to work on the store, and summer was kicking up for Mike, so he didn't either. But this would get them started. "Right now I'm gonna take in a flick. I'll hitch a ride back to the cabin, you guys have a long night ahead of you."

"I suppose you could call Mike, he'll give you a ride all night long, if you asked nicely."

That got Jesse's attention. "The two of you need to stop insisting that something is going on between me and Walker."

"You can stop playing this game, Ms. Bishop," Zak said, picking up debris from all the plants sold.

Lion spoke next. "I think the lady doth protest too much. Almost as much as Mike."

"Like the two of them are in cahoots to keep their little affair a secret by presenting a unified front of disdain for one another," Zak assessed.

"Shut up, you two. I've got a movie to go catch."

When she arrived back at the cabin, Jesse grabbed one of Walker's undershirts, got undressed, threw on the shirt that was hanging on the back of the bedroom door as a bathrobe and headed to the new bathroom. She peeked into Walker's bedroom and, finding it empty, knocked gently on the hallway bathroom door to reassure herself she was absolutely alone. To her relief, he wasn't lounging in the den either, despite the strong cigar scent that lingered.

Jesse pushed open the heavy door, then stood frozen on the second step as Walker's damp, naked body rose like a demigod out of the tub. She noticed the tidal waves spilling over the side of the bathtub, creating rainbow puddles on the floor with every sensual movement of his body. The only light was from the skylight, which illuminated every detail of his masculine frame. Walker stood in profile, one of his nipple rings throwing off light, his long mass of thick blue-black hair plastered against the gentle curve of his sculpted buttocks. His body was relaxed but she noted how tight and corded his muscles were. His smooth thighs dripped rivulets of water, while it seemed to cascade off his slim hips in slow motion. Her eyes moved up with wide-eyed wonder. The sparse hair on his body was as dark and black as the hair on his head. She took a long, lingering look at his narrow waist and washboard abs, her mind kept revisiting the fact that he was a deep cinnamon-gold all over. With his every turn and twist it ap-

peared his body just got sexier, the color more tantalizing, or his mass larger, his muscles more defined and
his hair glossier. It was as if he was preening and intentionally taunting her.

"Ummm, huh."

The clearing of Walker's throat jerked Jesse to full
attention, bringing her eyes to the smirk on his lips.
When the door to the bathroom opened he was bent
over retrieving his cigar. Giving her the moon. He was
so embarrassed he nearly burned his fingers. He turned
around, ready to hurl insults and expletives at his intruder and toss her out bodily if need be, but he caught
sight of her in his favorite old flannel shirt. Jesse was
swimming in the ugly, mud-brown thing that looked
more like chocolate cradling her skin. It was ratty, with
frayed edges that brushed the tops of her thighs. His indignation and embarrassment fled. Her brown eyes,
wide at first, like a doe's, filled with appreciation and
became clouded with a dark, sultry allure. The lust he
saw there caused him to stop and allow her to look her
fill. He became bold about his nudity as her eyes de-
voured him with a fierce hunger. How she wished she
could just kiss that look off of his self-satisfied face.

"Now I know how women must feel when walking
past a construction site." He blew a deep plume of
smoke into the air, which joined the steam rising off
his glowing skin.

"You don't know the half of it. Catcalls, whistles and very
vulgar comments. I spared you all that degrading stuff,"
she responded, trying to knock his ego off his shoulder.

"And yet you're still standing here, staring at me.
Unless, of course, you're gonna get in with me. And
since I'm still naked . . ."

"Sorry," Jesse muttered, finally dropping her gaze

and her things, and hastening out of the door into the den. She plopped down on the couch, threw the blanket over her head, mortified at her blatant perusal and unconcealed attraction for that man. The man she had successfully avoided every day, even though he pranced through her dreams every night.

"It did have a TV dream–scene quality to it, didn't it?" Walker asked, standing in the doorway between the two rooms. "All the steam and smoke and don't forget the soft light hitting me at the most flattering angles. And the soft, puppy dog moan that escaped you added the perfect soap opera moment. But, no, not a dream. You stood there, staring at me."

"It wasn't on purpose . . ." she whined.

"Come out from under there. I'm not going to have it out with a blanket."

She shot up to the arm of the couch with the blanket slung around her shoulders as if she was a kid playing superhero. Kneeling on the soft cushions, she yelled at his chest, "I've already apologized once!"

Unconsciously Walker secured the towel tighter around his waist. He was starting to get miffed at her indignation. *His* family jewels had been on display, and *he* was the one in a position of humiliation—why was she so pissed? He had been giving her the time and space. He wanted to be with her again, but he wanted to make sure she was ready and now here she was acting as if they were strangers.

"Could you just accept my apology graciously and move on!" she yelled, her arms gesturing wildly before her, flopping back on the couch and under the blanket just like a little kid.

She tucked the blanket under her folded arms, but the blanket sort of shifted and she could see him out of the corner of her eye. "What were you doing in my bathroom?" she asked with barely veiled hostility.

"Taking a bath, in what had once been my sweat room, in my home," Walker responded with similar hostility.

"You never take baths in there," she debated.

"You just finished it. 'Sides, Tak said I've been pushing myself too much this past week. He strongly suggested that I soak in steaming hot water."

"You should have told me."

"I don't need your permission to bathe."

"No, but as a courtesy . . ."

"Are you offering assistance again? I could use a good back scrub. It'll only take a minute to warm the water. And the offer for you to join me is still on the table." He took another toke on his cigar with a look of satisfaction. She was tempting him with her one leg hanging off the couch. He wanted to gently move his body over hers on the couch. Rain small bites across her exposed cleavage and run his hand just below the edge of the shirt where it hid her most precious secret. It even crossed his mind to go over to the couch, throw her over his shoulder and forcibly drag her into the tub so that he could see the wet flannel cling to her body. And then unbutton it with careful, unhurried precision, and full body-to-body contact. He would wash her from head to foot, treating her like a princess. Then he would pull her atop of him and devour her with kisses . . .

"I suppose I'm not the only one capable of being caught up in a moment," she said, dropping her eyes to his towel.

He was growing uncomfortable due to his very explicit daydream and she had been witness to that. "Happens to guys all the time. It's the wind."

She noticed him trying to regain his composure and break the spell by taking a more conspicuous pull on his cigar.

She pulled up the blanket to just under her nose, and he was struck dumb by her childlike behavior and innocent beauty.

"Come out from under that blanket," Walker commanded as he ground out his cigar in a nearby ashtray and moved stealthily in her direction.

Her body moved slowly off the couch. First he saw toes painted a faint pink, he glimpsed the delicate arch of her feet attached to beautifully defined legs that stretched out in front of his eyes. She stood up to her full height, put her hands on her shapely hips and she barely reached his chin. Before any more heated words could be exchanged he pulled her up against his body so that she could now feel the result of his daydreams. Her hands went up to his muscled chest, "I can smell you," Walker whispered as he nuzzled her neck, ". . . you want me, I can smell it."

Jesse squirmed and struggled but his grip held fast. He slid a hand behind her neck and turned her face to him. "I'm going to kiss you. Don't bite me and don't make me regret this, let me enjoy this. It's time you stopped running from me."

Jesse's mind silently screamed *No, no, no, no, I don't want you.* She gave a halfhearted attempt to get away from Walker. When he tightened the embrace she could feel all the things she had just seen, his chest perfectly sculpted, his legs encompassing both of hers, and she didn't have any words to describe what his manhood pressed against her stomach was doing to her. With the gentle pressure of his hand on her neck, the last of her common sense shattered like glass. His touch sent hot and cold sensations to the tips of Jesse's toes and back again. His lips barely brushed hers, but she felt as if she was being smothered. She could taste the cherry from his wood-tipped cigar. She could hear his heartbeats in between her own. His breath was warm against her skin and his lips pressed that much deeper. His tongue licked at her bottom lip and her body went limp in his arms. It lasted longer than forever as he tasted, tantalized and teased her into submission. He ended the kiss while sitting her on the couch.

"Now, that's more like the first kiss I imagined," he said.

Jesse wondered if he imagined them kissing often. "So, let's just put the other incidents behind us so we can get on to the part where we laugh about it. And, City, in the future don't try to avoid me."

Walker walked out of the room before she could deny and refute his statements. Why did he assume she was avoiding him rather than being out because she had a life? She would have to step up her game or else this man would have her sitting dumbfounded after every touch. She stomped over to the hallway and shouted at the bathroom near his room, "I hope you washed out the tub!" Then she marched back to the bathroom near the den and slammed the door behind her.

Walker, however, didn't hear her, as he was standing in an ice-cold shower mumbling to himself. Off in the distance he thought he heard a door slam, echoing his sentiments, just as he slammed his fist into the shower wall.

Chapter 25

He took a quick look at his watch, giving her a minute more before knocking. The bedroom door was flung open wide in his face and she charged into him. Jesse had been so caught up in leaving without being seen, she hadn't expected him to be standing right outside the door, so she slammed into the massive wall of unforgiving muscle. He grabbed her car keys and ducked her instinctive slap.

"*Now* what are you doing?" Jesse asked, following Walker down the hall. She felt like a child scrambling after an angry parent.

"Trying not to get hit by you anymore." He stopped abruptly and turned to glare at her. "Why do you do that?"

"Do what?" she asked, annoyed, walking into him when he stopped abruptly.

"Hit me so often. I swear everyone's gonna be talking about my abusive relationship with my live-in lover." He started moving again.

"What in the hell are you talking about? I'm trying to find out what you think you're doing with my keys.

Why are you hanging them back up when I've got places to go?" she asked, reaching to take her keys back off the hook.

"Because I got the lodge minibus. I figure if your *'friends'* travel anything like you then they'll need the extra room, especially your *'pregnant friend.'*"

"Where is it parked?" she asked, snatching the van key from his hand. "And stop using those damned 'quotation fingers,'" she said, imitating him. "I'm sure Katherine will be thankful for the extra leg room, she isn't tall but she likes to think she is."

"You're welcome," he responded, taking back the key, "but I'd be less worried with a man behind the wheel."

"Oh, do you know of one?"

"I've elected myself. I believe you've seen that I qualify. I've also made the trip often enough to make it a smooth and timely ride."

She took her keys from the hook. "Thank you, but no. I wouldn't want to keep you from your 'paying customers.'" She didn't want to have to listen to his smug comments during the entire ride to the airport.

He stopped abruptly, blocking her path to the door, and popped the keys from her hand. "It's no problem. If we take my shortcut you'll get to see a little more of the lodge property without losing any more weight, and I've got to make a stop at a large supermarket to get some stuff for the meal I have planned."

"You're making it difficult not to like you," she said, smiling.

"What? And let all that hard work go to waste?"

"I may want my enemies close but not when they look like you." The words had carelessly slipped from her mouth and she wished she could drag them back.

But the truth was the truth: she was more than attracted to him and by now it was certainly not a secret.

"Thank you for the compliment. Besides, I don't want you poisoning this guy Douglas's mind before I have a chance to win him over with my dazzling personality."

"And you just *'magically'* knew when to be ready."

"Your handwriting is immaculate." He smiled at her.

"You read *my* message?"

"It was on the *message* pad and it wasn't addressed to anyone in particular."

"In the future keep in mind, my business is my business," Jesse said.

"My house, my business."

And just like that he had her securely seat belted in the passenger seat. He put on some Neville Brothers while instructing her how to adjust her seat. The mellow tunes played lightly in surround sound and they were on their way.

The van followed the same rocky dirt road that she and Lion took on their morning walks. The brook that she often heard could now be seen with the shining rocks glistening in the soft morning light. In no time the road smoothed out and Jesse could see the lake that she and Lion sometimes fished at. The beauty of the lake did not escape her. She was fascinated by every gentle ripple caused by the wind and the bubbles that broke the surface from the hundreds of species of marine life that existed there. The van moved onto a paved road that ran along the far side of the lake that Jesse had never noticed before. She caught glimpses of great expanses of green, dotted with small clusters of trees.

"I never knew there was a road back here. You can't even see the bridge from the embankment."

"The road is a necessity without being an encumbrance, it doesn't detract from its natural surroundings."

"I don't think anything can trump Mother Nature. I've seen my share of manmade architecture and the things people's imaginations produce are incredible, but this, this just takes the breath right out of my body. Is this all lodge property?"

"No. Lake Ulo gidv is the border. This side is mainly preservation land."

"A reservation?"

"No, a wildlife preserve."

"Why the wordplay?"

"Indian trust lands are lands held in trust by the United States government on behalf of tribal governments or individuals. It gives the government power to come in and utilize the land without the residents being able to contest the actions. The idea was if the government was held partially responsible for the land, then monies and aid could be provided readily. That backfired, since the reality was Uncle Sam saying since you can't take care of all this land by yourselves, I'll take half and you take half."

"Doesn't look like ya'll are hurting."

"The reservation is just a small part of the preserve and we're protected by too many different levels of laws. So the Native nations that live here monitor the preserve, and live on it, it's their livelihood. They conduct tours, care for the animals, maintain the landscape and things like that."

"There's a lot of land."

"We have a lot of people. There are at least twenty-six different federally recognized nations that currently reside here. We're jointly headed by the Eastern Band of the Cherokee Tribal Council. But we open our gates to welcome whomever. That takes care of our dwindling population. But we do have a yearly fiscal budget."

"You sound very involved."

"I have a vested interest," Mike hedged, "I am *Ulo gidv*, tribal chief and regional director."

"I looked up *Ulo gidv*, it means sky wanderer."

"Or Cloud Walker."

Chapter 26

Jesse had spent some time researching the Native American influences and history in the region. She read up on the leaders of the nations but somehow confused the translation and therefore never made the connection between Mike and his name. The sky played a significant role in the history of the Cherokee people. It was believed that the first animals came from the clouds as well as the first man and woman. All of the Cherokee people could be sent visions from the sky, but only a gifted few could read the sky or clouds and communicate with those spirits. Majestic Cloud Walker was of that gifted group.

As head of council he helped his people to become independent of the government. They started businesses that would boost tourism, and soon owned tobacco stores, bookstores, boutiques and gift shops in Asheville, Sayer and Sayetteville. "We take the strengths of each of the nations and make them work for us. We hunt and fish and farm for our own needs," he said while driving along. It was hard for Jesse to tell how he was feeling. He seemed so nonchalant. "We take the time to learn about all the nations and add it to the schooling curriculum and celebrate the ceremonies as well. Originally the Creeks, Choctaws and Iroquois fought for the same lands. The wars were severe and bloody massacres, now we live on it together."

"'The ground on which we stand is sacred ground. It is the blood of our ancestors,'" Jesse said. Walker slowed the van over a particularly bumpy patch of road but looked over at Jesse. She smiled. "Chief Plenty Coups—Crow. Don't look at me like that. I did some research. I'm trying to grow on this sabbatical of mine."

"The Seminole and Chickasaw also have a strong presence here, they were part of the first 'Five Civilized Tribes.'" Mike liked talking to Jesse, finally admitting to her about his role on the mountain.

"What about Tak?" Jesse asked.

"He's a Texas-hybrid Indian and he's here confusing us with his triple accent. But he's very community oriented. He educates kids about medicine and a few of them will go to med school and one or two of them will come back here. It makes us less dependent on the *Unaka*."

"White men?"

"Right. And it makes it harder for them to take away land that is sustaining us. The land goes up into the mountains."

"Tax-free money."

"Not all of it. You know the government has its way of getting their money, like charging top dollar for supplies. They don't provide services until absolutely necessary and hold up hunting licenses, fishing licenses, insurance, or whatever else might be needed to properly run a business during the height of the season. Sometimes we have to hunt during an off-season, because of a flash flood or an early frost, and they'll come out and fine and arrest people. As if we don't care for the animals, like next year we aren't going to be the ones rounding them up, counting heads, mating them and giving out shots. Been fighting those bureaucratic bastards for years."

"Was it always like that?"

"It's always a battle. Just a different one from one year to the next for God's country."

Jesse leaned farther out the window to let the wind wash through her headful of curls, "God's country," she repeated. "I suppose I do feel closer to God since I've gotten here. Life is so much more peaceful. I could wander these woods every day and find something new each time."

"You ain't seen nothing yet." Mike talked for a while about the Blue Ridge and Appalachian mountain ranges, telling her about the 6,000-foot elevation, the year-round ice caps and the sixteen different hybrids of rhododendrons in bloom at this time of year. He offered to take her and her friends hiking near the trails at the edge of the spruce/fir forest.

"Actually I've hiked Mount Pisgah and the Richland Balsam Trail, to the peaks. I went to check out the Appalachian Culture Center. I had a nice time."

Mike felt that Jesse was still trying to avoid him, or more than likely, avoid dealing with the growing closeness between them. It gnawed at him that she rose early each morning and spent the entire day on some excursion, only to return very late, just to stay away from him.

"I plan on taking Kat to the Château Morrisette Winery for a cheese tasting, we'll skip the wine. I also

made an appointment at Newton Day Spa Hot Springs,"
she said, looking way too superior for his taste. Jesse bub-
bled on. "I have us scheduled for full body massages, ex-
foliating scrub, sea-salt rinse and forty-five minutes in the
springs. I've had Swedish and Shiatsu thus far, ohhh, I get
chills just thinking about it, the warm oil on my skin and
the feel of hands kneading the knots out of my joints."

Walker did too as images of Jesse in his flannel shirt
crept into his mind's eye. He could smell her crisp,
clean scent in the vehicle and he imagined her body
glimmering in a soft halo of light while she slipped
the shirt off her arms with her back to him. He could
see her long legs and full hips walking slowly into the
steam at the springs, when he felt a tap on his shoulder. "What?" he snapped like a dragon.

"Have you been?"

As a distraction he started in on her. "Spa sounds
like city . . ." He added a little Southern twang to em-
phasize his words. ". . . Round here we call 'em 'the
springs' or 'the bluff.' And of course I've been, years
ago. You won't find too many locals there anymore,
unless they're employees."

"I noticed. I've been twice already and it's mostly
rich out-of-towners. And I have noticed not a single
soul of color except the staff and me. It's a shame,
they have a great health-food regimen and vegan
menu. It's all about relaxing, relating and releasing."

"Exhaling," Mike said on a breath as he looked at
his passenger. Jesse had closed her eyes, and gave a
dramatic exhalation. His eyes went to her chest, which
was barely concealed by another one of his pristine
Hanes T-shirts. The large, dark areolas, perfect circles
that called out to be suckled, soft, smooth cleavage
rising with the deep breath pushing out against the

rounded neckline. Her breasts remained high, full, delectable mounds even after she let out the air.

"If I lived here I'd go every chance I got."

"You do live here, for now," he bit out against his own rising sexual tension.

"You know what I mean. It's like living anyplace— you never go do the tourist stuff where you live. You never have a real appreciation for it."

"Because in the real world we're all too busy living life rather than enjoying it." This was a rote argument he had often with his city clients who, while on vacations, hiss and spit fire because the lodge and cabins aren't equipped with enough voltage to sustain faxes, computers or video phones, and then wonder why they never get to see any of the beautiful countryside or woodlands. A year later, they're back with new resolutions but the same problem: in order to afford the vacation they have to work through it. She gave him a smile that put them on the same side of an argument instead of being adversaries. He smiled back, feeling much like he was floating around looking down on them. Mike was enjoying the carefree and revealing chat between them.

"The only thing I miss about the city, City, is West Indian food."

"Amen to that," Jesse said wistfully. She wanted to reach over and pull his hair out of the ponytail so she could watch it blow wildly in the wind like on that first night of her visit. His profile proud, his countenance softer, in his element he was beautiful.

"I could go for some oxtail, peas and rice and maybe some Potato Roti," Mike said.

"You got food on the mind, and me, I'm just feeling kinda deep right now. I feel like everyone should enjoy something like going to the springs. A real wonder of the world if you ask me."

"We enjoyed it before it became a 'spa' and cost you an arm, a leg and half a back, before any one person laid claim to it. We refuse to pay for something that should be offered to everyone for free."

"So what did you and your friends do to show how much you despised this practice?"

"What, am I in the truck alone? I told you we've been fighting the bureaucrats since the beginning. They have one excuse or another for cordoning off property that they want. So we show our displeasure by not giving them our money. Not utilizing the services offered and try not to allow our kids to go work for them. We want freedom from the white man rather than to be integrated."

"So if they offered discounts for living in the area you'd be opposed?"

"At the 1927 Grand Council of American Indians it was said, 'The white people, who are trying to make us over into their image, want us to be "assimilated," bringing the Indians into the mainstream and destroying our own way of life and our own cultural patterns. They believe we should be contented like those whose concept of happiness is materialistic and greedy, which is very different from our own way.' In other words, money can't buy everything."

"If that was a shot at me your aim is way off. I'm proud of my accomplishments as well as my culture."

Walker gave her a withering look. "I didn't mean for it to come out that way, it's just that nobody wants to embrace the Native American culture anymore. They feel we were disgraced in the history books and made to look like simpering weaklings. We took trinkets and baubles for Manhattan, and we got smallpox from some fucking blankets. We were massacred and murdered all over this country, and yet we were labeled Indian givers when we offered to share the land. They were the ones to shed our blood to get more and we defended and protected what we could. We come across as savages for our practices, for hunting, for killing. We seem like heathens for worshipping so many spiritual guides. We were made out to be idiots because we didn't speak or read English, or sit at a table with knives and forks or dress in useless clothes. Our history is as rich and important as any other culture, but we exist on these tiny squats of land dotted across the states in abject poverty.

"Our population is made stronger only by our numbers. We are a governing force for all the Native nations because we contribute productively to the American economy. In order to remain that strong we mustn't let them divide and conquer us any longer." He let the silence stretch on, while fighting his own demons.

"You wanted to get away from the mountain, when you were younger?"

"Like a bat out of Hell." He had to laugh at himself. Her smile was understanding.

Jesse sat back, soaking up the scenery as if she belonged. She wondered briefly how it would be to grow up with a family history as dramatic as that.

Walker watched her so closely that he almost drove off the road twice, trying to see what she was seeing. He tried to pay closer attention to the road. But when his thoughts strayed from his youthful desire to leave the mountain, it went straight to her physical presence.

Chapter 27

"Where do you want to stop for breakfast?" Mike asked.

She answered with a question. "Where you gonna take me?"

"I don't know. Lion and Zak have taken you to all the popular places. Did you have a favorite?" In all Mike's years living on the reservation, he'd seen less of North Carolina than Jess had seen in the four months since she arrived in March. He knew the history, had visited the museums on school trips and had been to some of the local tourist traps, but he never went shopping in a new grocery, or tried a different hardware store or ate at a variety of restaurants. He went with what was familiar. Mike found he rarely had to leave and when he did, he found he didn't like many places or, for that matter, many people. The mountain held all of his wants, needs and desires, especially now that this woman had appeared.

Jesse, on the other hand, seemed to love every nook and cranny of every place she went. He noticed she barely stood still anymore when having a conversation.

She could give directions like she had been living at the lodge all her life. Show her once and it was committed to some little supercomputer in her brain. Her stories were these exciting short quips about situations or sights that struck her as interesting. Most of the time, he would find himself shaking his head and smiling at the funny way she told a story or the hysterical messes she found herself in, usually involving bugs chasing her or a small animal staring her down. She was like a modern-day Lucy. And here he was in the place he grew up and couldn't think of one restaurant that suited this outing. He finally decided they could go to one of the chain restaurants in the airport.

"How about Duke's Gut Rot instead?" she asked, holding her hand out the window, pushing her fingers against the wind.

"Isn't that a bar?"

"No, it's a seafood bar and grill. But I hear they got moonshine, good, old-fashioned still in the back," she answered with a smile.

"Yeah, moonshine like paint thinner. Get you high smellin' it, drunk sippin' it, pass you out 'fore it's down your throat. For like five bucks my whole high school could drink. Sent someone to get us a jug of the stuff. Sat on some bluff, got plastered and woke up with dirt in my ears. Wasn't Duke's then either, and we're the ones who named it Gut Rot Moonshine."

"How'd you get dirt in your ears?"

"Don't know. Willow Reed woke up with vomit all over her shirt, we were never sure it was hers, and Dark Feather woke up in his sister's clothes." Mike smiled at the memory. Although he and his Native American compatriots were sick to their stomachs they were the ones to remove all the white kids' clothes and improvised the story that it was a wild orgy.

"So you had some friends."

"Yeah. Always one or two." He made a mental note to drop in to see Dark Feather's mother and put a card in the mail to Willow Reed, who was now Renee Wills of Seattle, Washington. "Someone to get into stuff with, remind you you're alive."

"I believe in living life."

"Me too, but sounds more like a death sentence, Duke's Gut Rot Seafood Bar and Grill. Sounds like a place you can order a side of salmonella with your clams. Where'd you hear about it?"

"A guy at the Roadkill Grill told me and Zak about it."

"Roadkill? So Gut Rot is nothing?" He noted the challenging look in her eye. "You got a death wish? This eating dangerously thing is one sick way to go."

"What, ya scared?" She smiled and her eyes twinkled and for a third time during this trip they almost ended up in a ditch.

"No. I just like my insides on the inside. But if you can handle it, so can I."

"Duke's it is." She stuck out a hand to shake on the deal.

"I survived your cooking." He gave a firm handshake.

She laughed like a maniacal kid, and it made her huge, round eyes sparkle. He never thought to say no because if eating dirt would keep that smile on her face he would do it.

Chapter 28

The ride to the airport was just as wondrous as their time at the restaurant. Jesse was interested in everything from the history of a town to the latest stoplight erected. She managed to get him to tell her about some of the stories of the Native nations in the area and the few kids who had befriended him while growing up. The more he talked, the more he realized he had made some good friends over the years. Their families still lived at the reservation, and although Sylvia, Digg and Tak kept him informed, he rarely checked in with anyone. He planned to start spending more time around the preserve and the reservation.

Jesse had gone on one of the walking tours and told Walker, "Those teenagers put no feeling into what they are saying. They drop the information on the table like heavy groceries."

"When I was young, a job was a job and we did the tour thing and taught the classes and all that. At some point I guess you feel like no one's really listening or they don't care. They just want the best pictures of their vacations to show their friends."

"Maybe now that you're an adult it may mean something different for you and you may have more to offer someone who hears it." She flashed that million-dollar smile and he smiled back. She paused for a moment. "Your grandfather . . . still alive?"

"No."

"What was his name?"

"Majestic Cloud Walker." The words just came without thought or direction. Jesse smiled and reached out to put her hand on his thigh. Walker let the warmth of her hand travel up his leg and seep into all the right places. "I was so different from the kids I was raised with. I was the chief's grandson, yet my parents ran away from the mountain. There was a lot of controversy about who should take over. But Majestic always made it known that 'the clouds would make the choice.' He didn't make it seem like it was gonna be me, but he made me feel like it was going to happen if and when the time was right."

"You said you did live with your parents."

"Yeah, but it wasn't until I went back to Majestic that I felt special. My grandmother died giving birth to my father, so Majestic was used to raising kids.

"Sounds all right," Jesse said.

"Nothing compares to life with Majestic. This ancient-looking man opens the door and all this smoke comes spiraling out of the house to encircle me. He reaches out to me through this cloud and I reach back, without really being able to see his hand, and he says, 'So, Mighty Cloud Walker, I have been preparing for this moment and am thankful that the ancestors have delivered you safely to me.' And immediately I felt surrounded by love and I felt protected and I knew he'd never let anything bad happen to me and that he was going to be everything to me." Mike cleared his throat, feeling slightly embarrassed by his outpouring of emotion. But he was compelled by the slight squeeze to his thigh to stop or keep going. So he did. "That's like my first real memory, seeing and hearing that old, weathered man reach out to me. I thought he looked like God, with long white hair flecked with jet black. His face like rawhide but buttery soft to the touch, and he never aged."

"It sounds like he gave you everything you needed. So why did you feel set apart?"

"The poverty on the reservation was really bad, but I lived in this big, beautiful old house with antiques, servants, elegant meals and three cars. And I couldn't do anything to help my friends on the reservation. When I tried, they gave me a hard time, telling me I think I'm better than them because of my fancy clothes and paper money."

"Some people like better."

"Kids like to belong. I worked my tail off to be like them, but no matter what I did, they always found some little reason to turn me away. To make me an outcast. We all learned English, but my hair was too short and my English made me sound like a 'pilgrim' or *Unaka*. I never felt like I belonged. I couldn't wait to be on my own. So I went away to college and spent my young adult life trying to prove something but never knowing what. Ultimately, after my grandfather's passing, I had to return here and take care of business. It's like running in circles. My grandfather always said, 'You cannot make the current of a river go where you want. Instead learn to flow with the current and it will take you where you need to be.'"

"Uh-huh."

"It means that you may not always get what you want but you will always have what you need."

"I disagree."

"You would."

Mike's grandfather had always tried to ease his childhood and teenage angst by insisting, "You shall rise above this to walk amongst the clouds. Should you keep holding to the pettiness of the earth it will take you long and hard to get there." Life on the mountain had been both frightening and fulfilling when growing up, it was a battle when he was away and a struggle getting back. He was searching for his place in the world, but looking at Jesse, he felt as if he had finally found his way. And one of his sole regrets was that his grandfather never did get to see him walk in the clouds . . .

Jesse dried his face and her own, and gave him a quick hug. He hadn't realized he was crying. He'd never told his story. He didn't know how hard it had been emotionally all these years to keep those memories locked away. But Jesse was there and he felt close to her and he thought about some of the times he did have with his parents and smiled. And that pretty yellow smell was all around him and he felt safe and comforted and as he looked back to the road ahead he realized this moment felt like the first time his grandfather held him.

Chapter 29

The Sayetteville/Asheville Regional Airport was alight with sunshine. The main concourse was a glass dome with water fountains and lush plants. The cream-colored marble-tiled floors had mirror shines. Every need was accounted for. A black lighted billboard boasted the various airport services; standard-issue ticket counters with the names of various airlines were in a line, with breaks for luggage. Walker guided Jesse by putting slight pressure to her lower back, while talking to her in soothing tones. That was enough to keep her moving and to make him want her again, as her body sort of molded itself to his hand.

"Wait, wait, wait," Jesse protested, planting her feet firmly into the carpet. His arms wrapped around her in a loose hug. "We're going to the gate?"

"Yes, how else do you expect to meet your friends?"

"We're going to the gate without tickets?"

"Yes. So if you've got a weapon or drugs on you get rid of 'em because we are going through an X-ray machine too, little girl," he said, patting her cheek.

It took close to fifteen minutes to clear the

security checkpoint because Jesse spoke to everyone who said hello.

"Why do you do that?" he asked with a smirk.

"Do what?"

"Speak to everyone, like they know you."

"Because they said hello."

"Everyone down here smiles and says hello, it's called being courteous."

She gave Walker a pointed look. "Not everyone, Mr. Walker."

Katherine Vitolli-Spiegel waddled up the short ramp toward them and caught Jesse in an awkward hug over and around her belly. Mike noticed how short Katherine was, compared to Jesse. She had dove-white skin that was even more noticeable on a face scrubbed clean of makeup, and her skin was aglow.

Doug carried two medium-sized bags toward the waiting party. "Look at me, saddled with the old ball and chain and a bun in the oven. I'll be old in no time. Marriage prematurely ages a man. It only looks like women live longer, because we drop like flies after marriage," Douglas added.

Kat playfully punched her husband in the shoulder. "Stop talking like that, you'll turn all of our friends off of marriage," Katherine scolded.

Pretending not to hear, he walked up to the only other man around. "It's called the three rings for a reason. Engagement ring, wedding ring and suffe*ring*."

Kat swatted at her husband, who ducked out of the way laughingly and pinched his wife's rear, making her squeak like a Chihuahua.

Mike guessed that Doug was a few inches taller than him. He appeared to be as lean as a swimmer. His height probably got him mistaken for a ballplayer all the time. His skin was a light sandy brown with an olive tint. His hair was a dark gold curly afro. Doug seemed very social, loud and friendly. It was easy to see why Jesse liked Douglas so much. He inspired trust. The two men bonded instantly over a lengthy, firm handshake and a masculine hug pounding each other's backs with the right amount of muscle.

"How does every man know the exact same secret handshake?" Kat asked in a mock whisper. "I bet little boys everywhere are practicing that right now."

"That's how men size each other up, it's a typical male ritual, almost like a pissing contest," Jesse answered smugly.

"Or a dog marking his territory," Kat said.

There was no denying that Doug was a man's man, like Jesse said. And Mike could see Doug's approval in a bouncing nod and half-smile. "Women shop, men pee. It's the law of the land. Keeps the cosmos in order."

Jesse threaded an arm thru Kat's. "Ohhh, and I have a couple of places we definitely have to hit."

"Hey, girl, where's the rest of you? You look great!" Kat pulled back to get a better look at her new slimmer friend.

Mike had noticed how Jesse's muscles seemed to have become more trim and toned, she was thick in a new way. She was still soft where it counted and round where it meant something. Her jeans hugged her ass in a way that made him sweat. When she stood still a little gap appeared at the waistband in back and he kept leaning forward when he walked behind her to see what he could see. The white T-shirt she wore was one of his new ones, it hadn't even touched his body yet, but he didn't take issue with it because she filled it out in a way that made his hands itch just to trace her form.

She sometimes wore it with nothing but panties while putting biscuits or pastries in the oven to heat before her shower. On the mornings he'd caught her like that, he'd silently watch from the hall. He'd watch every willowlike movement, soft and ethereal, her skin smooth, her ass round, high and protruding as she bent to put the tray in the oven. He would watch her reach up into the cabinets, sometimes propping a knee on the counter so she could reach higher and, to his appreciative eye, see more, which always left him with a hard-on. He would then take three large steps down the hall to his room and plop noisily onto the bed.

She often would carelessly call over her shoulder, "I know you're awake and up to something. There better not be no snake in my room and that includes you, Mr. Walker."

Mike pulled himself from his reverie when he saw Doug's large frame completely engulf Jesse in a hug. "I'm Mike Walker," he said, relieved that a real wife existed, and took Kat's hand and kissed it.

Kat glanced back at Jesse with an "I'm impressed" look.

"Don't be kissing on my wife," Doug said.

"Reign it in, big boy, that's just Southern hospitality," Walker explained while Kat batted her eyelashes.

"Walker is trying to prove he has some. Both of you stop looking at him like he's the second coming of Christ. I'm the one he's trying to impress"—Jesse turned to Mike—"and it ain't working, you forget I live with you."

"Living together?" Doug and Kat mouthed as Jesse went on.

"It's like the 'Real World' with him. It's always drama and he's like the moody artist." She cocked her left leg out, hips forward and chest pronounced, thumbs hanging from the belt loops and turned her back to him. He'd seen her take this stance pretty regularly since living on the mountain.

"I guess that makes you the tease," Walker said, walking over and grazing his chest across hers. Full body-to-body contact while his left arm snaked around her and his right between Jesse and Doug to get one of the bags. Now his body shadowed over her and then bowed down to her and, slowly, to her pleasure, moved back up her body. Jesse almost jumped at the feel of Walker's erect nipples brushing against hers, a picture of the little rings forming in her mind. But she refused to be backed down.

Doug was telling Walker they needed to go to the luggage round. "The woman packed for a month even though I told her four days."

"We might stay longer," Kat challenged.

"So, what, you can't wash your drawers by hand?"

"Haven't you seen the size of my maternity panties? It could take three days just to dry them," Kat volleyed.

"Men just don't get it. Don't try to understand, your minds just can't wrap around the complexity of it," Jesse said, walking down the beltway to Baggage Claim.

"Oh, so this is gonna be a boys-against-the-girls type of weekend," Doug assessed from a short distance away.

"That's okay, we men are ready for a battle of the sexes. We've got the strength," Walker added.

"Good, because we've got the brains," Kat said.

Doug fell in love with the minibus. He appreciated the spaciousness as well as the bevy of food and drinks. He put on the television even though he left the volume off and picked out a George Clinton CD to listen to. He asked Walker questions about the engine, the bathroom and the bar. He complimented the interior carpet, the leather seats and the windows. He even suggested that he and Kat get one, which she vehemently, but lovingly, vetoed. For Mike the ride back was enjoyable. He made a quick and easy acquaintance with Douglas and Katherine, which he normally found hard to do, but these people were salt of the earth. Doug and Mike spoke companionably for the first leg of the trip while the women held a cross conversation reminiscing about the week. The excitement of each conversation rose in volume to a frenzied pitch. Finally Doug and Jesse switched seats. Mike immediately felt the loss of her soft, feminine presence in the front seat. It seemed as though she moved miles as opposed to a few feet. Mike liked seeing her body draped all over the seat while talking to Kat. He had somehow managed to follow much of their conversation while talking to Doug. Jesse was telling Kat about the size of the cabin and its furnishings. She talked about her buddies, Lion and Zak, and all the things that they were involved in, and at least one hundred other things. The two women were like schoolgirls. He constantly glanced at her and admired her animated features. She looked so alive and vibrant to him, just like at breakfast. After a while he barely heard Doug because he became so engrossed in the movement of her lips or the sound of her laugh and the casual sexuality that vibrated from her very essence . . .

Chapter 30

On the ride back, Mike had gained even greater respect for Jesse. He'd seen her stand up to him, garden with Zak, dine with businessmen, smile and laugh with their wives, remodel the bathroom, and sit with Lion and read a dozen papers end to end while listening to opera. Sylvia adored her, Lila enjoyed her company, Tak and Digg poked and teased her mercilessly and she even had weird little Viona, from the community center, hanging around teaching her how to make pottery. And now she was sitting here blushing as her friends sang her praises.

"Yep," Kat said, "she joined her condo board, took their holiday party money and gave out Christmas bonuses to the staff and took them and their families all out for dinner. Let them enjoy how the other half lives. Even when the condo board fees diminished, Jess here didn't let it deter her, she took what they had the following year and dipped into her own pocket to make sure the bonuses were still nice."

"It just seemed like the right thing to do. All that

money for people with money, absolutely ridiculous. They needed to be shocked into reality."

Mike had confided in Douglas, telling him about the battle lines drawn for the property between the preserve and the state.

Newton Country Club was just another thorn in Mike Walker's side. They currently had him tied up in court for the rights to the lake and permission to erect massive stone walls on three sides, which he felt would mar the landscape. It was his land and that of the preserve.

"It doesn't seem right that they want to encroach on this wonderful landscape," Kat said, gazing at the lake.

"It's stupid to rip up the grass, trees and flowers that are here, just to replant them," Doug said, shaking his head.

Mike had enough money to keep them in court for years and he knew enough member secrets to keep them from playing dirty. A smile tugged at his lips. Mike glided the van to a stop in front of the cabin.

"Doug." Mike put a hand on the other man's shoulder. He gave a wink. "You ever smoke a hand-rolled Southern cigar?" The women snorted as Doug handed Jesse over into Mike's arms. He held her close, seeing the tenderness in her eyes. He had to release her immediately because he could already feel the stirring of his loins.

"You can smoke," Katherine said to her husband, tilting her head up and standing on tiptoe to kiss him.

"Thank you, love." He kissed her hard.

"I'll feel better once I've spent a shitload of your money."

"I don't care what it costs. Me and my new buddy

are gonna smoke one right now, before we unload the bus," Doug said with glee. And he and Mike headed around to the side balcony.

"So here's no-man's land. How do you like it?" Jesse asked.

"It's quiet."

"I said the same thing, it's a misconception, Kat. Give it twenty-four hours."

Mike had fresh cuts of steak marinating in an Italian wine and a balsamic vinaigrette mixture. He had gotten shitake mushrooms from Lakota Grocery, but had picked the onions, garlic, and green, red and yellow peppers from his own garden. There was also fresh corn on the cob from the preserve market that was stark white and big as a forearm. Douglas whipped up some stuffed Brussels sprouts with chopped greens simmered with bacon and turkey. He popped those in the oven with some panini bread Jesse had picked up in Clifton, which he seasoned with fresh herbs and spices and buttered with garlic cream sauce. Mike was at the grill when the ladies came back from a quick tour of the outside of the cabin, the rich, aromatic scents of dinner finding them on their stroll and delivering them salivating to the door.

"You know we missed lunch," Kat complained.

"No, you didn't, you had that yogurt parfait and granola," Doug said, kissing his wife's cheek as he carried a covered bowl out to the grill.

"Lunch requires meat or else it's just a snack in disguise. Why did you let him cook? We won't eat until it's as perfect as a painting. I'll starve waiting on that fool." Katherine plopped down into the nearest chair.

"You want some soup now? Walker always has some in the house, it has meat in it." Jesse whispered.

"Don't you dare feed her. She had a huge breakfast, twice, and then harassed the stewardess for lunch early, then ate the stuff you snuck to her in the van and then came out here with crumbs on her face from whatever she was hiding in her bag. Right, Snuggle Bunny? She'll be complaining she's as big as a house in a few minutes," Doug said while stirring his sauce and rubbing his butt on his wife. Kat slapped at it playfully.

Walker tapped Jesse's hand with a wooden spoon as she snuck a bite of food off the counter. Jesse turned on Mike with a spatula and they had a quick sword fight.

"Give me a man with a deep-down-to-his-toes, internal-struggle-type soulful look and I'm all his. You know, his full lips moist, slightly parted, eyes smoldering, Barry White voice asking me 'to come on over to his place' . . ." Jesse crooned.

"Oh, and after a long day of work, he'll run me a bubble bath, hand me champagne or wine, lightly scented candles and play Slave Boy to my Sexy Cleopatra," Kat added.

"And he'd say things like, 'Baby, your skin is as smooth as satin and, 'You walk with the beauty of a thousand queens.'"

"Oh, my God. That is soooo fake," Doug said, laughing while bringing food to the table that Jesse and Kat were setting.

"Really?" Jesse asked, looking into Mike's smoldering gray eyes as he helped Kat into her seat.

Douglas seated himself while Jesse stood waiting for Walker.

"Let's pray."

Doug was a bit surprised to see Jesse bowing her head in compliance.

"I can feel you staring at a hole in my scalp, Doug. Mr. Walker's home, Mr. Walker's rules," Jesse said.

"With an iron fist, babeee!" Doug said, giving his new friend a fist pump.

He spoke in Cherokee before translating into English, "Great Creator, allow Mother sun to always shine down upon us; allow Brother moon to always return for the ceremony; allow gentle winds to always brush across our faces; help us honor all that is part of where we are. And please do not strike me down for the words that come out of Doug's mouth."

Jesse barely heard the joke. She had grown accustomed to the musical intonations Walker used in the prayer. He seemed to have a new one each time she had finally learned the last one. And as sacrilegious as that was, it turned her on. Sitting with her eyes closed listening to the words wash over her, his hand brushing back her hair behind her ear . . .

"Look at Jesse over there swooning and my own wife, all goo-goo eyed at Mr. Sensitivity. See, he's playing y'all. Speak another language, show a little church, promise to take it slow. All the stuff a woman wants to hear. It's like an aphrodisiac," Doug said. He looked into his wife's eyes and said, "Your skin radiates like a pearl in the ocean when the sun is kissing the sky."

"See, Doug, when you take your foot out of your mouth, you say some really sweet stuff," Jesse said while cutting her steak into small, bite-sized pieces.

The first time Mike saw her slicing away like a meat grinder he stared in amazement. Now he started doing it too so that they were actually starting their meal at the same time. He even ate at a slower pace ever since she scolded him about 'scarfing down' his meals. "Yeah, for a guy that was pretty good stuff," Mike said.

"I guess you could say she brings out the best in me," Doug said, kissing his wife's hand.

Neither Jesse nor Mike responded. Mike was filling Jesse's water glass and she was busy giving his arm the once-over. Doug and his wife exchanged a knowing glance, each having caught on to the fact that the other two were unconsciously a couple.

Kat almost lost a Brussels sprout when she saw Jessica Bishop, entrepreneur, fixing the sides for Mike's plate. "Mike, that was an interesting prayer. Where does it come from?" Katherine asked.

"I was educated in both the Native beliefs and Catholic religion."

"That didn't sound Catholic. In fact don't Native American spiritualities worship more than one deity?" Kat asked.

"Yes," Mike said between bites.

"So wouldn't the two be contradictory?" Douglas asked, getting into the subject.

"Spirits are heavily enmeshed in both, so I still follow both. I believe in spirit guides and they are the ones who give me the prayers, and I believe in one creator."

"Yes, but Catholic spirits are considered angels and they leave. Everything is cut and dry in Catholicism, it even comes with a handbook," Kat noted.

"We have a handbook on a grander scale, it's called nature."

"How is that?" Doug asked.

"Majestic, my grandfather, believed that in order to

understand life you must understand nature. The animals behave like humans on a baser level—with their sexuality, child rearing, alpha males—and even bugs exist in a societal structure; flowers teach about reproduction; the trees, rivers and rocks hold history. Nature has all the answers. Spirits help to show you the way."

"I don't get how the spirits fit in," Doug prompted, hoping to get a better picture.

"'All birds, even those of the same species, are not alike, it is the same with human beings. . . .' 'The forces of nature are like the dreams that we have. We cannot control them but if we slow down we can hear what they tell us. When we cannot hear, the spirits will tell us.' My grandfather would remind me, 'Among us there have been no written laws. Customs handed down from generation to generation have been there to guide them. That is why council is so important.' So I never missed council, I listen and respect nature and care for Mother Earth and went to church. Letting the spirits guide me, not so easy."

"That must have been hard to deal with—growing up in a modern world and trying to fit in," Jesse said.

"That plus a thousand other things I don't even know about yet."

"How do you merge past with present, successfully?" Kat asked.

"I don't know. But when I do, it will be written in the clouds."

Jesse had leaned over, placed a hand on Walker's arm, whispered in his ear, and a perfect smile slashed his face. He gave her the sign for "thank you." Mike was still intoxicated by the intimacy he was sharing with Jesse. Every time her body swayed near him, he could

smell the familiar flower scent she wore. He wanted to
draw her out of her seat and onto his lap so he could
bury his face in her neck and hair and smell his fill. He
was assaulted by images like that all through the appetizers, soup and salad. She starred in the fantasies that
made him sweat and the dreams that left him hard.
Each thought of her in his arms accompanied surging
feelings of tenderness.

Chapter 31

Mike escorted Kat to the den, seating himself nearest the vent and pulling out a cigar.

Doug had the tray of desserts and Jesse carried the plates. "The meal was delicious, we should have brought you on as a partner," Doug said.

"I had no notion of Utopia until meeting Gideon, and since then I've heard him say the name umpteen times and then Jesse shows up and practically drowns me in it. Utopia boxes, bags, napkins, knives, forks, spoons, business cards, notepads, pens, letterhead, envelopes . . . And did I see a pin?" Mike asked.

"Always promoting," Douglas said.

"I've been meaning to check it out on the Internet but I never found the time. But the name has always been in the back of my mind. It's a very soothing, holistic thought. I know Utopia means 'perfect place,'" Mike said.

"Actually, it's supposed to be a 'place of ideal perfection' in governing laws and social conditions. I read once about the beauty of this imaginary place that only exists in the mind of poets. In Greek mythology they wrote about a blissful land called the Elysian Fields," Jesse explained.

"That's where old soldiers go to die," Douglas added.

"Warriors. And only warriors who die an honorable death during battle."

"Paradise," Kat kicked in between bites of dessert.

"No, you're confusing terms," Jesse said. "Paradise is defined as 'an intermediate place or state where the righteous departed souls await judgment or resurrection.' It's often confused with Heaven because it sounds nice but it's more like purgatory."

"Isn't purgatory 'God's Waiting Room'?" Kat asked.

"No, that would be Paradise, where you have done good on Earth and are pretty much a shoe-in. Purgatory is a temporary state or place of misery or suffering. You enter a sinner and suffer a punishment, make satisfaction and become fit for Heaven, exiting a saint. I think this idea comes from people who aren't really bad but could be better. They gave themselves a shot at redemption."

"You really know your stuff," Mike said.

"I have to. I named all our stores after religious, semireligious or mythical beliefs in the concept of eternal felicity. Can you imagine true ambrosia? Food of the gods? Something so indescribably delicious that it becomes more of a state of being than just a food? The idea is that our services provide a complete transition from this world to whatever your 'ideal' is. It transcends your immediate existence and carries your mind, body and soul to another place. A place of your own design, your own Utopia."

"Deep," Mike said, knowing that his Utopia would include the mountain and Jesse.

"I grew up with Roman Catholic parents. Church, God and state—all kinda intermingled. Then, as I learned about other religions and spiritualities I began to understand that in essence all of humanity is in search of this 'perfect place.' So when I chose the name for my 'perfect place', I went with the familiar. Concepts that endure through time and embrace all people. I think that's why my parents chose biblical names for us," Jesse further explained.

"Jesse is not in the Bible."

"Yes, it is, but he's a boy, not a girl. That's my Christian name, but you knew that."

"Jessica as your alter ego to hide your Superman."

"Jessica was Superman," Douglas interjected. "She did it all, especially in a field that she wasn't especially good at. And she made it happen."

"No, we made it work. Granted, I chose the most unlikely career for myself. I can't cook, I nearly failed restaurant school, no direction, no steady job, and I had no money whatsoever. But my best friend convinces me we have to do this. And I did everything totally back asswards, going against everything I learned in business classes." Mike felt the pride she and Douglas were emanating as if it were sunlight. "I had a plan and no money. I had an idea but no real knowledge. I refused to go into debt or have investors. I had a supply but no demand. I even had a location but no way to acquire and renovate it. Then Doug shows up with a pocketful of money and, lo and behold, we did it. I came up with an idea that we fully own and today have a thoroughly successful business that we love."

"And still, perhaps the currents haven't yet gotten you where you need to be." With those words he watched the animation drain from her face, the passion leave the conversation, and he could hear her walls of protectiveness go firmly back in place. "Don't do that," he said.

"Do what?"

"Get all you."

At that she smiled. "If I can't be me who can I be?" she asked innocently.

"You know what I'm saying. Don't shut down."

"That wasn't my 'shutting down' look, that was my pensive look."

"Uh-huh," Mike grunted.

"Seriously, I was thinking about a fortune cookie I read on the way here, it said, 'The universe isn't finished with you yet.' That's damn close to your river thing. Like I'm not all grown-up and out on my own like I thought I was. Like something big is coming to complete me and if ya ask me, Utopia was enough of a thing. It should have been the thing that took me into retirement."

"The money is a nice cushion, Jess. We have more than most at twice our age when they reach retirement. We're young enough to enjoy it. Do something else now," Douglas said.

Jesse nodded, feeling the contentment coming back.

"How many stores did you have?"

"One health food store: Ambrosia; one Kids Kwanza arts & crafts store called Earthly Gifts; two bakeries: Heaven Haven Bakery and Paradise Pastry; the Elysian Fields Café; three coffee shops, all called Cloud Nine; a restaurant called Elysium; the Acatour and Utopia," she said without hesitation or pause. "That isn't in any particular order. I was hoping to open a holistic healing center but that never made it to paper. The last idea was to expand the home-based offices, maybe open two more. Keep 'em small but essential." She noticed his mouth agape.

"Goddamn," Mike exclaimed.

"Religious, are we?" Kat asked.

"You never have to work again, do you?" Mike inquired. "How did you two do it? I know Doug gave you the start-up capital, but that's some corporation."

"My family. Although they keep me at arm's length, I still got my inheritance. It was more than enough to get us started," Doug offered.

"Why? If you don't mind sharing," Mike said.

"It isn't a thing, now. But at the time when my father married a black woman it was exceedingly scandalous. Some members of the family still feel that way, but as we keep moving forward, their thinking gets more progressive. Besides, they respect what I have accomplished businesswise."

"My dad tried to play it smooth the first time I took him to see a finished Utopia but the pride was practically oozing out of the man on the subway ride back to this little hovel of a studio apartment I shared with Doug at the time."

"After having met your dad, I can't imagine what ooze looks like coming out of him. I also couldn't see him in a tiny space." Walker said.

"You've met my dad?"

Walker gave her a nod and the rolling finger to go on. "Well, he rented a hotel room near Utopia, easy twice the size of my apartment. Utopia Hall was an abandoned factory down in the Village on the border of Chinatown. The city was practically giving them away in order to keep the squatters from getting them for free, or the drug dealers setting up a New-Jack-City type of thing. So we got it at a one-time auction. Doug and I renovated one floor at a time. Had family and friends kick in money, time, supplies and connections. Dad had connections with the city, he used to work construction. Most of it was done on a wing and a prayer. We had a restaurant, a large arcade and two medium-sized movie theatres and an arts-and-crafts area. It didn't look like much from the outside, but inside it was a one-stop family entertainment center," Jesse continued.

"And Jess worked right alongside the guys. I remember thinking how slow the work was in coming but it was dang reliable and inexpensive. Jess lifted a hammer every chance she got. Learned anything and everything," Doug bragged, pulling his wife closer in the crook of his arm. Kat was dozing off from a combination of dessert, pregnancy and, of course, hearing this story too many times to count.

"Sounds like you had a lot of people working on your dream," Mike said, thinking of the types of dreams she would have now, wondering if a simple life with him on the mountain would be enough.

"Utopia alone was six years from paper to profit," Jesse stated matter-of-factly. "Then we changed the entire business to strictly catering. On any day of the week the place is packed with parties, weddings, banquets, bar mitzvahs, bat mitzvahs, sweet-sixteens, cotillions, fashion shows, talent searches, book signings, roundtable discussions, political fund-raisers, whatever. You name it, we've held it. It seemed like we never stopped working. Back then I couldn't wait to sit down. Now I have nothing to do and I can't wait to get up."

"And now you wanna fill the time working on the shop downtown for Lion and Zak." Walker said.

"That's the immediate plan. And after seeing Viona's work, I want to see about a workshop for her. The ceramics she does are phenomenal, and she and Lion could share the space and . . ." Jesse's enthusiasm boiled over.

"We'll talk about it, Jesse Ruth." Walker said.

"I could use your help, Cloud."

He loved when she used his name. It came off of her lips like a song and settled in the depths of his soul. She might be ready to fly with the Eagles one day soon.

Chapter 32

Doug and Jesse decided to take a stroll outside before turning in. Mike went to stoke the fire, and check on Kat, who was no longer asleep.

"Jess wrote me. She told me some guy named Steele taught her how to throw a knife," Kat said. "Doug would probably be safer staying put. That knife is about nine inches of serrated, bone-slicing metal. Her tongue alone could reduce an oak to sawdust." His cigar was out but he kept it in his lips because Jesse's taste lingered on the wooden tip. "I've seen her practice. She's good. From the technique I'd say he was special forces, military or covert operations," Mike guessed.

"He must not have known how lethal she is without a weapon," Kat quipped.

"That woman can get anything from anyone."

"I've seen her hypnotize men and women. They just get stupid around her. My husband is one of them." The baby started doing a dance and Kat tentatively rested Mike's hand on her stomach, he pulled back and she laughed at him. He watched the baby move and stretch beneath the skin. "All her dealings with men are on her terms. In business she is treated as an equal by strong men and walks on the weak ones like Jesus over water. As a person she's a role model and as a woman she's the ultimate package. Self-made, self-reliant, self-centered. You either love her or hate her."

"You always loved her?"

"Nope, couldn't stand the bitch," Kat said with a smile. "She's an exotic, full-bodied, supersmart, totally-in-control beauty. I was not in her league to compete for Doug's attention. And lucky for me I didn't have to. I had to look at her separate from her relationship with him to see them as individuals and not pieces of a whole. And in the end, I respected her strength and resilience. Despite her weird quirks. How'd you get past all her idiosyncrasies?" Kat asked.

"You mean like the way she eats, sleeps and goes about tackling things so aggressively?"

"Yes."

"I like her the way she is."

"She's changing. She's trusting, she has faith in you," said Kat.

"Yeah, I bet," Mike said.

"She doesn't compromise and that's why her and Doug get on so well. He doesn't have to think for himself when she's around and she gets everything the way she wants. You see, they don't fight, he hardly challenges her, and she never asks his opinion. He's a big kid and she lets him be that," Kat said.

"And you, how did you tame the beast?"

"Like *I* have the ability to face this power-suit-wearing, shit-talking, massive-wall-of-China of a woman. *She* came to *me*. And now she's this normal person to me, with hairs out of place, mismatched socks and insecurities running over."

"Insecurities—Jesse? Convince me, 'cause since I've known her, I've seen her face it all and do it all and come out on the other side smelling yellow."

Kat didn't know that yellow had a smell, but she wasn't about to ask him. "Jessica Bishop doesn't believe in failure."

"No one wants to fail. And I can relate to the pressure," Mike said, thinking about the pressures in dealing with the preserve, the reservation and being chief.

"Okay, here's another one, her weight."

"What about it?"

"Well, now she's thrilled, but for years she's wanted the body she has now. She's always dreamed of Victoria's Secret curves."

"I like her full-figured curves. She's built like a real Southern girl. But if she keeps shrinking I'mma tella sumthin'."

Kat swatted at Mike as he helped her slide her feet to the floor and rise from the couch. He picked up her shoes as he followed her slow progress to her room. "First of all, her weight suits her, second, her skin has a healthy glow, next, her hair is full, also her eyes are bright and, most important, she smiles more often. All very positive changes so, if you say anything stupid and ruin this for her, I'll kill you."

Mike thought about the transformation he saw in the Ice Princess. "I told you I like her the way she is, inside and out. Muscles, weight complexes, idiosyncrasies, jokes, red hair, all of her nuttiness I can take." He pulled on the unlit cheroot.

"What happens if she keeps changing anyway?"

"Then I suppose I'll fall in love with that person too."

"So, now that you've told the least consequential person, why not go tell her?"

"Because. You don't hit as hard."

"Give it time. I just got here."

Jesse had gotten a good head start on Doug and was now playing hide-and-seek in the woods. Up ahead, Jessica must have stopped because there was an eerie silence before the nocturnal creatures got back to work. Her footsteps resumed and scared the animals and him. Doug stumbled along and grumbled. "Damnation and brimstone, this was dumb. Where's the light switch, Jess?" Her torch lighter blazed to life, illuminating her features in an artistic, music-video way. She was leaning with her back against a tree on some rock-type steps. She was just past a nice-sized clearing where he pictured himself hosting a nice barbecue.

"It's a lot more dangerous walking the streets of Bed-Stuy than it is out here."

"You obviously don't remember the *Friday the 13th* movies. Jason died in a place like this."

"I'm sorry, Doug, for leaving you like that."

"What, are you crazy?" He grabbed her into a tight hug. "Where do I start before the real Jessica gets back?" He pushed her back and then pulled her into a bear hug. "Okay, thanks for apologizing, I don't think I've ever heard those words pass your lips. And, wow, if you want we can work out something with Utopia that will work for both of us. We're family, you and your parents were always there for me and then for Kat, even though Kat has a family, a large one at that, six sisters . . ."

"Doug. I don't want to go back to Utopia. I didn't

leave spur-of-the-moment, I just needed an excuse to come at the right time. You were right all along. It wasn't the same working there anymore. It won't be the same because we're different now. Utopia isn't Utopia for either one of us anymore."

"So I guess it's time to make a new one," Doug said with a smile as he threw an arm over her shoulder. "I'm sure Walker will be glad to share his with you."

"Shut up, punk." She ran back to the cabin. Douglas took off after her and three seconds later found himself wheezing and coughing in the dark. "I'll kill you as soon as I finish dying," Douglas hissed. "And, believe me, that man is into you!"

"No, he's not." Her voice came at him from a thousand different directions. He was glad she hadn't abandoned him.

"Yes, he is," Doug said, stopping to bend at the waist and trying to breathe. "He's head over heels. I know a man in love. And if I was a betting man I'd say you were falling . . ."

"The only thing I'm falling into is a bed." Jesse watched Doug's slow progress, from behind a tree, making sure he was okay. She came out of the shadows on the steps and helped Doug. "Pant, like you're in labor. Use your Lamaze training." As she stood holding him up, Jesse wondered if maybe Douglas was right, if maybe Walker would allow her into his Utopia. Life on the mountain was serene, beautiful and productive in its own way. Until this point in her life, she had been striving for the "American Dream." Working to fit the standards of society. Here the only standards were the ones she set for herself. The ones that made her feel good and appreciate each breath, the ones that brought her closer to being with Mike.

Chapter 33

Jesse returned to the cabin perspiring from her early-morning walk with Lion and a stack of papers under her arm. Zak had taken Doug and Kat up to the lodge for breakfast, and Mike had just returned from an early-morning repair call and was standing in the kitchen drinking water when Jesse came in. He relieved Jesse of her unwieldy bundle and gave her a quick peck on the lips as if it was the most natural thing in the world. He walked away, ignoring her dumbfounded expression, but then she regained her feet. Jesse moved into the kitchen and the mixture of sweat and spandex had him seeing double when she leaned over him to open the recycle bin. Mike caught her by the wrist and placed a delicate kiss on the inside of her arm.

Jesse slipped into another world. He held out her arm while licking his way past the crook and blew air up her arm to her shoulder and then into her hair, making the area between her legs moist with anticipation. Mike kissed her and Jesse tried not to allow herself to be swept up into the whirlwind of his affection.

He caught a handful of Jesse's hair in his hand and pinned her to the counter, exposing her neck to a sensual assault of love bites. Her breath started coming in gasps as she felt his arousal and for a moment, she rubbed herself against him, the desire to have him growing with each second. She started to pull at his clothes and he yanked at her spandex shorts. Mike turned her around, pressing himself against her ass with lazy insistence.

"I'm filthy, let me get cleaned up first . . ."

He silenced her protests by gently turning her head and licking her lips. He pulled off her top and threw her sneakers clear across the living room. He divested himself of as much of his own clothing as possible while giving her lingering kisses. He turned her back around and gripped the muscles of her thighs while placing sultry kisses between the warm valley of her breasts. She ran a hand down the side of his face and back, urging him not to stop, her nails leaving light marks.

He leaned her back and parted her thighs while kissing his way down her stomach. He was planning to love her with his tongue, he wanted to taste her and take his time with her. But as he took a step back to get her shorts off, she slid to the floor and ducked under his arm and headed for the shower. When he went to follow her, he heard the front doorknob turn and grabbed up as many of their clothes as he could, and then ran after her into the smaller bathroom. She turned on the spray to WARM and beckoned him in.

"Sex, shower and shave, I knew I loved your mind as well as your body."

"Save time and water," she quipped. He divested

himself of the remainder of his clothing and the last of hers, their bodies hot and wet by the time she wrestled him into the shower. With warm hands Jesse gently pinched at his nipple rings until the dark buds tightened around the shining silver. She took one in her mouth and sucked.

The slight jolt woke up all the other sensitive areas of his body craving for her attention. He liked seeing her look so hungry for him.

Jesse then found herself pinned helplessly to the wall and being loved in a slow fashion. He kissed her with lips that barely grazed her skin. Every light touch was felt in each nerve ending all over her body. She was afraid of wanting him so much. She began the first in a series of orgasms with his fingers deep inside her, driving her to the crest and shooting her into the blinding light, and then building on that release immediately toward the second. He was kneading one of her breasts with a firm hand while his tongue rapidly darted in and out of her belly button, trying to keep pace with the three fingers probing her body as his thumb played with her erect button, sending her trembling body surging forward on the swell of the second orgasm, allowing Jesse only enough time to take in a few deep breaths before working on a third. He was driving her higher and higher to another explosion with his face now buried within her folds. She had her leg up on the side of the shower, her back against the cool tiles, her body too hot to distinguish between the heat of the summer and the fire he was shooting through her with his talented tongue. He was gently sucking at her labia. She moaned breathlessly as he took confident claim of her clitoris in his mouth, swirling it with his tongue, drowning in her fragrance. Jesse felt the heat build in her spine and the mind-blowing explosion rocket through her while Mike intimately kissed her, drinking his fill. She had her hands in his hair, her body undulating into his face when she gasped her release.

He stood up and kissed her with a desperation he had been holding in check, his discipline deserting him, as he moaned and licked her chin, her neck, her lips. She kissed him back, sinking her tongue into his mouth, taking a liberal taste of herself. She let her tongue wander down his body as she lowered herself to his groin. She took what she could of his length in her mouth, her fingers massaging his thighs. He fell against the shower wall from that first shocking warmth, her doe eyes looking up at him with a silent message. He groaned as he put a hand into her hair and shuddered when she took him even deeper in her mouth.

His head lolled back under the spray of water as she moved her tongue along his length and gently cupped his balls, causing his breath to come faster. She stopped and then took his balls into her mouth, her tongue paying homage to them, then licking along the ridge. His elongated member stood out perfectly parallel to his body and Jesse took a firm hold, stroking it as she loved those secret areas with her mouth. He didn't think he could take too much more of her warm, wet mouth on him when he felt her moving into unexplored territory. Her mouth had again slowly taken his girth and he let out a groan that got trapped in his throat as her fingers continued gently kneading his balls, and then slowly moving further behind them. Initially his mind resisted out of panic, but intense pleasure soon followed; he crested just when her finger passed over the threshold, sending his seed coursing fast and hot out of his body, and into her eager and willing mouth.

He pulled her up and pressed her into the wall. "You are going to drive me crazy," he growled into her ear. Jesse's breasts were flattened to the wall as his hand came up to cup one breast. "You're about to see what that little trick did." He stepped out of the shower, rummaging around the pile of clothes, and returned with a condom. He groaned as he rolled it over himself and entered Jesse with languid care. Her head snapped up at the mass of him, despite the fact that he had just cum. The tight walls of her body sent a shiver up his body and he almost lost control. Her body moved sensually against his, he was sweating at the effort it took not to slam into her and spill his seed. Jesse leaned back, luxuriating in the new angle they discovered together. It was almost his undoing when she pulled away and turned around to face him. He lifted her and she instinctively wrapped her legs around his buttocks. Now, he could feel and see the desperate need, the vulnerable passion etched in her beautiful face. He thrust with the intensity she demanded, both lost in the quest for fulfillment.

Mike took her from the shower and placed her up on the counter, never leaving her body. He ground into her mercilessly and she begged for more. He was closing the chasm fast when she looked into his eyes and convulsed around his throbbing manhood; he gave two, then three, then one more thrust and his body went rigid as he leaned until his head touched the mirror behind them, pulling her into him with an iron arm around her waist. The intensity was maddening and the sweet agony of his orgasm dragged on in several long jolts. Jesse couldn't believe that a mortal man could bring such an esoteric explosion to her body. She crumpled in his arms. They held each other for what seemed like an eternity.

"Do you think they heard us?" she asked, worried about the five or six voices she could make out once the water was off.

"They'd be deaf not to."

"The shower could have drowned us out."

"We'll find out when we walk out of here."

"We are not walking out of here together. I don't want them to know."

"Why not?"

"Because they won't understand our relationship. Doug and Kat will tease me and make a big deal of it. Try to get us down the aisle before they leave. They act like everyone has to be married to have sex and that you have to be married to live happily ever after." Jesse finally looked at him and saw his features darken and become hard. As dangerously attractive as he looked, she definitely felt a coldness reverberating off of him. It was time to leave, their moment was over.

Mike left first, not caring who saw him. He walked bare-ass naked into the room across the hall to dress. He couldn't hide the hostility he felt because of what she'd said in the bathroom. He secretly hoped everyone heard because he wanted more of that, he wanted more of Jesse Ruth Bishop. He wanted her to face up to what was more than just attraction between them. He was in love with the woman and wanted everyone to know it. When he walked into the living room he saw Zak, Lion and Tak leaving, and Jesse leaning on the kitchen counter, wearing his clothes, drinking his unfinished bottle of water. She smiled her enigmatic smile and he thought maybe he had misunderstood what she had said earlier, maybe she meant they should develop their relationship in their own way, without her friends pressuring her. She did say they wouldn't understand their "relationship," so at least she acknowledged something was there.

Jesse tried to sort out her emotions. She loved what they did to each other physically and appreciated the mental challenges he presented, but Jesse was fearful that it was too soon to bring her walls down. As soon as Douglas and Kat left, she would sit down and tell Walker that she couldn't have anything more than a physical relationship with him. But if he wasn't willing, then she would have to do without.

Douglas was putting together a salad while Kat caught Jesse up on all of the New York gossip. From what Mike was hearing, he could tell Jesse had several questions about her ex-boyfriend, Eric. In fact, Jesse had so many questions about his situation that Mike thought this might have been a more serious relationship than Jesse had let on.

"I'll send a nice basket with my congratulations and call his office when I'm back home for the birth . . ."

Mike was getting jealous of Eric and he thought, *Since when did she start considering New York home again?*

"Have you seen your mom and dad?" Kat asked.

"Yes, I spent a day with them. I plan to meet Naomi there after your baby is born and spend a week. Mah kinda spurred Naomi into calling and I kinda took that as a way to mend some fences," Jesse said, feeling good about her talk with her sister.

"It does seem that Ma Bishop has a hand in everything. I'm surprised she hasn't had a talk with Mr. Walker, yet." Kat said.

"No one said she didn't," Walker said as he walked in and as they began setting the table for brunch. He was finally glad to be a part of the conversation again. But more importantly, he now had Jesse's full attention. "I've met Ma Bishop. I missed fishing with Big Joe and Gideon because I had lodge business that morning, but I did get to meet them the afternoon they left.

"When was this?" Jesse asked.

"What?" Mike asked, perplexed, while seating Kat at the table.

"When exactly did you meet my parents? And why are you only copping to this now?"

"Two weeks before Gideon went to New York. He brought Phaedra too. He said your parents agreed to come to the cabin for the weekend and he wanted me to meet them."

"And Phaedra? And you acted like you needed me to tell you about them, when you'd already met them."

"It was a short visit. I can't say I *know* them, just

met them. And if you haven't noticed I'm not all that talkative."

After a nice meal, Walker had questions about Jesse and of course they each had a story for an answer. She finally had to set the rule that no one could tell stories about her when she was out of the room. The day flew by and the guys opted to go fishing and leave the girls to their own devices. Jesse took Kat to the spa. They spent the day getting the full salon treatment while talking about baby mania.

It was late in the day when the women returned to the cabin, refreshed, to the smells of baking, grilling and frying, although the cabin needed to air out from the overwhelming odor of fish. The dinner conversation was light and lovely. Cheap wine and beer were the men's after-dinner drinks of choice, and Mike was thoughtful enough to make nonalcoholic Mint Julep Iced Tea for the women.

"So you run a catering business, but you used to only cook enough not to starve to death," Mike picked.

"And I'm not the least embarrassed by the fact. Doug's the cute cook and I'm the money man."

"You were more than that." Doug pulled himself to one elbow on the arm of his chair. "Listen, this chickadee has this ability to pull apart any dish. She can recreate any recipe. The only time she misses ingredients is if she doesn't know them. But due to her year working with Gideon, helping his business off the ground, she was able to travel abroad, tasting cuisine, being pampered, seeing exotic locales and learning the ins and outs of food and wine wherever she went. She constantly sent me spices and seasonings and told me the dishes they came from and how to prepare each one, down to about how long something should be boiled, baked, simmered, even dredged. And, for all her talk, she cooks all right. I knew way back then that me and Jesse were destined to be together for the rest of our lives."

"Yeah, the rest of our lives . . ." Kat said with fake malice.

"You talk like she lived with you," Mike said.

Kat made a face and rolled her eyes.

"You're kidding?" Mike asked.

"I don't live with you, Kat!" Jesse gasped.

"You might as well have. You still have a bedroom in our apartment."

"It's an office with a couch in the attic," Jesse defended, "and it's your husband's office."

Kat rushed to explain. "He never uses it. He barely uses the office he has at work." She turned to Mike. "I put it in when Jesse and I were trying to get to know each other. I wanted to be interested in what interested them. Turns out you can't fake that much interest. It's a good thing Jesse has other interests."

"Opera, the ballet, newspapers and tea," Mike said, lighting a cigar.

"Don't you mean coffee?" Doug asked.

"No. Tea," Mike answered.

"I kinda got off the coffee. Out here they have so many varieties of tea, I couldn't resist. Most of them cure one thing or another and there are so many that are caffeine free," Jesse explained.

"So, Doug, tell me how you two met," Mike asked.

Katherine knew that Jess and Douglas had been friends since junior high school. He had moved in with her family in high school when he lost his parents. Then they enrolled in the same restaurant school. Doug cooked and baked with finesse while Jesse struggled and cursed. Doug could balance numbers only if they were in a book on his head, so, Jesse, with her skill for numbers, came to his rescue. Together they strengthened each other's weaknesses and each managed to graduate by excelling in one area and doing well enough in the other.

Kat held out her glass. "Mike, fix me another drink, please, I'm feeling a might parched. The Mint Julep is good." She batted her eyelashes and brought her hand to her throat like a real Southern belle. He refilled her glass from the pitcher beside the swing, sans the Kentucky Bourbon. Jesse took the empty glasses inside and Doug closed his eyes like a man who was peacefully nodding off. "Now, tell us something else about you, Mr. Walker, Mike," Kat corrected after catching the look from him.

"I was born on the mountain, lived here til I was two, with my grandfather. My grandmother passed before I was born. I lived with my parents in Chicago for two years. I came back to the mountain and lived with my grandfather up until I went to college. I was raised Cherokee, I went to Northwestern for journalism. Told my grandfather I would tell the story of all the great Native Americans, living. I would rescue our tainted past and make the culture worthy again. Truth was, I changed my major to law the day I set foot on campus. My area of expertise became business law. I passed my bar at the tender age of twenty, didn't even have the diploma in hand yet. I worked for two firms, Southern Arms and Montgomery Group."

"I heard of them, they're both famous, I studied a couple of their cases about eight years ago," Kat said.

"And what do you do, Kat?" Mike asked.

"Librarian. It's not as boring as it sounds. I work in periodicals and conduct classes on the proper use of materials. So, did you like being a lawyer?

"I was part of the army of attorneys buying up different parts of defunct corporations. I had money, power and knowledge, and not an iota of sense. I just did what I was expected to do."

"I spent my life doing what everyone told me. I'm number six out of seven girls, both my parents are alive and until I got serious with Douglas, I always did what was expected." Kat took a sip of her drink. "That's what I admired about Jess. She does what she wants and sometimes that comes across as cold," Kat concluded.

"My grandfather was like that. He never questioned his destiny. He was born here and he died here. He said leaving the mountain left him open to too many trials. He said, 'A man with too many paths is a man with no direction.' He died trying to keep these mountains and this land under the banner of the Native Americans and he fought a good fight with only half the education I have, a third of my resources, and none of my connections. I wasn't here the day he died. I'd visit as often as my parents had visited me when they were alive, and I listened respectfully as he told me all the stuff I didn't hear but needed to know. He wasn't worried, though. He told me, 'The mountain and the people will be in your path one day and there will be nowhere else for you to travel but up the mountain and into the arms of the waiting people.' Now that I'm back, it seems like each day some of his words float down to me, remind me of the next step on my path up the mountain. I don't feel so bad, because he once said, 'In order to do battle in the elements you must know the elements.' I was one of the bad elements doing bad things. I know the guys I'm up against, I can fight in their arena. I was trained by them and I've fought on their side. I'm prepared to fight them to the death for my land."

"This is your mountain? So, you're really the Chief?" Kat asked.

"It is and I am," Mike said. He had always taken the title in stride, but now it was his next step on an undiscovered road, and he was ready.

Chapter 34

Jesse spent the following day entertaining Douglas and Kat, introducing them around and taking them on a short hike up to a small casino where Kat fell in love with blackjack. Afterward, Kat lay down for a nap after lunch and Jesse took Viona with her on some errands.

Viona was quickly becoming Jesse's sidekick. The girl talked to Jesse about everything teenagers found important. Viona had made herself a cozy home at the community center, using one of the second-floor storage rooms for a bedroom. Jesse was honored when Viona invited her up one day to look at some of her drawings. Jesse saw the sparse room and instead of feeling bad for Viona she complimented the girl on her creative use of sheets as curtains and blankets as art hung on the walls. Jesse would pick up odds and ends for the room without it looking like charity. Jesse told Viona it was her way of paying for the ceramics classes even though they were offered free. Jesse said, "In order to hone your talent you had to work for it. You should be paid for sharing it."

Mike was thankful that Viona had a positive role

model. Since her aunt died a year ago, the reservation had been responsible for the girl. Luckily for Mike she was resourceful and, other than making sure the community center was operational, the girl never asked for anything. Mike thought about Viona on his short walk with Doug. There was no breeze but thankfully low humidity. Mike, being respectful of the dry ground and grass, refused to light his cigar as they walked. Mike was enjoying Doug's unique brand of friendship and looked forward to their time bonding, whether it was during cleanup duty or cooking or the nightly cigar hike, they managed to find good company in each other.

When Mike talked with Gideon, Gideon constantly talked about himself, his work, his family, and one day settling down with Phaedra and her family. Lion would worry one subject to death and Zak was like a kid with ADD, Sylvia was a gossip and Lila was a mother hen. Digg and Tak were better as a package. With Doug, the conversation was very give and take. Doug's questions were well thought out and required a minimum of four sentences to respond to adequately. Sometimes Doug would give a look that made you want to better explain a statement or give more details in order to clarify. Doug's answers to Mike's questions always gave another hint into his personality and usually made him laugh. There was no direct Twenty Questions drill and he never felt as though he was being pushed. "Despite popular opinion, I'm not a spy. However, Big Joe has asked that I find out your intentions toward his virginal daughter."

"You're out of your mind, Doug," Mike said.

"I've never seen her like this. In just these few days

it's plain to see you aren't just any man, but the man she wants. So even if you can't promise happily ever after, just keep her as happy as you can, for as long as she'll let you. It's nice seeing her happy."

"You've never seen her happy before?"

"I have, but I haven't seen her happy for a while, and I've *never* seen her happy in a relationship before. I mean Utopia dominated everything around us. It dictated our lives and made us willing participants in our own enslavement. When I met Kat, I knew that a time would come when I wanted to be free of it. Shit, I was the one who begged to get out, but Jesse's the one who actually did it. But that's the way it always is. She makes a decision and I get onboard."

"You sure this is what you want?"

"Oh, yeah. This is definitely for the better. I've got a baby coming, my wife got a promotion and my partner's in love with a chief." Mike gave Doug a little shove. "Yup, this is the right thing for us. But, you know, there was a time when all we ever talked about was the business. I had no life outside of Utopia, but I was okay with that, since me and my best friend were doing exactly what we wanted. But, I don't know, I guess I woke up and it just wasn't what I needed to fulfill me as a person. I needed something else, something more."

"True love will do it to ya," Mike said, his own life changing because of his growing love for Jesse.

"It wasn't Kat. At least she wasn't the only thing."

"Then what changed?"

"You'll have to ask Jess."

That evening Mike had rounds to make, not just at the lodge but for the reservation and preserve as well. As he drove back to the lodge he wondered what could have changed Doug and Jesse's lives so drastically.

Mike woke the next morning in desperate need of another shower session. The entire night he was plagued with images of Jesse in her underwear. The pink panties, the red women's boxers, day-glow orange boys' shorts, six different styles of black ones, a blue pair, a few flesh-colored ones, and the yellow ones with the smile on the front. He left the cabin early to check in at the lodge and then headed over to the reservation. He called the cabin all day but no one picked up the phone. Finally he called the front desk and was told that Doug was hanging around waiting for him, and that Jesse, Kat, Sylvia, Lila and Zak were in Asheville taking one of Viona's pottery classes. Mike picked up Tak and the three men headed over to the reservation. They smoked cigars, told dirty jokes and talked sports. But in the recesses of his mind were thoughts of Jesse.

Jesse and her gang returned with Viona, and found that Mike and Douglas had planned a huge barbecue for the last evening of their visit. The guest list had grown so large that Mike called up to the lodge and asked the staff to stop by to give a hand moving tables and bringing out grills, and invited them to stay to eat. On the menu were Grilled Shark Steak, Roasted Wild Duck with Rosemary and Thyme, Buffalo Stew, Venison Burgers, fresh grilled vegetables, greens, Guhitligi salad, deep-fried onions and pitchers of spiked Kool-Aid. Doug and Mike managed the food with help from whoever offered.

"Sweetie, why don't you use the platter I made in pottery class?" Kat asked, holding up a passable dish in subdued colors.

"Is it safe to eat off of that thing so soon?" Doug asked, looking suspicious.

"Of course," Kat squeaked. "Maybe I should have done what Jesse did with hers."

"Jesse, where is your work?" Mike asked.

"Smashed into a million pieces in the back alley of the community center," Kat answered like a kindergarten tattletale.

"What?" Doug jumped in.

"I let off some frustration, the old-fashioned way, with organized violence," Jesse said.

"Why, what do you have to be frustrated about?" Mike asked.

"None of your damned business," Jesse snapped back. Jesse walked toward a group at one of the tables. But Kat and Doug were pretty sure what frustrations Jesse was trying to work out.

Some of the lodge guests joined the party, bringing chess boards and cards. It was a festive evening of eating, dancing, socializing and drinking. However, Mike tried to make it an early evening, fairly rushing people off to anyplace but his backyard. Thoughts of Jesse were wearing on his attitude, which in itself was never the sunniest, his own frustrations having grown watching Jesse dance with men, women and children with abandon. She ate on her feet and socialized with everyone like the natural hostess she was. Mike helped the staff clean up. Doug took Kat to bed, because the air on the mountain seemed to have her ardor up and he was taking full advantage of his amorous wife.

When Mike was able to go inside, he walked straight to his bedroom, only to find Jesse sprawled out in his bed in just white cotton underwear that barely covered her round, gorgeous ass. She was facedown, spread-eagled. He was tempted by the idea of just sliding on top of her and giving in to his urges, but he knew she was really tired. He shrugged off his shirt and decided to sleep in his jeans next to her. He placed his hands on her to roll her to one side of the bed and then stumbled back into the rocking chair in the shadows looking at the way her curly hair laid out on the crisp sheets.

"God, what are you doing to me?" He admired the way her breasts pressed into the bed and wished they were pressed to him the same way. He loved how her legs were so very soft, strong and long. Without realizing it he started stroking himself, first just trying to adjust it to a more comfortable position, then putting his hand inside his clothing and rubbing it. Mike watched as Jesse pulled a pillow under her body and began slow gyrations against it, her moans music to his ears, rising and falling like an aria.

He noted her waist had the perfect curve, her back smooth. When she turned on her side, he could see the front of her naked body, head to toe. Mike's hand was stilled by her unbridled beauty. He'd found her attractive since the day she arrived, but now she appeared otherworldly and perfect. He visually took his fill of her exposed breasts, remembering how they tasted, how they fit the palm of his hand. Turned on by her lips, her thick eyelashes jumped slightly on her evenly tanned skin. She turned on her back and once again the urge to just climb on the bed and be with her seized him.

One of her hands glided over the mountain of her breast, stopping to caress a peak, first gently, then with more urgency. His free hand gripped the arm of the chair in order to stop himself from reaching out to help her out. Her other hand continued over her slightly rounded stomach down to the V of his torturous desire. Her entire body lifted up as she slid a hand inside her pristine white cotton panties. They were so thin that he could see the dark brown of her pubic hair.

Mike watched her slide one finger in and then a second. The moaning intensified as he watched her fondle her breast. Mike had a tight hold on his manhood as he sat in the shadows watching his private, X-rated show unfold. As much as his conscience was screaming at him to leave, the voyeur in him wanted to see her orgasm. Jesse picked up the pace, her hips riding her fingers; she bucked against her hand as her head twisted from side to side, begging her own body to come. When both of their bodies reached a fever pitch there came a series of grunts, gasps and other half-swallowed noises, through bit lips and clenched teeth from the bed and the chair.

When her breathing slowed and Mike's returned to normal, he saw the sheen on her body. Now his heart ached to crawl into the bed with Jesse and hold her in his arms. He thought about how vulnerable she could be emotionally and didn't want her shying away from him or, worse, hitting him. So he waited in his chair, watching the rise and fall of her breasts, and listened to the sounds of her even breathing, until it looked like she had fallen soundly back to sleep, before quietly standing and walking to the door.

"The next time, there will be an audience-participation fee," she whispered, still splayed and open to him.

He looked back, his body already responding. "Next time send out an invitation and you won't have to go it alone."

Chapter 35

Mike woke up preoccupied with thoughts of Jesse. If he wasn't reenacting one of their intimate moments, he was worried about her emotional state. He was worried if seeing her friends and hearing about home would send her running back to Utopia and the City and away from him. Doug asked him what was going on, but Mike had no grasp on the situation. He was a man divided. He wanted Jesse but he also wanted what was best for her. Mike left to go on his rounds, assuring everyone he would be back in plenty of time to see them off.

He had a business to run. He had supplies to order, shifts to schedule and paychecks to issue. Paperwork wasn't boring to him and he knew he'd be finished in enough time. However, interruption after interruption came knocking at his door or jingling his phone, and so he never made it down to the cabin. The pool filter was blocked, the restaurant refrigerator was leaking, the toilets on the west end of the second floor kept flushing and two of the horses managed to escape the corral. It seemed that everyone was out in the field and Mike had to take care of most of the problems, and he did so while vocalizing every hostile thought that walked into his head.

Tak stopped by his office and told Mike about himself. Mike then turned his anger on Tak. Tak was a man of many words and he gave Mike plenty of them, including the words "sexual frustration." But Mike wasn't feeling very reasonable and he wasn't yet ready to make apologies for his behavior or excuses for his mood. Still, he listened to the Texan because he needed both him and the sheriff to help him locate some lost campers. Mike left a message for Jesse to apologize to Doug and Kat for his absence.

Jesse took her friends to the airport and hugged and kissed them good-bye. Not wanting to be alone, she went to the lodge and had a late dinner with Zak, Lion, Lila and her family, and Viona. She passed on dessert and took a few laps in the heated pool before returning to the cabin. Her body had reached a new state of nirvana after her swim. The den held a pleasant chill despite the warm night, so Jesse set a small fire. Between all the physical activities during the day, her late dinner and the warmth surrounding her, Jesse quickly passed out on the couch.

Mike arrived two hours later, his body muddy and sore from pulling two four-wheelers and three drunken twenty-year-olds out of two-foot-deep muck in the woods on the farthest end of the property behind the cabins. He put off a shower in favor of a soak in the tub, his shoulders already protesting the day. He walked back toward the den at a slow gait. As he stretched out his hand to the cellar door he heard a light snoring coming from the couch. He looked over and spotted Jesse. In the firelight she glowed a beautiful copper, her hair falling in soft ringlets around her face. Mike went over to straighten the sheet that had gotten tangled in her legs. She buried herself in the cushion and a soft moan escaped her. Mike reached over and gave each sock a little tug to remove them. Mike found himself studying the fine lines of her body, caught up again in the fantasies that she was offering. He removed her bra without removing the T-shirt and peeled off the soft denim in three slow, tantalizing moves, her black-mesh thongs singing songs of ecstasy in his veins. With a light snore emanating from her, her body was draped over the couch in the perfect position so that he could slide on top of her and enter her without disturbing a single hair on her head. The real-life image in conjunction with the powerful urge drove him out of the room and straight to a cold shower for a quick release.

Mike spent the following day on rounds and making apologies to his staff for his foul mood. Even with a full schedule his mind returned again and again to Jesse. She was as surly as he was, and taking her over his knee for an old-fashioned whooping sounded better than an apology. He was tired of her ignoring him and he was determined to make her talk to him. He'd expected that with their intimacy, they would grow closer emotionally and she would open up to him more. He was certain she had feelings for him, but to what extent, he wasn't sure.

All day long Jesse tried to sort out her feelings for Walker. She knew that going back to keeping him at arm's length was impossible. He had touched her heart. She had come to recognize and accept the love she felt for him. But she still worried that it was too soon to give herself when she was just getting back so much of herself.

That evening, when Mike walked into the kitchen, sitting at the breakfast bar, looking serene and demure, was the object of his frustrations.

She was quietly making dessert and he went over and helped. She was scooping in cups of vanilla-bean ice cream when Mike pulled out a bottle of cognac. She smiled in appreciation and he began creating two perfect cognac sundaes. After the ice cream was gone they drank just the cognac and sat up talking. She talked more about her siblings and he talked more about his job as chief. He watched her lovely body stretch toward the ceiling with catlike fluidity. She unfurled from the couch, desperately clutching at the warm and fuzzy feelings that she felt from their chat. She also felt a deep physical closeness to Walker. When she said good night he saw that she wasn't too steady on her feet. At the door he picked her up and carried her to the bed. He left the door open a crack so he could hear her if she woke up, and heard her soft snores within seconds. Mike went to clear up their dishes in the den but once he sat down on the comfortable couch, his cognac-leaded limbs refused to let him up. He fell asleep as soon as he was settled in.

Mike's sleep was usually light and this night was no different as he caught a glimpse of the familiar scantily clad body sneaking down the hall to the kitchen. Jesse's heart jumped into her throat as she looked up from her scoop of homemade cookie dough and saw Walker with an elbow over the side of the couch giving her a smug look. She marched down the hall to tell him to "keep this to yourself" when she saw the look of wanting in his eyes. The T-shirt and thong remembered too late as he grabbed her wrist and pulled her down on top of him.

He hungrily looked her up and down. "The way you're dressed is inviting me to do a lot of things."

Trying to keep her cool, Jesse responded in her most cool voice, "I didn't send out any invitations, yet."

"This show is on me," he countered.

"Let me go," she growled.

"I can't tell what kind of game you're playing but let's kick it up a level."

"I'm not playing a game."

"I know you're doing something, and you have tempted me for the last time. I need this to be taken care of or some other poor, unsuspecting soul is going to feel my wrath. People are ready to quit just because I can't get off. Even when I do, I'm still filled with wanting you because you looked at me or touched me. So let's finish what we started."

Jesse could feel her own body responding to his. The warmth between her legs was getting hotter with each word from his sexy lips, but still she couldn't help but laugh.

"What am I, a joke? You think I'm joking, little girl?" She rolled her eyes and took tiny nibbles on her cookie dough till it was gone. He was affected just by the way her mouth moved. He snatched the spoon and threw it across the room. "You see what I mean, you tempt me by doing stuff like that. You rub your body on me when you pass, you wear my clothes, your perfumes are on my skin, you are so feminine without trying, you get this 'do me' look at least twice a day . . ."

When she ran a hand over his groin, he grabbed it and pressed it to himself, wrapping her fingers tightly around his penis, guiding her hand. She smiled and he refused to let her go, he did not want her to stop.

His hips bucked as she began a slower pace, she was wielding incredible power and he was trying to show control. He was looking into her eyes in a challenge and she was getting more and more excited. Her own hips ground into his leg, looking for the perfect spot, the rough fabric of his khaki shorts providing a welcome friction. The arch of her back meant she was hitting that perfect spot. He started to reach for her to help her climax, when she slapped his hand and waved a finger.

"No, no, no. You said I started this game, then we play by my rules." She managed to get his shorts off, but in the process they went tumbling to the floor, her hands tangled in her T-shirt over her head by the time they were sprawled on the rug, inches from the fireplace.

"I think I told you already this is my show. I'm not in a mind to be repeating myself."

He lowered a dark head to her breast and he began laving one nipple with a slowness that Jess could not endure. Her body twisted beneath the warmth of his mouth; one hand held her arms above her head because she was attempting to break free. His other hand was punishing her hip, keeping her pressed into the carpet. Mike was denying her her natural response, he held his body an inch from her, tormenting her, making her want him that much more. He started working her other nipple, gently biting and pulling, suckling deep draws and then blowing across the dark cherry-brown peak. This time her chest arched up to him.

"That's it, baby, come to me," he urged. He released her hip and Jesse's arms came free of the shirt. He put on the condom he had in his shorts pocket. She wrapped her arms around his neck and brought him close to her. She slid him inside of her without the use of her hands, wrapped her legs around his back and impaled herself on him to the hilt, surrounding him with her liquid tightness. He used all his strength to keep himself in check. His arms were being tested, the muscles taut, veins bulging—all that chopping wood had paid off.

With one arm, he held her body several inches above the ground with pride. He was ready to explode after the fourth stroke so he reared up like a horse, pulling her that much farther onto him, now sitting up, his hands hooked under her arms and on her shoulders.

Jesse could feel him growing inside of her, each stroke going deeper. She silently pleaded for him to lay back, and she lifted herself with his help all the way out, so that the head of his dick was visible and slid back down, rotating her hips so that he felt all her walls clinging to his hard staff. Each time her hips moved in a suggestive circle, the friction was hotter, her pussy wetter, his endurance tested, his nerves taut. She quickened the pace to a fever pitch, and Mike was helpless to stop her. Finally Jesse lifted herself almost all the way off of him, hovering like a tantric angel, her juices leaving his erect penis glossy.

When she lowered herself onto him it was as if somehow she had gotten tighter. His body flushed as her eyes raked over him and yet somehow never broke contact. The slowness was a form of torture that had his senses fighting for more. Each time he lifted himself to greet her, she teasingly danced away. He was intoxicated by the creamy, thick wetness and the tightening tunnel she encased him with. She leaned forward, both hands on either side of his face, her breasts brushing the hair on his chest, and started a quick tempo of punishing thrusts. Faster and deeper with her own moans coming in tandem with his. He palmed her ass, lifted his hips to meet her, shoved himself into her as far as he could go and finally, breathlessly heralded his completion like a banshee in the wild. He tried not to crush her when he flipped them both over and yanked the blanket from the couch on top of them.

He gathered her close, wrapping his legs around her and burying a hand in her hair, massaging her scalp until his little hellcat lay purring in his arms. As soon as he felt her eyelashes flutter closed against him, he settled into a deep sleep that for once was void of taunting dreams of Jesse.

Chapter 36

Jesse had plans to spend the day shopping with Viona, Lila and Sylvia. Each of the ladies needed a well-deserved break from the rigors of daily living. It would also help Jesse keep thoughts of Walker from taking over her mind. There was nothing wrong with thinking about him but she didn't want to be consumed by the thoughts. Mike threw himself into work. It wasn't that she was cold toward him when she climbed into the SUV and drove off, it was that she seemed so calm, while his world had been turned upside down. The feel of her body pressed against his, the look on her face when she reached ecstasy; he wanted nothing more than to spend the day giving as well as he had gotten, but after lunch he accepted the fact that she would willingly give him her nights. He left work early to prepare a special evening for her.

Mike was sitting on the porch when she finally drove up. He helped her out of the truck and pulled her into his arms for a kiss that melted both their bones.

"I'll be back after my rounds. There'll be a small

storm tonight. Don't lock the door this time." He kissed her on the cheek and hurried away.

Jesse sighed deeply and went in, the silence closing in on her immediately, and she didn't like the feeling. She left the lights off and headed to the back of the house; maybe what she needed was the sanctuary of her big bathroom in order to realign her chi.

She didn't need any light in order to identify the smell of fragrant flowers all around her. Fire crackled from the hearth. The glimmer of the oil lamps cast a beckoning glow. On the floor she walked on a bed of multicolored petals. Candles stood flickering on every available surface, a thousand little flames dancing all around the room. The waterfall was making a harmony with the light pitter-patter of the rain that began falling on the skylight.

A broad smile spread across her lips as she looked at all the sensual items Walker had displayed around the room. On a tray next to the tub were a dozen long-stemmed, chocolate-dipped strawberries and next to that was a tall glass of sparkling wild-berry juice, with a bottle chilling. Incense burned in every corner of the room so that a subtle apple scent floated through the air. On the mobile brass towel rack hung a plush yellow bath towel with the word "KING" followed by "JB" with a gold crown over it. A blue velour, full-length, hooded bathrobe hung on the back of the door, and with it was a blue satin men's nightshirt with a neon-yellow handkerchief in the pocket that said, *"Yours."* She laughed at his sense of humor and was flattered that he already knew her so well.

On the radio stand she found a tattered paperback called *The Tao of Pooh.* She pressed PLAY on the radio and the sorrowful soul of Billie Holiday poured through the speakers. Jesse closed her eyes and swayed with each earthy note. Even the breaths the songstress took spoke volumes.

She didn't know how long she danced and basked in the glow of the room when she *felt* his presence. She knew he never made a sound when he entered a room.

"Let me run you a bath," he said from close behind her, turning on the tap. He began stripping off her clothes, she could feel the hunger in his eyes. "If the water is too hot, tell me." He lowered her into the tub and the steam rose up around her.

"You joining me?" she asked, watching him peel off his fringed suede top, showing gleaming muscle through the steam.

"Not just yet, lean back some."

She sank down into huge white bubbles that foamed in the water and rested her neck over the back lip of the tub. He poured half a cup of apple-scented oil into the bath and then he used a pitcher to pour water over her hair. He used a firm-bristled brush to scrub and stimulate her scalp and then ran his fingers through her curls as he rinsed. Walker didn't speak as he worked, but Jesse could hear the low rumble of his humming along with Billie. As he rinsed and rewashed her hair, she dozed off.

When her eyes struggled open some minutes later, he was using a loofah sponge on the bottom of her feet and the back of her legs. He handed her a strawberry and tantalizingly scrubbed her with sea salt from neck to toes. Walker let out the used water and added fresh water into the tub. The temperature in the room stayed warm, the steam continually rising from her skin, the music touching, and Jesse felt transcendent. Not like a spoiled princess but like a mythical, spiritual creature.

Walker again added the champagne-colored, apple-scented oil to the water. He stood up and Jesse got a clear look at his hard body, wet with bath water. The ends of his black hair curled up his back as he shook his long hair loose of his heavy braid. Jesse imagined wrapping his hair around her hand and yanking him into the tub. Through slitted eyes Jesse watched Walker unbutton, unzip, wiggle and struggle out of his wet jeans. They fell with a thud to the floor around his muscled legs. Jesse sank down in the water until only her nose and eyes were left above the water.

"I don't have anything you haven't already seen." He lowered his massive frame into the huge tub with her. They sat comfortably facing each other. He found he was enamored of the way her lips moved, enthralled by her body language and also the things she spoke about, the passion in her eyes, the happiness in her voice. "I heard you mention working in the garden to Zak the other day. Starting a garden is no small feat." To Mike that sounded like a long-term goal. Like she was setting down roots and he liked the sound of that.

"I enjoy manual labor. I loved doing the bathroom, I think I can handle a garden, although I won't get started until after the work on the store in town is done."

He didn't question her declarations, he wanted her to think in terms of a future, he wanted her to think of their future. Mike began feeding her strawberries again, each bite drawing her closer and closer to his body until she found herself practically stretched out on top of him. Jesse felt herself drowning in his smoky gaze. His eyes asked for nothing but offered her everything. He slid her onto his lap, pulled her face close to his and licked a drop of sparkling juice from her lower lip. He sucked on it with fervor, his hands massaging all over her body.

Jesse had come to him like the moon that fits perfectly into the sky. He covered her lips with a long, hot kiss until her lips fell open, his tongue touching hers. When he drew his tongue back, hers followed. He struggled to reach for the condom he had placed near the tub on the floor, and was shocked to feel that Jesse stilled his arm.

"Not this time, Cloud," she whispered into his ear and then pulled back, looking deeply into him with a pleading and vulnerable gaze that nearly broke his heart and dragged at his insides.

He closed his eyes and pressed his forehead to hers, exhaling slowly. His soul hummed with the profoundness of what she'd just given him. He then lightly licked and nibbled on Jesse's ear, murmuring soothingly, while lifting her just enough and lowering her gently onto him. He fluttered kisses along her jaw, then down her neck, and back to her lips, until his shaft was completely inside her. They both shuddered at the skin-to-skin contact. Neither could remember the last time they'd made love to anyone without barriers.

Jesse gasped against his mouth, his size seemed to have increased. He watched as her face went from shock to pure ecstasy. Mike wanted to always give her that look. They moved together in an ancient rhythm that put small waves in the water, a rhythm between all lovers, but uniquely special to them. His hands held her waist, his knees parted, her buttocks brushing his thighs, his hips rising up to meet her in tantalizing movements. He was determined to watch her soar to complete fulfillment.

He brought her body fully down his shaft and slowly up, then held her a teasing distance away, giving several shallow strokes before twisting his body in such a way that he could slide himself along the contours of her womanhood with different amounts of pressure. He watched her with fascination as she writhed in pleasure when he pushed himself deeper into her. He lowered his head and kissed the tips of her dark cherry nipples. She gripped his shoulders and whispered his true name as he suckled the hardened pebbles, giving the right amount of attention to each one just as the other felt bereft. He filled her more as his own excitement increased.

Jesse then gripped the side of the tub, feeling as if she would leave her body. Her breathing labored as she tried to move faster, but as he drove deeper into her, he forced her hips to remain moving at his agonizingly slow, sensual pace. He whispered tender words as her body tensed and bucked against him. He slid a hand between them and stroked the tender bud between her legs until her responses drove him right to the edge. All at once he saw her body strain and arch. With a loud sob, she turned her face up to the skylights, eyes shut against the shattering of stars and the crash of orgasmic waves. Mike shamelessly grinded his manhood even deeper into her, sinking his fingers into the generous flesh of her ass. Her hands wrapped around the back of his neck, pulling him toward her, as they shared an urgent kiss.

At the onset of her second orgasm, Mike was forced to succumb. Even the rain seemed to hesitate and listen as a low rumble began in his chest. He moaned, hissed and sank his teeth into her shoulder and whispered her name like a prayer. Jesse was spent and tears were running down her cheeks when she sank heavily to his chest. After a while, Mike stood and carried Jesse's exhausted form into the den. He laid her down in a large blanket kept warm right in front of the fire and slipped in next to her.

"I am going to be so embarrassed tomorrow," Jesse said.

Laughter erupted slowly from his mountain of a chest. "You sure will. I think people in Asheville may have heard you."

"Please, be quiet." Jessica's voice sounded far away.

Mike looked at Jesse with a tilt of his head, his eyes the same silver-gray of a shiny dime. His lashes, long and thick, blinked slowly. He raised one eyebrow but said nothing. He reached past her almost into the fire and pulled out a container. He put the contents in his hands and smoothed the warmed honeysuckle oil on her back. "I always thought you smelled yellow."

"Yellow?" she repeated, luxuriating in the feel of his strong hands manipulating her muscles.

"Yeah, like on a bright sunny day. Not the outdoors, but like the sun itself."

She hummed as he moved his hands down her back. "So you've smelled the sun?" she asked with a smile.

"No, but I haven't a better way to describe what you smell like. I've been smelling yellow stuff for months and only you have that special scent. I hope you like this."

"I like."

"Talk to me. Tell me anything."

Mike continued to massage her, taking care to linger on the scars that seemed to cover several areas of her body. All of them small and insignificant, as if they had help healing, and eventually fading so that they were barely noticeable.

"I was attacked about three years ago." Jesse rolled her shoulders to help release some of the tension. Mike stayed quiet as he rubbed more oil into her shoulders, silently coaxing her to continue. Jesse took a deep breath, "That scar, where your hand is now, that's from glass. If you noticed, I have marks on my upper thigh, my shoulder and calf. Here on my stomach . . ." Jesse turned over to show Mike the long, thick scar that reminded him of an appendix scar. This one too was smooth to the touch and just a shade darker than her suntanned skin.

Jesse was shaking now, tears brimming in her eyes. Mike wanted to hug her, but he was sure she would jump, out of fear, since she wasn't with him at the moment. She was three years in the past, on a New York City street.

"I was leaving Utopia and I left my pocketbook, even though I had my briefcase and a coupla bucks I still decided to go back. I walked the few blocks from the train and . . . I didn't see him, he shoved me from behind into the alley. I hit the ground so hard, I was stunned. He went straight for my skirt, ripping and tearing at it. I hit him three or four times and then he showed me the gun . . . I tried to crawl away . . ."

Jesse stopped and he handed her some water, Mike wrapped the towel over her shoulders and began brushing her hair. She smiled as if she just remembered he was in the room. She lay back down, pulling the towel around her, her head in Mike's lap. She curled up in a fetal position.

"He grabbed my leg and I kicked him in the face with

the other one. That's when he shot me." Mike's hands paused but Jesse continued. "I never really wanted kids, at least not for a long time. With my job, I didn't have time for a relationship so family was way off, I figured I'd never have children, but to have that bastard decide for me . . . I watched my own blood pouring out of me. I tried to stop it . . . I would have died there but a cab driver, or someone, driving by heard it and just drove down the alley." She stopped and breathed deeply.

"You seem tired. Why don't you try going to sleep now?" Mike had a hundred questions, but they could wait. He planned to put her to bed and go outside and kick some trees, maybe chop wood in the dark, just anything to let out his anger.

"Don't you wanna know the end?"

"There's no more. You're here, with me. It's over and although I can't protect you from bad things, I'll always be here to help you through them."

She was trembling again but he could see the angry flush of her skin. "He didn't get what he wanted, but he took things from me that were way more valuable." Jesse had tears streaming down her face and the words scorched him like hot coals.

"You can't let him win. You can't look at it that way."

"He still haunts my dreams. But with each day he becomes a more distant speck on my radar. One day he'll just be gone."

Mike wasn't sure if he should speak anymore. He wouldn't remind her of the nightmares that had her screaming into the night. A chill ran down his back and he was looking at the Ice Princess again. She built her fortress to keep others out. He didn't want to be one of them. "Tell me the end."

"Robert Derins. Found dead on the train. About

four stops from where I was found. Another woman identified him as the man who raped her. Article said he was called Cruise because he would cruise a neighborhood, stalk three or four targets . . ."

"Does it help you and your family cope?" Mike asked.

"You're the only one who knows, from end to end, what happened." Mike looked at the few very faint scars on her neck and on the top of her back on glowing brown skin that begged to be kissed. "My mother urged me to get help, Douglas wanted me to *talk* about it. Thankfully my attack was kept out of the news. I didn't want to talk about it. I don't want to relive it every day. I don't want to live like a victim."

Jesse yawned and Mike pulled a blanket on top of their nude bodies, wrapping his arms around her. He wanted to tell her he wasn't going to be a crutch, rather someone she could lean on, but she was already sinking into a deep slumber.

Jesse's mind was only briefly at peace before the scene in the alley replayed itself. The open black caw, the oily shadows that became a man and converged on her, blocking out any light, the pain ripping at her stomach, her arms, her back, but this time she didn't scream out or fight. No, this time the shadow man was snatched from behind and he evaporated into a puff of smoke. She saw the silver eyes piercing the darkness of the alley and felt herself pulled into the sunlight. A golden God stood holding out hands spread wide in a field of green grass, blue skies and a rainbow of flowers, his face to the wind, with hair that imprisoned the shadows and billowed with surreal movement. He'd delivered her to a place that smelled yellow.

Chapter 37

The next few days flew by in a blur for Jesse. Her nights were filled with peaceful dreams. She felt free, unhurried and unburdened. When Mike hinted toward commitment, Jesse retreated to her emotional tower. But Mike was always there waiting for her to descend. He taught her to ride a wild horse, bareback, and showed her hidden spots to pick herbs. He constantly cooked and they almost always ate out of doors. Walker worked long and erratic hours so she had plenty of time to devote to developing her friendships.

She went with Zak and Lion to the flea market where they had a booth, and she helped Viona at the community center. She also got to begin work on the storefront she had bought in Asheville. She worked in the lodge office a few times a week making plans and budgets. She would visit Lila, and watch the kids so Lila could rest or work. Jesse would also go shopping with Sylvia. And now she understood peer pressure. Sylvia's impetuous youth was contagious and she could talk anyone into just about anything. Jesse had several day-glow colors of nail polish and purchased sandals to match. Sylvia also talked her into getting a henna tattoo, when Sylvia sat for her third authentic one. The girls helped her to empty out the last remnants of the expensive, ill-fitting clothing that no longer belonged in her life.

Then Mike invited her out for dinner and dancing. Their first "formal" date. That Friday evening, Mike arrived decked out in a trendy Hugo Boss suit of charcoal gray, his hair pulled back into a neat braid down his back. His breath caught when his date opened the door on the first knock, his witty comment caught in his throat. Jesse stood in a pose that would put Joan Crawford to shame. She wore a full-length, wine-colored satin gown. The style was modest in that her body was fully covered but when she turned around he saw a flash of leg through a chiffon split that went up to her thigh. The back of the gown was so low that he could see the dimples of her lower back winking at him. She pulled a faux fur wrap around her and picked up a small matching bag.

"Are those bells?" she asked of herself, and then kicked her foot to the side so he could see the little noisemakers on the t-strap of her stiletto heels.

"Rings on her fingers, bells on her toes, she will make music wherever she goes," he quoted from a children's nursery rhyme.

Their evening was the epitome of romance. Dinner was succulent and, as a true renaissance man, Mike Cloud Walker could two-step his way into any woman's heart. Mike loved watching Jesse's body move in the sexy cutaway gown. It flattered and teased at him visually, her voice and smile filled with laughter tantalized, her dancing mesmerized, her body enticing him. He couldn't wait to get her alone.

During one of the breaks she leaned over and whispered into his ear about how many different ways she wanted to make love to him, with his suit on and off. Mike made haste and led his beautiful date out the door.

Jesse woke with a blissful feeling. She had made love to Mike three times before she felt sated. And she knew he was content as well. She wasn't the least bit worried that she was alone in bed. The clock said it was 5 AM and the sky was just beginning to grow lighter. He probably had to answer some early call. She slipped into her favorite brown shirt and padded to the kitchen for a bite to eat. With a muffin in her hand she went to the den to get a book. Her eyes lighted on a tray laden with goodies and her stomach betrayed her with a loud rumble.

"It's finger foods: coupla cucumber sandwiches, crackers, cheese, fresh-cut vegetables, Wahuwapa Wasna, homemade spinach dip, fruit and juice—thought you might be hungry. You didn't get a chance to eat much. I know I didn't."

"You kept asking me to dance."

He sat at her feet as she picked around the platter and ate ravenously.

He didn't remember it happening but when she leaned over to get the sparkling cranberry juice she was in his arms. And just like in all of his dreams, it seemed she'd leapt into the flames and did not get singed, she'd tamed the wildfires that burned and put out the inferno that kept everyone at a distance. It was lovemaking in its purest, most unadulterated form and he never wanted it to end. She responded to his every touch and he was touched in places he had long thought dead. Her kisses lingered but when she stopped he only wanted more. He allowed her to dictate the pace, it was her moment to reaffirm life, to reestablish the path of her new life.

He followed her and matched her until he couldn't stand it, the words were real and leaving his lips faster than his breath. "I love you, I love you, love me back, please stay with me, I love you . . ." he cooed, entering her. She said nothing but he saw her body language change. He held her back, so he could look in her eyes, and saw that she was crying. But behind her tears he saw the stars in her eyes.

The thunder in her ears blocked out all sound, her throat was thick with unspoken words from her heart, sparks seemed to be in the air all around her. She was melting into him, losing herself and, although she was scared, he was there, with his golden body bared to her, his hair keeping the shadows at bay, the smell of yellow all-encompassing. Mike kissed her and pulled her close, he touched, and stroked her with his lips, his hands, his body and his being that reached to the core of her, all the while whispering the words of love he'd been inspired to say for weeks now.

Her soul was accepting his and it was the sweetest feeling he'd ever known. Jesse's body moved with him, her crying becoming a silent plea for him to love her. He saw her lips moving and he thought that she was forming the words he'd been wanting to hear, words that would plunge him into a deep warm abyss. The thought of hearing them drove him closer to the brink of ecstasy. He moved inside of her as if to coax the words out of her.

Jesse's body opened beneath him like a flower to a

bee, her lips begging silently, wanting him. Mike looked into her eyes, his soul drowning in them. It was as if she could see deep into him, past his pain, past his defenses . . .

The room fell away from their sight and there was nothing but each other floating in the hold of a force more powerful than themselves. Neither wanted to let go, the feeling was filled with every touch, every kiss, every climax they had experienced together—all came crashing through them as their bodies communed and their hearts connected on a higher level. They were lost in a whirl of profound rapture that entwined them forever.

Mike wasn't sure how long he slept or even if he'd slept, but the phone was ringing. It shrilled over and over again, yanking him from his glory. Jesse was over the couch like an Olympic pole-vaulter, all he saw was her (his) shirttail flapping in the wind.

She came back minutes later, breathless. "Look, that was V, she needs my help so I'm going to the center." He watched as Jesse pulled on denim pedal pushers and a white tee. "Keys?" she asked.

"Suit pants pocket, bedroom door," he said grumpily. Just like a kid, Jesse flung herself into his arms, kissing his face noisily. "I'll see you later."

And once again it felt as if she had increased the distance between them, but this time it was different. The spirits had spoken. And as if he needed tangible proof, he'd already seen it. A tiny bell with a red curl laying next to a wayward black strand and a strip of leather fringe.

Chapter 38

Lila stood behind the desk with her glasses perched on the edge of her nose.

"Here she comes," Sylvia said, scurrying to her post. Jesse walked up to the desk feeling elated and tired at the same time.

"Sylvia, hush," Lila admonished.

"Well, can I ask her why she hasn't been around all morning?"

Lila handed Jesse her messages. "I was with Viona. She called early this morning, thought she had a burglar, turns out some boy who has a crush on her has been hanging around. I told him to take her to breakfast and I taught her first class."

"Oh," Sylvia said. "I thought maybe you were getting a jump on wedding preparations."

Lila lightly tapped Sylvia on the arm.

"Who's getting married?" Jesse asked. Both Lila and Sylvia went back to pretending they were working. "You two are not referring to me. He hasn't even officially asked and I certainly didn't officially say yes."

"Well, Tak said that Digg said, that the spirits

have finally spoken," Sylvia said, with another glare from Lila.

"What are you going on about?" Jesse asked, now utterly confused.

"Apparently the chief's been all up and down these mountains trying to get a sign from the spirits," Sylvia said.

"In Cherokee tradition a marriage must be approved by the parents, particularly the mother. And then a priest, or Ani Kutani, is consulted. He gathers two roots and says a prayer over them, facing the east, and if the roots move together, then the couple can move forward."

"So, what, nobody has to ask the woman?" Jesse asked.

"Who would say no to the chief? He's chief, he's rich, and he's smart and sexy as all get-out," Sylvia answered.

"Sylvia, go get me a copy of the specials."

"Why?"

"Just go," Lila said more firmly. When they were alone, Lila continued, "I think Cloud is planning to ask you soon, especially now that he has the signs. To him and to most of the people of the mountain, signs are as good as a binding contract. He's put the cart before the horse and he wants to make sure that when the horse is ready, the cart is all set. You see, a sacred spot must be selected for the ceremony and blessed for seven consecutive days and then a sacred fire must be lit. So in his mind, he has plenty of time to talk to you."

"Where is this sacred spot?"

* * *

Jesse's feet hit the dirt as soon as her SUV came to a complete stop. It seemed no one in the circle moved a muscle and yet she knew they felt her approach. The forest was crackling with energy all around her. Mike was sitting amid the circle on a log, dressed in elaborately decorated, traditional ceremonial skins. Most of the people present were older men whose faces were vaguely familiar, although she was sure she had never met any of them. She moved toward the outer circle, which was mainly elderly women. No one moved to intercept her, but she froze when she heard Mike's voice as if in prayer.

His back was to her and he spoke in the musical Cherokee tongue that had once sounded meaningless and harsh. Now those same haunting melodies became words as they reached her ears: "honor," "kindness," "harmony," "endurance." And then she could distinguish phrases: "Bound by your word," "Things have a purpose," "Treat with respect." She didn't need to move closer to hear him more clearly, she just needed to close her eyes and let his words wash over her.

"Treat with respect all things," she repeated first in English, then in Cherokee. "Listen to guidance offered by all of your surroundings; dreams, quiet, in words or deeds of others." Again she spoke in both languages and Mike would cease speaking until she was done. Those in the circle cleared a path as if to allow for the energy between them to flow uninterrupted. In the end, she spoke in Cherokee, her mind forming the words in Cherokee, her body feeling weightless, the warmth of the forest cradling her, bringing her into the fold. Mike became encircled in an aura of yellow light, but she felt no fear. "Practice inner calm. Reflect on endurance, dignity and reverence. Practice modesty in all things. Know the things that contribute to your well-being, and those that lead to your destruction. Treat all people with respect. Give thanks and honor all living things, live each day as it comes." Jesse alone finished speaking.

Mike turned to the east, north, south and west. He offered different herbs, and the fetishes: her hair and bell, his hair and torn fringe. Each was held up in each direction. He placed on the ground seeds to bless his home with fertility, he swept his arms high into the air to carry his thanks to whisper in the ear of the creator, and to the center of the earth he offered nothing, for he was just a humble man and must bow down when he can do no more.

It seemed that the fires in the center of the circle started of their own volition, people moved from everywhere in bright costumes coming to the circle, music started and voices lifted in song. Mike stood waiting for Jesse's eyes to open, for her to return from her Spirit Quest.

And in the style that impressed and confused Mike time and time again, Jesse turned and headed back to her truck.

If he expected her to stop running from her fears it was time for him to do the same. He was the grandson of Majestic Cloud Walker. A historic chief who brought many Native nations back from obscurity to rise up under one banner and make their voices heard. He was the grandson of a great man who harnessed the power of the spirits to bring pride to a people and present them to the world. As Mighty Cloud Walker it was time for him to do the same. Jesse had helped him touch his heritage with bare hands and embrace it once again. He walked after her. When they got to her car, Jesse turned to him.

"Cloud, I love you." Her words were supported by the sincerity he saw in her brown eyes. He was weak with longing. He knew that no matter how long he lived, he would never tire of hearing those four powerful words from her.

"But you have a responsibility to your people—the people of this mountain. Shouldn't you be shouldering that first? You didn't even ask me before doing this."

"I'd like to shoulder all of this with you," he answered.

Jesse smiled at the gorgeous giant of a man with the changing gray eyes. "When I got here, I was just a vessel moving through life, gliding on a current of others' wants and needs. I don't know if I'm ready for that kind of mission. I'm still trying to understand where the river is taking me."

A smile lit his face. The dark planes and lines that once seemed so formidable and intimidating seemed like rays of the sun to Jesse. Cloud understood. He left the mountain once for the same reason everyone does, to prove that you are your own person. He wanted to build a life on his own needs before taking on the responsibilities of others. At this point in his life, he was bereft without the mountain. It was his heritage that gave him strength. It was the spirits of the mountain that gave him life and made him a man. He knew that she, too, had to leave to see what had already been written in the sky.

"Just know that I'm not going to stop you or ever try to hinder your growth." Cloud opened the driver's side door, looking at Jesse and remembering the day the impossible vixen drove this monster beast over his daisies. He got in and started it up.

"Don't you have to stay?"

"It's a seven-day festival. I got time. I think you're the one in the hurry. But let's have something to eat before you go. How about Roadkill Grill?" He got in and started the car up. Once Jesse was inside, he put her hand on his leg and pulled her across the seat to sit under his arm. He'd miss the feel of her. The taste of her. And that yellow scent of hers. But he didn't despair. The spirits said his mind would become focused, his path clear. And it was. The spirits had said he and Jesse would be together. They never specified when, but the spirits were fussy that way. He'd give her all the time she needed.

Chapter 39

Cloud Walker spent his time between lodge business and resurrecting himself as chief. It was not an easy task. Although the casinos were running at capacity, all the stores turning a profit, the hunting licenses being issued in a more timely manner, there was always more to worry about. He sat in on more than his share of meetings with one government agency or another and worked in conjunction with the other council leaders to get bills passed and laws honored that would help their cause. He walked into the lodge expecting to see Lila or Sylvia hard at work but instead spiked purple hair was aimed directly at him. "Viona? What are you doing here?"

"My homework," she answered, looking up briefly.

"You're early," he said, looking through his messages.

"Clerical half-day." She squinted at him as if trying to make a decision. "Jesse wrote me. Wanna hear it?"

"Not necessarily . . ."

"She said she saw her ex, Eric and his new fiancée. They make a nice couple but she could use some meat on her bones. Doug and she finally decided to sell Utopia and she's selling her condo . . ."

"Where is she moving to?" Cloud's curiosity shot the words out of his mouth like bullets.

Viona quickly scanned the letter again as if she hadn't already read it a dozen times. "Doesn't say, but she plans to call when she comes down to visit her parents in a few weeks. And Kat had a baby girl named Allie." Cloud already knew about little Allie, Doug had called him first thing with the news and requested a box of cigars.

"Ummm . . ."

"Yes, Viona."

"I feel funny asking you for stuff. But Jesse said if I needed anything I could come to you."

Viona had taken the statement literally. She had moved into one of the staff rooms at the lodge. She claimed some boy was always hanging around and that it kinda freaked her. Cloud took her to school each morning on his way to do rounds. Saturday and Sunday evenings, she manned the desk. And on those evenings when Lila was around she made them all sit down to dinner together and Viona was always seated across from him.

"So what do you need?" he asked, putting the phone messages in the boxes.

"Advice. The boy who's been hanging around the community center is kinda cute . . ."

Viona talked a mile a minute, her scrawny teenage body shifting position constantly.

A smile crept across his face. These were the moments of fathers and daughters and here he was having one with Viona.

"What?" she asked suddenly aware of his smile.

"Let's talk about this over McDonald's, I'm starved."

"Oh, most def," she said, gathering her books. "Let me call Sylvia."

As she made the call, Cloud swelled with pride. Viona was smart and strong. A survivor in spite of the odds, who used the resources of the mountain to sustain her, and here she was asking him about boys.

"Let's go. So his name is . . . Why are you smiling?"

"I think you're doing great, Viona."

"Grown-ups are so weird. So anyway, I was thinking maybe you could meet him. And maybe he could come with me to your naming ceremony. It's cool you're going to be anointed after your grandfather. Another Majestic is quite cool. Sylvia's grandmother thinks you'll fill his shoes and then some."

Cloud Walker felt the lightness of being that came with deeds well done. Having taken over as chief was as right as loving Jesse and letting go. "Thanks, so finish telling me . . ."

"Oh, right, so, I want you and Lila to meet him . . ."

November was almost over and Cloud sat on his porch listening to the sounds of the forest. He always felt as though his nights were especially created for time alone with Jesse. So, during the gloaming of early evening he tended to feel the pangs of loneliness. Jesse had been gone since September, living her old life. He wondered if selling her condo meant she had found her path.

Jesse sat on the porch admiring the inky darkness of the North Carolina sky. The sounds of the country were all around her, the fresh air filling her lungs. Two months of New York were more than she needed. She loved visiting her friends, seeing Allie born and even having lunch with Eric and his fiancée. But she had felt claustrophobic riding the subways, and saddened by the sight of so much refuse on the street. There were homeless people begging on every corner and it seemed that everyone was rushed and it was loud twenty-four hours a day.

She went to movies, plays, concerts, restaurants, and any number of events to keep herself occupied, and she slept less and when she was able to sleep it was fitful. She avoided going out alone at night and was very alert to every face around her. It was taxing her nerves. The only good to come of her trip was spending time with her sister. They shopped very little and instead attended several art shows that Naomi had been interested in. Naomi was knowledgeable not only about the works themselves but also about the artists and art history. They spent plenty of time discovering what other things they had in common, but when Jesse was alone she felt hollow inside.

It had been only two weeks since selling the condo and temporarily moving into the cottage behind her parents' house, but already she was much more at ease with herself. Her father and sister were heading across the tall grass in the crisp night air.

"How early you planning on leaving?" her sister asked.

"Too early for the likes of you," Jesse answered.

"But not for me."

"Daddy, I've already told you I can handle this. I don't need a bodyguard."

"What about an extra set of hands to help you

pack?" Naomi asked, holding out her hands and taking a seat next to her sister. Jesse clasped them in her own.

"It really isn't much. I'll be fine." Naomi shrugged and went into the cottage, leaving her father and Jesse to talk. "Yes, Daddy?"

"I won't take much of your time but it seems you love this man. And you two seem to be well matched. You get mouthy, he gets mouthy, you're nice, he's nice, you run and he patiently waits for you to stop running. Then you let him hold you, even if you don't hold back and he looks in your eyes and you can swear he sees your bones. And he likes them the way they were, the way they are and the way they will be. Not too many people get that." Big Joe Bishop kissed his daughter and walked back through the tall grass.

Early the next morning, Jesse arrived at the cabin. At 5:40 the sun hadn't bothered to make an entrance to announce a new day, but she was certain Mike Cloud Walker was already halfway done with his first set of rounds. Jesse opened the door and went straight to work getting herself reacquainted with the cabin and unpacking. She'd gotten into a good rhythm when she felt a distinct temperature change in the room. The wind rustled the curtains in the window and the air took on a strange lightness. Jesse could feel his presence in the doorway.

"You trying to slip in and out without sayin' 'hey' to anyone?" Cloud's voice was like a welcoming beacon directing her home. But Jesse wanted to find her own way.

"I planned on stopping by Lila's and then having breakfast with Lion."

"That would leave a heap o' folks a mite disappointed."

Cloud moved into the room but walked along the perimeter. It was as if he were tracking a skittish animal. "You look good, Ms. Jesse Ruth."

"Thanks," she said, feeling breathless, his intoxicating scent finding its way to her. "What are you doing home?"

"Waiting for you," Cloud said, her heady fragrance riding on the breeze.

"You knew I was coming?" Her hands stilled finally.

"I wait every day," he said, moving closer. "There is a saying: '*Nav doyi amagesv akati nidoha.*' It's from the Lord's Prayer. It's the part that says, 'He leads me beside still waters.' Even when the river does not move, the creator will take you where you need to be."

Cloud placed a hand on her shoulder, giving a slight squeeze. "'. . . I have seen that in any great undertaking it is not enough for a man to depend simply on himself.'"

"You should have been a therapist."

"Philosopher. *Isna-la-wica.*" He rubbed her cheek with the back of his hand. He turned her around to face him.

"Until you landed on my mountain Lila had to act as a surrogate me to the outside world. People who didn't know me were afraid of me."

"And women?" Jesse asked with a quirk of her head.

"They come to me."

She looked up into his eyes, feeling the warmth from him pass through her. He pulled her into a loose embrace.

"I need people." He kissed her neck. "I need you." He kissed behind her ear. "I need the mountain. My great undertaking is still under way, I still have growing to do. I know you do, too."

He kissed her until she swooned at the sensations threatening to drown her. "Now, I'd like to ask you, would you be my wife? And for the sake of formality, here's your engagement gift." He presented her with a Ziploc bag.

"What's this?"

"A smoked venison sandwich."

She took a large bite. "I love the walnut spread. This sandwich thing could catch on," she said, taking another bite.

"It's Cherokee custom for the groom to present his intended with meat, it represents his role as hunter and provider."

"And the woman?" she asked.

"Bread, to represent home and farmland," he answered.

"That is so stereotypical . . ."

"Humor me because we both know I don't hunt." Cloud's laughing eyes confirmed that here is where she wanted to be. Here there would always be warmth, love and freedom."

"Here." She handed him a piece of the crusty, flakey bread and then took another bite of the sandwich. "That's me saying yes. You got a drink in the other pocket?"

"Let me check. No," he answered, holding out a velvet box and simultaneously going down on one knee. "But I do have respect for your culture and customs."

Jesse could care less about the beautiful ring in the box, because he'd already given her his heart.

Epilogue

Chief Cloud Walker moved silently through the house on moccasin-clad feet, looking for the smallest little Native Americans in the household. He flung his shoulder-length hair into his face before creeping up on them behind the couch. "Boo!" he shouted, and little shrieks, screams and yells went up all over the house. Three-year-old Tsuwe and her twin brother, Kaliwehi, scrambled up the stairs to the second floor with Cloud Walker in pursuit. Along the way he found seven-year-old Tangy hiding behind a door. Children were running everywhere and causing a blissful mayhem.

He paused at the door of his wife's favorite room. She was snuggled in the corner of the well-loved family sofa with her feet up on the steamer trunk they used for a table. Jesse was trying to understand the "new math" being taught in high school, when she looked up at her husband and gave a loving smile.

Jesse put down the book and watched her husband's seductive eyes while he poked a toe at a bundle on the floor.

Ecru's voice rose from outside. "Uncle Gideon,

Uncle Gideon." He was a tall, thin fourteen-year-old with the voice of a grizzly old man.

"Uncle Gideon is here," six-year-old Callum said.

"Oh. He can help me with my math," Viona said. "And maybe he'll take me to the football game," she added, pulling her books together and racing out of the room. Reed, an eleven-year-old girl, unraveled from the floor and took off in Viona's wake.

Jesse closed her eyes and listened to all the happy sounds of her brother greeting the children. She imagined herself standing on the top of the tower watching all of the kids far below.

"It won't work, you know." Cloud Walker's voice was low in her ear, his breath warm and welcoming, his kiss tender on her neck.

"What?"

"You can't hide, there's too many of us. We're scaling the walls like Ninjas. He laughed a maniacal laugh and stretched out on top of his wife.

She had loved the room ever since her wedding day. It was the largest one on the second floor with a panoramic view. Old, comfortable, not antique, furniture gave it an atmosphere that brought the whole family together every night before bed. Books, toys and the occasional stray sock littered the floor. It was a bright, happy space.

"I'm not trying to get away, I'm trying to get a better view." She bathed in the silver twinkle of his eyes while basking in the sunshine of his smile. "There's a lot to keep up with. A bird's eye view every now and again keeps things in order and me sane."

He kissed her with a passion that made what little sanity she had left walk out the door.

"If you could handle me"—she poked him for

making fun of her—"then you can handle these five little people."

"You must have lost a couple. On last count, there were seven."

"Oh," he said, kissing her neck with reckless abandon and slipping his hand under her shirt before any children returned.

"Oh," Jesse said with a smirk, enjoying their moment alone and feeling the fission of skin-to-skin contact.

"Oh? Oh, what, wife?" Walker stopped kissing her so he could focus on what she was about to say. "Please go on."

"Well, at council they asked if *we* would take one more."

"Jesse, we're up to our ears in kids and kid stuff, you just said there's seven. Soon we'll need a school bus to get around."

"Majestic, when I told you this house was too big for the two of us, you said we could fill it any way we wanted to."

"I was talking about parties, guests, Bishops and Spiegels. You've got Gideon and Phaedra and their kids. And they have one on the way. Viona's with us. Your sister and Tak are moving back in another three months."

"I told you he'd hate Paris," she said smugly.

"It was a great fashion program. He wouldn't have let her pass it up," Cloud said between nibbles on his wife's jawbone.

"Every kid needs a home, a place to plant roots, a place to feel safe, and we've inspired so many people to take in foster kids or adopt." He answered by licking between her breasts, eliciting a moan of surrender.

Cloud then sat up, pulling Jesse up with him. "You don't have to sell me, I'm thrilled to have so much family around me, I grew up an only kid. So, tell me about our new addition."

"Well, his mother is trying to finish her college degree, and he's only two months old and he's Blackfoot Native . . ."

"Wing? Missouri Watson's son? Oh, my God, tell me it's Wing!"

"Yes. Between your connections, my reputation, how well our kids are doing and the fact that Missouri knows us, they pushed for the placement. They're gonna let us have Wing."

"I'm gonna be a father! I get to mess this one up from the ground up!" He kissed his wife all over and then some, his love apparent in the house they had built and the family they had created. To most, it was just the biggest house in the realm, with the most unusual family, that welcomed everyone. It was a place to complain, run away to, make friends, solve problems, veg out, work, study, play, meditate and just relax. But to Jesse Ruth Bishop it was a kingdom on a mountain that resided in the land of Utopia.

She closed her eyes as her husband clucked like a rooster, reorganizing bedrooms to accommodate the new addition to the roost. She saw him standing there the day they were married, the words from his mouth magical. And she saw it all: the history, the ancestry, the love, the family and, of course, all of the little clouds, hovering over their home. She looked at her husband, his hair falling in thick waves to his shoulders, his skin bronze, his eyes gray and, hearing the kids outside, felt completely and totally at peace.

About the Author

J. S. Hawley currently resides in Queens, New York, while being employed by the Department of Homeland Security. Aside from reading and writing profusely, she has managed, as a single mother, to raise two daughters, ages thirteen and four.

She performs at poetry readings when her schedule permits and has coached her daughter's cheerleading squad. She has participated as a speaker and poet in several events for DHS and has worked as an EEOC counselor/mediator. She has also been involved in recruitment, community outreach and career days as well as in the PTA. Through all of this she fights Discord Lupus.

Her inspiration has always been her family and the kindness of strangers.

Jacqueline appreciates comments and feedback. Feel free to contact her at JSHawley@hotmail.com.